DESCENDING

Holly Kelly

Clean Teen Publishing

Descending

Edited by: Cynthia Shepp

Cover Design by: Marya Heiman

Typography by: Courtney Nuckels

Clean Teen Publishing
PO Box 561326
The Colony, TX 75056

www.CleanTeenPublishing.com

Content Disclosure

For more information about our content disclosure,
please utilize the QR code above with your smart phone
or visit us at www.CleanTeenPublishing.com

CHAPTER 1

Deep inside the belly of the Kraken, Kyros had the beast right where he wanted. Enveloped in blackness, he sank to the floor of the stomach wall and inched his way to the side. Despite the fact that he kept his mouth and gills closed, he could taste the soured and rotten flesh of the beast's last meal. He tried not to think about the fact he was swimming in vomit.

Lifting his sword, he sprang off the wall. His blade slashed through flesh, organs, and muscle. His tailfin drove him forward, spilling him out into the open sea. The water clouded with blood and stomach fluids. This was not the most appealing way to slay a Kraken, but it was effective—if you avoided the teeth on the way in. Thank the gods Krakens had extremely slow digestion. This would never work with a Leviathan.

Shouts of relief echoed through the sea. The town of Volosus had a new hero. Crowds of fellow Dagonians formed a semicircle of packed bodies pressing forward to get a good look at the dying beast. The colorful tailfins of the females outnumbered the grey fins. They'd lost a lot of males in this sea-monster attack.

The Kraken lay groaning on a bed of crushed homes. The beast's eyes dimmed as crimson clouds billowed from his wound. His mouth gaped open, his jaw askew. Red wisps of blood flowed out, only to be sucked back in as the creature took his last breaths. Finally, the breathing stopped and bloody tendrils rose around his long, jagged teeth. The beast's body spanned the entire width of the village—most of which he'd destroyed. If only Kyros had been called earlier. How the village warriors thought to kill this monster themselves was beyond understanding. Even the most skilled of warriors found it difficult to slay a Kraken. Kyros glanced around; the villagers looked haggard, broken.

A rounded Dagonian fluttered his fat, stumpy tail, inching his way through the sea toward Kyros. "Thank you, most honorable warrior." He smiled, flashing perfect, white teeth framed by a jovial face. "This monster's been terrorizing us for days. He killed my best soldiers, yet you alone defeated him. Thank you again."

The Dagonian reached out and offered Kyros his hand. Kyros's glare stopped him. The man clenched his fist and pulled it back. Clearing his throat, he gave him an apprehensive smile. "I invite you to celebrate with us." He turned to the crowd. "Men, have your females prepare a feast."

"Stop! No one move." Kyros narrowed his eyes at the Dagonian. "And you are…?"

"The mayor—Eleon, son of Demokrates." He cleared his throat, his eyes avoiding Kyros's glare.

"Why did you wait days before calling for help?" The venom in Kyros's voice tainted the water.

"I…uh…we didn't want to bother you with our problems."

"You mean—you were too proud to admit you couldn't handle your problems." Kyros narrowed his eyes and clenched his jaw. "Was it you who finally came to his senses and called me?"

The mayor's head bobbed up and down.

"That's a lie." A shout came from a Dagonian in the crowd. "I called you." A fit, young soldier swam forward, his hateful glare on the mayor. Other soldiers followed, anger echoed in their faces.

"Who are you?" Kyros asked.

"I'm the spawn of the devil," he answered.

"Who?"

"He's Azeus," the mayor said, frowning, "…my son."

Kyros approached the young Dagonian, who looked or acted nothing like his father. "Did your father ask you to call me?"

"No, on the contrary, he threatened to disown me if I did. He couldn't admit he was wrong. Even when his own soldiers were devoured, he insisted he had everything under control."

"Are there any soldiers left?" Kyros asked.

"Yes, my unit is still alive. My father wouldn't let me lead them against the beast. I guess he didn't want to lose his only son. But these unfortunate souls…" He nodded to the stunned survivors. "I guess their family members were expendable."

"Is this true?" Kyros shouted to the people. "Are there any to collaborate this soldier's story?" The villagers had fear in their eyes, but several nodded in agreement. None spoke out for the mayor.

Kyros turned to Azeus. "You do understand, as an elite guard, I outrank everyone in this village—including your father."

"Yes, sir," the young lad answered.

"I order you to arrest your father and place him in lockdown until trial."

"No!" the mayor shouted. Azeus's guards surrounded him. "How could you? Son? Will you betray your own father?"

"You betrayed your people by betraying their trust. You let soldiers die, for your pride's sake only. I am ashamed to call you father."

"Azeus, as the mayor's son," Kyros continued, "and because you have shown such fierce devotion to this village, I hereby appoint you mayor in your father's stead. You will remain in position until such a time as elections can be held. Do you accept my appointment?"

Any doubt Kyros might have had appointing a young man to such a high level of responsibility flew from his mind as he saw the weight of responsibility settle over the lad's countenance.

"I do."

"I cannot stay longer," Kyros said. "You have much work to do caring for the survivors and rebuilding the village. I will be checking up on your progress. First of all, I suggest you get rid of this Kraken's body before a larger creature comes to feed."

The lad nodded. "Thank you, sir. You've saved us, despite my father's ignorant pride."

Kyros nodded back.

As Kyros swam over a mountainous rise, he looked back on the scene of carnage. The town lay in ruins. It would take them a long time to rebuild. Tethered to three blue whales, the body of the Kraken left a scar across the sea floor as they dragged it toward the drop off. The creatures of the deep would have a feast on that carcass.

Kyros didn't look forward to his new destination. It was even more unappealing than this scene.

Xanthus had summoned him.

Kyros had dreaded this meeting since he'd first heard his best friend was searching for volunteers—for a mission a hundred times worse than tearing through the digestive system of a Kraken. These volunteers were expected to live among the humans and guard a mermaid. Either of these things alone would be unpleasant enough, but together...

What was worse, the mermaid was Xanthus's new wife.

Regardless of being Xanthus's best friend and most loyal companion, Kyros shrunk from such a job. He wondered how, in Poseidon's realm, Xanthus would find others willing to perform this task. Dagonians loathed mermaids—at least, they used to. Sara was the

Descending

first mermaid to be born since Dagonians killed the last of them two thousand years ago. If the stories were true, all mermaids were cruel, selfish, and self-absorbed creatures. Why Xanthus would want to marry such a thing was beyond Kyros's understanding. Perhaps the siren had bewitched him. If that were the case, Kyros may just have to figure out how to break the spell and save his friend.

But, to live among humans? He couldn't think of anything worse. Word was Xanthus was looking for five soldiers to guard his wife. Perhaps he was finally putting his extensive fortune to use.

Kyros raised his face. His body shot straight up, racing to the surface. He had one place to go before the dreaded meeting. A place he hadn't been to in a hundred years. He broke through the waves and flipped two times in the air before slamming his back flat against the water. He relished the pain; this burn was more tolerable than the painful memories he was about to confront. But he needed to face them. He needed a reminder of what the land-walkers had done to him. What they'd taken from him.

The journey took him merely two hours, swimming at twenty knots—it felt like much longer.

He considered passing his childhood home without a glance, but thought again. He was exhausted from fighting the Kraken, and even more so from witnessing how one man's pride could wreak such devastation and destruction. Besides, if his parents knew he'd passed by, he'd never hear the end of it.

Swimming toward the village at dusk, he frowned when he realized this village probably looked much like the last one—minus the rubble and stench of blood.

His house stood on the edge of town and looked just like he'd remembered it—a hollowed-out, lumpy dome of multi-colored coral that grew in size every year. His parents were predictably old-fashioned. Where most families were building stone homes, with sea-glass windows and marble floors, his parents were happy with the house they'd found and hollowed out eight hundred years ago.

Kyros had to admit that it was plenty big. When his parents had first moved in, it had been barely big enough for the two of them. Now it could hold a large family. Too bad he was the only child they had left. Eros, the god of procreation, had not been kind to them—only two children born to them in eight hundred years.

"Kyros! How come you didn't tell us you were coming?" asked an excited voice, interrupting his thoughts. His mother swam toward him and wrapped her arms around his chest. Her brown eyes sparkled. He looked down on her loving face, her long, red hair haloed naturally around her head. She'd long given up on keeping up with the latest hairstyles. She said they were far too complicated to braid and a waste of time, anyway.

"I'm not staying long," he said. "I was just in the area."

She raised an eyebrow. "Our village is not in danger, is it?"

"Not at all. I was just passing by."

"Oh good. Come inside. Your father will be happy to see you."

"Happy to see who?" His father swam in from the reading room. He was a large Dagonian, longer than Kyros—nearly as long as Xanthus. With genes coming from both his parents, Kyros had ended up somewhere in the middle—about seven and a half feet from head to fin.

"Who is this stranger?" His father scowled.

"Oh, stop being silly," his mother said.

"I'm not being silly. We see so little of him; he may as well be a stranger."

"You just saw him five months ago."

"Five months is far too long. My friends have their sons by their side—helping them fish during the spawning season, helping them clear out the human debris that seems to get into every crack and crevice, and helping their fathers home when they've had a bit too much pod juice. Not to mention, their sons get married and give them grandchildren."

"Dear, stop hounding him. He'll marry when he's ready." His mother flitted around the house, batting small fish out the windows and closing the shutters.

"So, what has brought you here?" his father asked.

"I just needed a reminder."

"A reminder of what?"

Kyros sighed, predicting his parent's reactions. "Xanthus is going to ask me to accompany him to the surface."

They both gasped at the same time. "Whatever for?" his mother asked—her face as white as whalebone.

"He recently married a mermaid."

Their eyes grew wider.

"That *is* surprising," his mother said. "I didn't realize King Triton had more children. But I still don't understand. Mermaids don't usually live on the surface."

"No, but Xanthus does—at least for a while. He has it in his head he needs to singlehandedly convince the humans to stop polluting our seas."

"Sounds like a fool's errand," his father said.

"Yeah, I've tried to tell him."

"So King Triton is worried about his daughter and wants her protected?" his mother asked.

"Yes."

"Why come home?" his father asked. "What do you hope this trip will accomplish?"

"Dear…" His mother frowned.

"I'm going to be around humans for a while, and I don't want to forget," Kyros said.

His mother bit down on her lip as his father asked, "Forget what?"

"How much I loathe them."

CHAPTER 2

Kyros swam forward. He could still taste his mother's tears. The memories he'd stirred up were hard on her. She'd never gotten over her daughter's death. What parent ever did?

He approached the island. If it was as he remembered, not much more than a sandy peak topped with a mound of seaweed and crabs.

He knew nothing would be left of the crime—not a clue to what happened that fateful day a hundred years ago. In his mind, he could see it clearly…as if it had happened yesterday.

Kassi had gone missing—longer than usual. His twin sister had given their parents fits. She was always wandering off, exploring. But she had never stayed away overnight—until that dark day.

The whole village had gone to search for her the next morning. Everyone else searched the sea, but Kyros had known where to look. He looked on the tiny island.

She'd brought him there once before, confiding in him that it was her favorite place to be. She'd even pulled herself onto shore—against his protests. But Kassi never listened to him, and that time was no exception.

She'd wanted to show him what happened to her hair when it dried. She lifted a mirror to watch her reflection. Her long, black hair blew in the wind. Her eyes sparkled as a smile crept across her face. Her hair curled and puffed over her head like lumpy coral. He couldn't help but laugh at her. She looked beyond ridiculous. Kassi laughed too, giggling so hard she nearly tipped over. Even now, he smiled at the memory as sadness squeezed his chest.

Today, Kyros surfaced again. The island looked different—barren, lifeless—as if a curse were upon it. He approached the atoll and remembered exactly where he'd spotted the keel of the boat—just fifty yards offshore. A familiar sickness twisted his insides as the memories flooded back. No human had ever sailed to the island before. But years ago, on that dark day, there they were.

Kyros hadn't hesitated to surface. He cared not that the humans would see him, that he was breaking the law by showing himself to them. The need to find and protect his sister was overwhelming, a desperation.

The smell of blood assaulted his mind as his vision of the past played from his memory. The humans were shouting—two men. They scrambled around a net. Kyros had no idea what they were saying. One of the men cried out when he saw Kyros, and they both looked at him in horror—their voices now silent. Kyros examined the scene.

He couldn't see his sister, but it was too strange a coincidence that she was missing and humans were there, in her favorite place. A net hung over the side of the boat, jumbled in a tangle of seaweed and flopping fish. The scent of blood saturated the air. Then he saw something that shouldn't have been in a fishing net. Long, brown hair tangled around the thin, interlocked ropes.

Kyros dove under the water, swimming straight down. Turning sharp, he shot back toward the surface. He broke through, traveling at top speed, and crashed down on the ship's deck. The humans screamed and ran inside the craft.

Kyros dragged his body across the wooden surface, to the motionless lump hidden in the net. The wind blew icy across his skin, the cold penetrating deep into his body, as the reality of the situation speared him through the heart. His sister hung lifeless, her eyes still bright, her head caved in above her temple—her blood fresh. A metal rod lay nearby, smeared with her blood. The former chill he'd felt was burned away by his sudden fury.

At sixteen years old, he was not yet full-grown, but he was still larger than either of the human murderers. They might have screamed. Kyros had no recollection of it. The only scream he heard was his own—a mixture of pain, anguish, and rage as he mercilessly tore them apart. When they were dead, he returned to his sweet sister, cut the ropes, and carefully pulled her body from the net.

The next few months passed in a blur. The village elders must have disposed of the ship and the bodies.

They never mentioned it. No one ever spoke of the humans or Kassi again, but from that day on, an invisible barrier existed around the island. No one went near it.

CHAPTER 3

Xanthus's home came into view between mountains of surrounding coral. Kyros clenched his fists at the unusual sight. He'd been to his best friend's home a thousand times, but it never looked like this. Normally, colorful fish abounded and surrounded the building, weaving in and out of the columns. Not anymore. Sharks of every shape, size, and species circled the structure.

He shook his head and growled, "Mermaids."

Kyros swam toward the entrance. A great white shark cut him off and opened his jaws wide. A low, rumbling growl vibrated in the creature's chest. Kyros reached for his sword just when Xanthus called out, "Amintah! Let him through."

The shark didn't flinch; he didn't even move an inch.

"Please, Amintah, let my husband's friend pass." A sweet, melodious voice brushed Kyros like a caress.

The shark snapped his jaw shut and turned, swimming around back toward the voice. Just as Kyros was about to move forward, the shark's tailfin snapped back, flicking his nose, causing his eyes to sting. He rubbed his nose as he swam forward.

The shark swam toward a blue-eyed mermaid with her arm locked around Xanthus's arm. Her black hair floated around her head. Her face was beautiful, and her blue eyes striking. The small, intricate image of a conch shell glowed across her cheekbone. It was below her right eye—Triton's mark, showing he'd claimed her as his child. Anyone who harmed this mermaid would feel the sea-god's wrath.

Reaching out, she brushed her hand over the shark's side as he passed by. "I'm sorry, Kyros," she said, speaking English. "Amintah is a bit protective of me."

Kyros narrowed his eyes, scowling at her. What audacity, speaking to a man as if she already knew him! Xanthus needed to teach his wife her proper place.

The light in her eyes dimmed when she saw Kyros glaring at her. She looked back to her husband as her cheeks filled with color.

"Sara," Xanthus said. "Why don't you go on in and get us some drinks?"

Her brows pinched together as she bit her bottom lip. "You want...drinks?"

"...in the kitchen, first cupboard on the left." Sara nodded, turning to swim away. Xanthus snagged her back and pulled her in for a thorough kiss. With the light back in her eyes and a smile on her face, she swam toward the house. Although swim would be a gross overstatement. Kyros had never seen anyone swim quite like that. Actually, his friend, Timotheus, might have—

after a rock slid off a cliff and struck him on the head. Kyros chuckled at the similarity.

Xanthus frowned at him, but couldn't quite hold it. The corners of his mouth pinched down, as he did his best to suppress his smile. "She's still learning."

Kyros turned to Xanthus as realization dawned. "No," he breathed. "She…?"

Xanthus nodded. "…grew up on land."

"So…Hades. I wondered how you got mixed up with a mermaid when you were supposed to be capturing humans."

"Yeah, you wouldn't believe how surprised I was to find her—a daughter of the sea, living on land, *with* a tail. Lucky for Sara, she hid it well. She didn't even know *what* she was. She thought she was a malformed human. But now that she knows the truth, she's really starting to blossom."

"How could she hide such a thing?"

"She rode in a chair with wheels and covered her tail at all times. She was quite careful."

"Why didn't Triton help her?"

"He wasn't aware of her existence until recently. But now that he knows of her, he's extremely protective. Which brings me to the reason I brought you here."

Kyros shook his head as they swam inside and went into the library.

"Listen, I know you don't want to help." Xanthus spoke to him in Atlantian. He obviously didn't want his wife to hear this conversation.

Kyros scowled. "No, I don't." He didn't say more, having no reason to make this easy for Xanthus.

"But you are the only Dagonian in the sea I trust completely. Besides…" Xanthus paused.

"Oh no." Kyros whipped his head around. "You are not going to bring that up."

Xanthus raised an eyebrow.

"I just knew you would."

"But I didn't…"

"You were going to. Don't deny it."

Xanthus pressed his lips together.

"Okay, so you saved my life. I owe you." Kyros drifted over to a large book on the desk and read the title, "The Mer—A complete history". *Figures.*

Kyros sighed. "So, what do you need me to do?"

"Right now, I'm recruiting soldiers to guard Sara."

Good luck with that. "And you want my help."

"Yes, I want you to accompany me to Panthon Prison."

"What?" Kyros jerked around, knocking a stone figure off the desk. "Now, I had to have heard you wrong. After what happened, do you really think any of those guards will help you?"

"Not guards…"

"Not…?" Kyros scowled, and then the light went on in his head. "You mean Pallas?"

"He's one of them."

Kyros had to admit, Xanthus's plan was bold.

Descending

"I never did think a husband should have to pay for his wife's crime. This will not sit well with the council. I expect they will be angry when they find out you've released prisoners."

"The council is too busy arguing amongst themselves to be of any worth anyway."

Kyros smiled. "This might not be such a bad idea. Who knew the great and honorable Xanthus would ever side against the council? There may be hope for you yet, my friend."

Xanthus laughed. "Falling in love with a mermaid has made me reexamine my whole honor system. So, you'll come?"

Kyros spotted Sara peeking into the room. She approached when Xanthus smiled gently at her. She grinned back, handed him two purple tubes, and left.

"I'll come." Kyros frowned, looking at the tubes in Xanthus's hands. "You really need to teach your mermaid the difference between pod juice and sea-slug repellant."

Xanthus sighed. "Yeah."

⚡ ⚒

Rocky spires towered over Panthon Prison. Sharp-eyed guards armed with harpoons circled each point, guarding the giant, stone structure. The building stood imposing and impenetrable. Incarceration here was a death sentence. Starvation—the executioner. The most heinous and dangerous criminals were sent here, which was why this was the only prison Kyros and

Xanthus would need to visit. Xanthus insisted only the most capable of warriors were fit to guard his mermaid. And a skilled warrior was never sent elsewhere—no place else was formidable enough to house a lethal soldier.

Kyros followed behind Xanthus as they approached the prison. Two guards at the front door drew their swords. Kyros knew them by name and reputation. Titus was the one with a barracuda-sized bite out of his tailfin. He was a sneaky little backstabber. The other guard, Bemus, was a follower who was always looking to get on the good side of the most powerful men around. He was loyal only to himself. Both of them sneered at Xanthus. Kyros glanced at his friend, wondering how he felt about this animosity. Just weeks ago, these guards would have been stumbling over their words in an attempt to speak to Xanthus—the legendary Nightmare of the Deep.

Not anymore.

Xanthus had married a mermaid. He had become the enemy, and Kyros…Well, after today, he'd be considered one as well. Great, just what he needed—more enemies.

"We've been ordered not to let you pass." Titus clutched his sword and swam just above them in a show of intimidation. Kyros nearly laughed at the attempt.

"I have orders for you of my own." Xanthus ignored the posturing and passed them a scroll. "King Triton has signed for the release of these men for a special mission."

Descending

Titus snatched the scroll from Xanthus's grip. "We'll see."

His eyes flew back and forth across the paper, growing wide. "But these men are prisoners—here 'til death. Their crimes are of the most serious nature."

"You mean their wives' and daughter's crimes."

"No, *their* crimes. It was their responsibility to prevent the actions of their wards."

"I didn't come here to argue with you," Xanthus said. "I came to collect these men."

Titus turned and whispered to Bemus. Bemus nodded and entered the prison. *What in Hades are they up to?*

"I'll need to speak to the warden first," Titus said.

"No, you need to let…" Xanthus began. Kyros rushed Titus before he finished. Titus thrust his blade toward him at his approach, but he deflected, circled around him, and had his dagger at the guard's throat before he could even blink.

"Xanthus," Kyros yelled.

Xanthus had already rushed through the door. "Yeah, I know," he called back.

Kyros could feel Titus trembling in his grasp. "So you think you could order their deaths while we wait?"

"I don't know what you're…"

Kyros increased his grip, cutting off Titus's airway. "Don't lie to me. If I hear one more word come out of your mouth, I'll silence you forever."

Kyros loosened his grip to let him breathe. Titus

squirmed, groaning, "You cannot have the prisoners."

"You think you can defy King Triton?"

Kyros could feel Titus reaching for his belt. *Oh please, don't be stupid.*

"I won't need to defy him," Titus said. He raised his dagger in one hand, pulling on Kyros's arm with his other as he turned. Anticipating the move, Kyros jerked against the guard's arm, slicing his jugular vein in the process. Titus stiffened for a moment as blood clouded the water. Kyros could almost feel the horror emanating from him—he knew he was going to die.

When he went limp, Kyros felt a twinge of regret. To die because of stupidity, now that was a tragedy. "You just had to do it," Kyros said, shaking his head. He pushed his body away, swimming into the prison. Holding his sword up, he was ready for more resistance.

The guards looked up at his entrance. They glared at him, but made no move to intercept. Kyros raced toward the cells, passing by Bemus, who was being pulled along, unconscious, by another guard. Kyros tasted the rot and filth of the prison. It got stronger and fouler as he swam into the heart of the buildingprison. Despite the decaying conditions, he smiled in anticipation of freeing the prisoners on the list. Xanthus had trained Kyros alongside these men.

The first one they'd retrieve would be Amar. It was a dark day when they were ordered to bring him in. His wife had committed adultery—a crime punishable by a lifetime in prison. Amar was blamed for not keeping a tighter rein on her and for shaming his family. And of course, because of the idiotic law, his wife remained free.

Kyros smiled as he saw his old friend's face.

"I will not go," Amar said.

What in Hades?

Xanthus turned to Kyros. "He refuses to come with us. He says he'll not shame his family further."

"So you would rather refuse the order of a god? That brings its own shame, you know."

"I must serve out my sentence. That is the only way to restore honor to my family."

Kyros scowled. Amar's family came from the Persian Gulf—a more radical group of Dagonians inhabited that sea. Kyros had never understood the culture. But he had an idea how to get around his reluctance.

"How about we agree to return you to the prison as soon as the mission is fulfilled?"

Xanthus frowned at him, but Amar seemed to take heart. "Will you give me your word?"

Kyros would rather not, but he knew it was the only way. "Yes, I give my word. But do you give your word to see this mission through?"

"I do," Amar said.

"Okay," Kyros replied. "Who's next?"

"Pallas," Xanthus answered.

"Good choice."

"Why don't you retrieve him?" Xanthus asked. "I'll go after Drakōn."

"Drakōn? Good luck with that. Pallas will be——"

"Did someone just call my name?" A voice came from down the dark hallway.

Kyros swam forward. "Now why would anyone want to talk to an eel like you?" he asked as he swam up to the bars.

Pallas grabbed the bars and pulled hard, slamming the door against the lock. "Come in here, and I'll show you who the eel is."

Kyros approached the cell door. Pallas's haggard face appeared in the barred window.

"Why don't you come out here?" Kyros asked.

Pallas's eyes narrowed at his words, while his glare filled with enough venom to stun a whale. "Is that a joke?" he growled.

Kyros smiled. "Not at all. You have a mission to perform. Xanthus has secured your release."

The anger melted away as he sank to the floor. Kyros was sad to see Pallas's condition. Darkness circled his hollow eyes. He had lost weight, and his red hair and beard floated in clumps around his head. He looked defeated. Kyros much preferred him angry.

"No one leaves Panthon," he whispered.

"Today, four of you are. Triton's orders."

A hint of a smile lightened Pallas's face, but it didn't quite reach his eyes. He wouldn't believe he was being released until they were in the open sea with Panthon Prison at their backs.

The building shook as thundering crashes and

angry bellows echoed from down the corridor—sounded like things were going better that expected with Drakōn. Kyros had expected him to put up more of a fight.

"Is that Drakōn?" Pallas's voice rose.

"Yeah, Xanthus is releasing him."

"Wow, what kind of mission are we going on?"

"I'll let Xanthus explain. We need to get Straton."

Straton had only been at the prison a month. But from the looks of him, you'd guess he'd been there years. His daughter had killed a council member's son. Straton was paying for her crime.

In the end, Xanthus had five seasoned warriors— Amar, Pallas, Straton, Drakōn and of course, Kyros.

They swam toward Xanthus's home, over the rugged Calibrian Rise. Being that the former prisoners were all on the brink of starvation, they immediately took to hunting. They circled an entire school of barracudas— decimating their numbers in minutes.

Pallas took his last bite and pushed the fish carcass away. "So, Xanthus, what kind of mission requires the help of convicted criminals?"

The others gathered to hear the answer.

Xanthus hesitated a moment before speaking. "I need you to guard my wife."

"Why does your wife need a guard?" Straton asked.

Kyros folded his arms across his chest. *This is gonna be good.*

"She's a mermaid." Voices erupted in surprised

confusion.

"Tell them *where* this assignment will take place," Kyros said, smiling.

All eyes were turned to Xanthus. "On land."

"No," Drakōn gasped.

"How?" Pallas asked.

"Triton," Xanthus said. "My wife's father is willing to give you all you need, including human legs——"

"No!" Drakōn interrupted. "There's no way. I'd rather go back to prison."

Kyros raised an eyebrow.

"How long is this assignment?" Pallas asked, his arms crossed over his chest.

"Triton has given me as much time as I need to accomplish my goal," Xanthus said.

"What goal?" Straton asked.

"I'm attempting to convince the humans to stop poisoning our seas."

"And how do you expect to accomplish that?" Drakōn inquired, narrowing his eyes.

"Anyway I can," Xanthus answered.

"After this impossible assignment, are we to return to Panthon?" Drakōn asked.

"Triton ordered your release," Xanthus said. "There was no mention of returning."

"The council will want us back," Pallas said. "When your mission is over and we return to the sea, they'll send soldiers to hunt us again."

"We'll worry about that when it happens,"

Xanthus said. "For now, you're free."

"Yes, it appears we are, but what a price for freedom." Pallas shook his head, looking over to Kyros. "I'm confused as to why *you'd* agree to such a…vile assignment. You weren't a prisoner."

"My reasons are my own, Pallas."

"Xanthus," Drakōn said, "you should have told us before we left what we were expected to do."

"Do you truly think to go back to Panthon?" Xanthus asked, looking around. "Do any of you *want* to return?"

No one spoke.

"Okay, so you all accept this assignment," Xanthus said. "I'll hear no more complaints, and I'll tolerate no insubordination. Under no circumstances will I tolerate any unpleasantness toward my wife. And if any of you do not protect her to the best of your ability, I will send you back to Panthon in the most painful way possible. If you are negligent and she's harmed, I'll send you to her father."

Kyros sickened at that thought. Triton had lived many millennia. If anyone knew how to inflict eternal misery, it was he. And the Dagonian who was sent to Triton for punishment would likely suffer not just for Sara, but for all his children killed by Dagonian hands. Kyros glanced around at the others. They looked as terrified at the prospect as he did.

Darkness descended on them as they approached Xanthus's castle. Kyros looked up. Sharks—thousands more than before—circled the building. There were so many that their shadows nearly blackened out the sun. His blood chilled at several monstrous forms swimming among the sharks. He moved in close to Xanthus.

"Are those…?" Kyros couldn't finish his question.

Xanthus's eyes widened. "Yes. Megalodons." His voice rasped like dry sand.

"How did her father coax them from the depths?" Kyros asked.

Xanthus raised an eyebrow. "He can be persuasive when he wants to be."

"Suddenly," Pallas whispered in Kyros's ear, "life among humans doesn't seem quite so unappealing."

Kyros looked around. The soldiers pressed in closer to Xanthus.

"Looks like you've got an infestation," Drakōn said.

"Hades, I've never seen anything like it," Straton said.

"Triton's protective of his mermaid, isn't he?" Pallas asked.

"No more than I am," Xanthus answered. "I just don't have sharks at my beck and call."

"No, you have something much more dangerous," Kyros said.

Xanthus turned to him. "What?"

Kyros smiled. "Us."

CHAPTER 4

Honolulu, Hawaii ~ Federal Courthouse

Sweat trickled down Gretchen's back as she cradled a sleeping child in her arms. Her fingertips brushed over the little blonde curls. Jami Tollman was a beautiful child with a precarious future. And right now, her future was balancing on the razor's edge of the American justice system. But Ms. Gardner was on the job. As her intern, Gretchen had heard her boss rehearse again and again. The argument was fierce and compelling. There was no way she could lose. However, stranger things had happened…but not this time. The fates wouldn't be so cruel to this little girl.

Gretchen looked up at the clock mounted on the cinderblock wall next to the security station. They'd been there for only half an hour. It'd probably be another thirty minutes—unless the judge ruled quickly. She caught a strong whiff of cigarette smoke as a boney woman with greasy hair stepped up to the security stop. The burly guard gave her little notice, his eyes on a man behind her dressed in shackles and escorted by two police officers.

Gretchen held little Jami tight. This was no place for a five-year-old girl. If life were fair, she'd just be getting home from kindergarten, returning to a loving mother. She would bake her cookies and ask how school went as she hugged her and pressed a kiss to her soft cheek. When her father came home, she'd run up, he'd lift her up above his head, twirl her around, and drop her in his arms, telling her what an amazing child she was.

But life was rarely fair.

The doors to the courtroom opened and people began to push through, like cattle escaping the coral. Gretchen found the person she was looking for. She sucked in a breath and held it as her heart froze. Ms. Gardner looked downcast. When she saw Gretchen watching her, she shook her head, confirming it didn't go well.

Gretchen had to force herself not to take the child in her arms and bolt out the door. That likely wouldn't go over well. Kidnapping was a serious crime. Well, beating a child almost to death was worse or so she thought.

Ms. Gardner didn't say a word to Gretchen. What was there to say, other than, 'we lost'? Instead, she approached little Jami.

"Jami, sweetie." She sleepily opened her eyes.

"Can I go home now, Ms. Gardner?" she asked, her pudgy hands rubbing tired eyes. Gretchen knew she wasn't talking about her father's home. She wanted to return to the nice family that took care of her and treated her like a princess—the one hoping to adopt her.

"Jami, the court's decided your daddy feels terrible about what he did, and they think you'd be better off living with him."

Jami didn't seem to grasp what was said. She sat in silent stillness.

"Come on, sweetie," Ms. Gardner said. "Your daddy's waiting for you."

Jami's head bobbed in a nod as she slipped off Gretchen's lap. She stood there, not moving for several moments. Then, like a flash, she was running toward the front door. After a short, stunned second, Ms. Gardner and Kyle, her assistant, went running after her.

Gretchen caught herself before shouting, 'Run Jami, run!' She might not have said it, but she was definitely thinking it—praying she could getaway. But where would a five-year-old girl escape to?

It was only seconds later when they returned—Kyle carrying the screaming, flailing child in his arms. "You can't make me go back! I don't want to live with my daddy. I want Mommy Jill. Let go of me!"

"Ms. Winters." Gretchen's head snapped up at the sharp tone of Ms. Gardner's voice. "What were you doing? Why did you just stand there like an idiot when Jami ran? You didn't even attempt to catch her. You were the closest one to her."

"I…I'm sorry. But this is wrong. How can we send her back to that monster?" Gretchen stammered. She clenched her hands to keep them from shaking—or wringing someone's neck.

"What do you suppose we do—short of letting a five-year-old child run loose in Honolulu?" Ms. Gardner asked.

"I don't know. We just can't let her go back to *him*."

"Listen, Gretchen, I understand how upset you are. I'm feeling quite angry at the justice system myself. But we have no choice. The judge has made his decision, and we have to respect that. Whatever happens is on *his* conscience now. I've done all I can."

"Whatever happens, *Jami* will have to live with it—if she survives," Gretchen answered.

"Get your filthy hands off my daughter." Gretchen looked back to Kyle. Jami's father was yelling as he wrestled his kicking, screaming daughter from the assistant's grip. Mr. Tollman yanked Jami free and pulled her to his chest. She seemed to give up the fight as she held still

"Don't worry, baby," he said. "Daddy won't ever let you go again."

Gretchen strode forward, not stopping until her nose was just inches from Mr. Tollman's. He jerked back, surprised at her for a moment, before he sneered. Anger burned Gretchen so hot that she felt as if she might spontaneously combust. "Mr. Tollman," she whispered, "you may have won this, but if you hurt your daughter again, you will regret it. You might as well take a gun and put a bullet in your head."

"Gretchen!" Mrs. Gardner clamped down on her arm and pulled her back. "What in the world are you doing?"

Mr. Tollman stumbled back into the wall—his

daughter hanging loosely in his arms, his eyes locked on Gretchen's.

"Nothing," Gretchen answered. "I'm not doing a thing."

Gretchen turned away and strode purposely toward the exit.

CHAPTER 5

Gretchen crushed the corner of the red, tasseled throw pillow in her fist. "I don't know what I was thinking," she said. "I wasn't thinking actually. Someday, I hope to be able to practice law. I can't be threatening people. I especially can't be telling them they should put a bullet in their head."

Dr. Yauney's demeanor remained calm, as always. Gretchen had never seen him surprised, upset, or unhinged. The seasoned therapist was as steady as a rock. "Yes, that may have been a bit over the top. What was going through your mind at the time?"

Gretchen swallowed the lump in her throat. "I kept seeing pictures of the girl's battered, little body. They played through my mind, over and over again. He did that. He hurt her. He could have killed her, and he the one person in the world who should have protected her. How can a person do that to a child? How can they do that to their own daughter?"

"Are we still talking about your client's father, or are we talking about your birth mother?" Dr. Yauney asked.

Gretchen wanted to scowl at him, wanted to be

angry. But she couldn't. She didn't have the energy. Her face crumpled. "I don't think I'm going into the right profession. I can't be objective. I have too much emotion tied up into dealing with victims — especially children."

"What would it take to change your emphasis?" Dr. Yauney glanced down at his notebook.

"I'm pretty far into my internship," Gretchen said. "Still, it might be best to change it now. It'll only be harder when I'm already a practicing attorney."

"Gretchen. I'm going to tell you something I think you need to hear." He put his papers down, linked his fingers together, and peered at her over his wire-rimmed glasses. "I don't think you should make this decision at right now. There is obviously something upsetting you."

"Well, yeah. I threatened a man in a court building. I have been off my game lately." She gave a weak smile.

"I think you were struggling before the courthouse incident. Why did you decide a month ago to resume meeting with me? You seemed to have moved beyond the issues of your past. You'd been so happy, so carefree. But the woman I see before me is troubled and unsure. I would just like you to tell me what happened to change things."

"Nothing happened. I have a boyfriend who loves me, I have a wonderful internship with one of the best attorneys in Honolulu, and I have the money to pay all my bills with enough left over to have fun on the weekends. My life is great."

"That sounds wonderful, but I'm sure the internship comes with its own stress."

Gretchen hugged the pillow to her chest. "It can be stressful." She sighed. "I just wish Hal would listen to me."

"Is this the boyfriend you are so happy with?"

"I am happy. At least, I used to be. Things were better when Sara was here."

"Your best friend." Dr. Vincent spoke it as a statement.

"Yes. We were as close as any two sisters. I could tell her almost anything."

"I think it odd you two only met a year ago, yet you both act as if you'd been friends for years."

Gretchen shrugged. "We just connected. I can't explain it."

"How long ago did she move away?"

"It's been a month."

Dr. Vincent's brows crinkled. Wow, a reaction.

Gretchen's eyes widened. "You think I'm back in therapy because my best friend got married and moved to the other side of the world?"

"Are you?"

"Now that would be ridiculous. I'm a grown woman. Why should the fact my best friend left..." Gretchen couldn't continue. A lump got stuck in her throat, and she clutched the pillow in a vice grip. "I'm scared," she whispered.

"What are you afraid of?" Dr. Vincent's eyes

warmed with concern.

"I'm afraid it's all going to come crashing down. The world I built, I mean. The relationships I've made. I love my life, but always in the back of my mind, I know it could end. I've witnessed the other side—the evil, cold, and dark side. It gives me nightmares even now."

"It might help if you'd talk about it."

"I've tried."

"Yes, I know. Your previous therapist was wrong to dismiss your early memories. Whether or not they happened, they were real to you."

"He thought I should be committed."

"He was wrong. You are a smart, capable woman. Smart enough to take another look at those memories and begin to process and understand them."

"I may be smart enough, but I just don't see the point in dredging up the past. I have such a bright future. Shouldn't I be focused on that?"

"Absolutely. But should you ever decide to delve into the past, I'm a good listener."

Gretchen smiled. "Yes, you are."

Dr. Yauney looked up at the clock. "Before we end here, I want to have you do something for me. During the next week, I want you to brainstorm reasons you feel out of control. You might want to retrace your steps and figure out when things started to look bad. Will you do that for me?"

"I take it you think I already know the answer."

"I *know* you do. You just need to open up your

mind to it."

⚡ ⚡

An hour later, Gretchen stepped into the law offices of Donnellson, Gardner, and Cole. Things had been strained since the horrific day at the courthouse. She and Ms. Gardener initially worked well together. But after…?

Yeah. It hadn't been pretty.

The cool air-conditioning raised goose pimples on her skin. The receptionist looked up from behind a mahogany desk, and her eyes widened. "Ms. Winters… um, Ms. Gardner would like to see you immediately." Her eyes darted toward the door leading to the offices and back to Gretchen. A look of pity was written clearly across the girl's face.

A lump formed in Gretchen's throat. "Thank you."

She walked back through the wide hall. The nameplate—Andrea Gardner, Attorney-at-Law—shone from the door at the end. Gretchen stepped down to it and knocked softly.

"Come in."

Ms. Gardner always exuded an aura of true professionalism. Her suits were pressed so crisp you could cut a pineapple against it, she wore her make-up simple, always perfect, and nothing *ever* upset her.

Today, she was upset.

Gretchen stepped inside and closed the door.

"I got a call from Jami Tollman's caseworker. Her

father fatally shot himself. Jami has been returned to the foster care system."

"No," Gretchen breathed.

"Yes. Apparently, he took your advice. According to Jami, he slapped her after she spilled a glass of juice. Then he calmly walked to another room, pulled out a gun, and shot himself in the temple."

"But I…I…" Gretchen's stomach soured.

"Listen, I know you didn't mean what you said. You were upset. But word has gotten back to the judge in this case, and now I'm in the hot seat. I am being asked to dismiss you or face a reprimand."

Gretchen could feel her heart crumble in her chest. She couldn't think of anything to say or do to repair this. There was nothing she could do. She stood, her limbs trembling.

"I'm sorry, Gretchen. I *have* to dismiss you. You can clean out your desk after you speak to Detective Baum."

"Detective Baum?"

Ms. Gardner nodded. "He's waiting in the conference room."

Gretchen breathed deeply as she stepped toward the door. She hesitated, turning back. "Ms. Gardner, is Jami…?"

"She's back with the same foster family. They've already started adoption proceedings."

Gretchen cracked a weak smile and left the room. The door to the conference room stood open. The detective had his back to her when she entered.

"Hello, Ms. Winters," he said, looking out a window.

"Detective?" Her voice sounded steadier than she felt.

He turned toward her. His face was round, he had a shadow of white whiskers sprinkled across his jaw, and his eyes pierced her. "I have a question that's been plaguing my mind. How is it you tell a man if he hits his daughter again that he should put a bullet in his head, and low and behold, he hits her and does just what you told him to do?"

"I don't know, sir."

"This case doesn't add up. This man was messed up, but he'd never shown any suicidal tendencies. And here I have a young, wannabe attorney who seems to be able to predict the future."

"Maybe I'm psychic, and I was doing my best to warn him."

"You're not psychic."

She shrugged.

He stomped forward until he towered over her. "Something smells in this. And that smell is you."

"Are you charging me with a crime, Detective?"

He tightened his jaw so severely that she could almost hear his teeth grind.

"I didn't think so."

"I could hold you for forty-eight hours for questioning."

Descending

"But you'd have to show probable cause for holding me. My guess is you don't have that, or you'd be bringing me in now. Detective Baum, I did *not* personally threaten Mr. Roberts. I'd never met him until that day in the courthouse, and I have not seen, nor spoken to him since. I cannot in anyway be found at fault for his death. Unless you think I have some magical power of suggestion, you have nothing on me. Now do you have any intelligent questions to ask me?"

His blood seemed to literally boil beneath his skin, making his face all red and blotchy.

"I didn't think so." She turned and strode through the door. Ms. Gardner stood leaning against her doorframe. She'd obviously heard every word. Giving a weak smile, she said, "I wish we could keep you on here. You'll make a great attorney one day." With that said, Ms. Gardner returned to her office and shut the door.

Gretchen didn't have much to pack: a picture of her parents and brother, a picture of her and Sara at a rugby game, and her lucky shark's tooth necklace. Everything else in the office was provided by Ms. Gardner. Gretchen placed her few treasures in her purse and headed out.

The walk was a short one. Her apartment was just a mile from the law offices. Her building was a tall, brick throwback to the eighties, but at least it was well maintained. She glanced up to her apartment from the sidewalk below. The curtains were pulled shut, but she was almost positive she'd opened them that morning.

The only other person with a key was Sara. Hal had kept bugging her about giving one to him, but she'd made the mistake of moving too fast in her last relationship. She didn't want to mess this one up, so they'd agreed to take things slow.

Maybe Sara was here. Perhaps this day wouldn't go down as the worst day of her entire adult life.

She jogged up the stairs and tried the door, but it was locked. Sara had always been a bit paranoid. Perhaps she'd locked it.

Gretchen used her key and entered her apartment. The place was a mess. There were clothes strewn across the floor—a short, pink skirt, strappy, white sandals, Hal's favorite jeans, and a lacy, yellow bra…

She stopped herself before she started yelling. Hal's keys sat on the coffee table. How did he get into her apartment? Did he steal a key?

Laughter came from the bedroom. *That cheating, lying, thieving…*Gretchen's whole body began to shake. She wasn't sure if it she was about to go into a crying fit or a homicidal rampage. She sure didn't want to cry, but then killing her cheating boyfriend would not make things any better—as an intern, she'd seen up close and personal what prison life was like. But she'd better find a way to diffuse her temper, and she'd better do it fast. Hal's hairstyling bag—the greatest treasure of Honolulu's up-and-coming hair designer—sat unguarded on the floor next to the sofa. And it was filled with the highest-quality equipment money could buy—worth thousands. Should she? She looked toward the window. It was three stories down to the pavement. She could easily toss it out and have her revenge. He wouldn't be able to work until he replaced his tools.

She relished the thought, but sighed, knowing she couldn't do it. Darn her for having a conscience. Why should she? No one else seemed to.

It only took one trip down three flights to carry the bag and all his and the slut's clothes down to the street. She placed them on the sidewalk next to Gus, the neighborhood transient. He gave her a toothless grin as he sat on the curb. She smiled back, her spirits immediately lighter.

When she got back to her apartment, she knocked on the bedroom door. She heard a thump and scrambling. "Hal," she called out. "I took the liberty of helping you remove your items and carried them downstairs for you. You don't need to thank me. It's the least I can do for all you've done for me. They'll be waiting for you on the sidewalk beside Gus."

"What?" he shrieked.

The door flew open and he stood there, wrapped in a towel. "Not my bag too."

She nodded, smiling.

"You left it next to a homeless guy?" he shrieked at her.

She raised an eyebrow.

He wasted no time, streaking through the door.

He was soon followed behind by a red-faced,

strawberry-blonde female in another towel. She slinked around Gretchen as if she expected her to strike her. The thought *had* crossed her mind, but she was already in enough trouble today. "Hello," Gretchen greeted. "I left your clothes by the curb too. Good luck getting them back from Gus. He's partial to women's clothing."

"You're insane," the woman cried as she flew down the stairs.

Gretchen shut the door, sagging against the frame.

Okay, this was definitely the worst day of her adult life.

Stepping into her bedroom, her anger boiled. Why couldn't she find a decent man? Why did every relationship she had go up in flames?

She stripped the rumpled sheets off the bed. They were her favorite, satin, and worth a week's pay. Balling them up, she stuffed them into the garbage. She got out her spare cotton ones and made up her bed.

Hitting the bathroom hard with cleanser, she disinfected it from ceiling to floor. She knew she was probably overdoing it, but she couldn't help but think that everything Hal and his slut touched was contaminated. She used an entire can of Lysol just to be sure.

She left the bathroom door open while she showered—she didn't want to succumb to the fumes. The water soothed her, the stream caressing her body. She spent a long time under the spray, until it turned cold.

Descending

She thought about calling Sara as she slipped on her robe, but frowned when she did the math. It was only five o'clock in the morning in Bermuda. She'd have to call her tomorrow.

Late that night, she finally climbed under the cotton sheets. They felt like sandpaper against her skin. She tossed and turned until she finally fell into a restless sleep.

A sweet melody glided through the seawater—drawing her forward. Gretchen swam, her legs kicking out hard as she followed the voice. It was beautiful, like an angel, but chilling. She looked down through the surface of the water to see light coming from below. Diving down, she found the entrance to a tunnel. Soon, there was another sound mingled with the first. She could hear it as she neared; it was harsh and high pitched…She broke through the surface of a dark cave, slapping her hands over her ears at an ear-piercing wail.

It was little Jami. She sat, crying, on a rocky shore. Her howling voice echoed off the walls of a sea cave. A woman stood nearby, one who radiated cold beauty. Gretchen's stomach sickened at the familiar face.

"Hello dear." The woman smiled, evil glinting in her eye.

"What are you going to do to her?" Gretchen asked—her voice weak and trembling as she looked at the terrified girl.

"Does it matter? She's nothing to me."

"Please, just let her go," Gretchen begged, tears

burning her eyes.

The woman's laugh was like ice. "If you insist."

Gretchen and Jami's screams mingled as the woman pitched Jami forward into the water. Gretchen reached for her, pulled her sputtering face up out of the water, and crushed her to her chest.

"Ms. Winters," Jami wailed. "Please help me; I don't want to die."

"I've got you." Gretchen held her tight in one arm as her other hand grasped the rocky water's edge. She looked around for an exit, not able to bring Jami out the same way she'd entered. She was much too small to hold her breath that long. But there didn't seem to be another exit.

"Where did the mean lady go?" Jami asked.

Gretchen looked around, horrified. "Let's get you out of the water." She pushed her up to the rocky shore. A scream pierced Gretchen's ear as something pulled Jami down—her cry cutting off as her face submerged. Gretchen tried to hold on to her wrist, but she wasn't strong enough. Jami slipped through her fingers.

Gretchen dove down, attempting to catch hold of her again and pull her back. She could see Jami's horrified face grow smaller, smaller, going deeper and deeper, until she disappeared.

Gretchen shot up in bed, drenched in sweat. Her body trembled. "It was only a dream," she whispered over and over again as she sat and rocked.

CHAPTER 6

Kyros barely made it to the toilet before he lost last night's dinner. Who knew walking on legs would make him so sick? It didn't seem to bother the others. They'd taken the transition without any problem—well, other than being repulsed by their new human bodies.

Kyros just couldn't handle the way the legs made him feel. The rocking back and forth from one foot to the next and the jarring he got from each step made against the hard floor. Hades, just thinking about it made his stomach turn.

He dove into the indoor pool and entered salty bliss. He didn't even mind the excruciating pain of the change from human to Dagonian. It was worth getting his fin back. These daily swims seemed to be the only relief he could get. Swimming in the water was heaven. He closed his eyes and imagined he was back in the sea. He would have made an actual trip to the sea if he'd had time, but he was on call for babysitting duty.

An hour later, he could see Straton standing above him through the rippling surface. "Kyros, Xanthus wants to see you," his muffled voice shouted.

Kyros grunted in reply. A few minutes later, he staggered out of the pool room.

"Your land legs still making you sick?" Straton smiled.

"Shut up."

"Kyros." Xanthus's voice came from the kitchen. "We're in here."

A foul stench assaulted Kyros the moment he entered the kitchen. "Oh gods. And I just got my stomach settled."

"Lucky you," Xanthus answered. "Hades, I don't think I'll ever get used to human food."

Sara sat across from Xanthus and ate heartily. "You know, most people love my cooking."

Kyros covered his nose and mouth. "Yeah, well, that's the problem."

"What?" she asked.

"Cooking." Kyros said. "Dagonians don't cook. We hunt, and we eat what we've caught. Animal meat heated and burned beyond recognition—well, it's like…I don't even have anything to compare it to. But it's worse than rotting flesh."

"Ugh. Now I think *I've* lost my appetite." Sara scrunched up her nose. "You asked for it."

Kyros turned to his friend and coughed. "You did?"

"I'm trying to get used to it."

"Impossible," Kyros said. "There's no getting used to that." He gestured to the plate filled with dead meat.

"Perhaps I should try feeding you vegetarian food," Sara said.

"Veget...you mean plants?" Kyros asked.

"Yeah."

"Dagonians don't eat plants," Xanthus said.

"I give up." Sara stood. "Just eat your live fish in front of those politicians you want to impress. They won't think *anything* of it. Oh, and don't forget to rip the fish's head off first. I'm *sure* they won't mind." Sara stomped out the door, mumbling to herself.

"I'm going to pay for that later," Xanthus said.

"Pay for what?" Kyros looked around.

"Sara's mad at me."

"Mad? Why?"

"Kyros, you have a lot to learn about women."

"Yeah, well, Dagonian women are different from humans...and mermaids for that matter."

"Right. But..."

"But what?"

Xanthus shook his head. "I don't know what to do. Sara's not making the adjustment well."

"Her adjustment on legs?"

"No, no. The legs are fine. I don't know what the problem is. Perhaps she's just having difficulty adjusting to her new home."

"She's not the only one," Kyros said.

"I know what you mean. Look, I've got to travel tomorrow, and I'll be gone for a few days. I'm going to need you to keep a close eye on her. Make sure she doesn't do anything stupid."

"Like cooking dinner for all of us?" Kyros shook his head at the thought.

"No, like putting herself in danger."

Xanthus paused for a moment, looking like he wanted to speak. Out of respect for his friend, Kyros waited.

"Listen," Xanthus said. "I know you don't like Sara, and I understand why, but you need to know how much she means to me. If anything happens to her…I don't think I could survive it."

Kyros paused, stunned by Xanthus's words. He'd had suspicions Xanthus was under the mermaid's spell. Why else would he choose to destroy everything he once held dear—his honor, his status, his reputation…? She'd even convinced him to move to Bermuda when he should have been moving closer to Washington DC. Xanthus's words now seemed to confirm Kyros's suspicions.

Xanthus turned to leave.

"Xanthus."

He turned back. "Yes?"

"I do have one question."

"What's that?"

"Why did she choose to live here?"

Xanthus shrugged. "I don't know." He sighed. "Sara insisted this was where we needed to be. She doesn't seem to understand it herself. But she was adamant."

"And you let her make this decision because…?"

Descending

"You wouldn't understand."

"No, I think I understand perfectly." Because the little mermaid had his best friend in her beautiful clutches, and she could bend him to her will.

CHAPTER 7

Deep in her cave of lost treasures, Aella held a small mirror. The golden handle burned cold in her grasp. She trembled as she admired the most valuable treasure to be brought to her mountains of plunder—the Mirror of Theia. And it had been within her reach all these years. If only...

No, she wouldn't regret. Now was a time for celebration.

After fifteen years, she had a chance. The fates had finally showed her favor. They were giving her the opportunity to right a wrong she'd perpetrated years ago. She could finally rectify her mistake.

She spoke in a commanding voice. "Show me the one who would destroy me."

Her reflection shimmered as another beautiful face came into view—a woman. Dark hair framed her delicate features; her eyes glimmered—filled with deep secrets and regret. And she was near. The gods were undoubtedly on Aella's side this day.

She gingerly placed the mirror on a carved, wooden chest. Sprinting to the water's edge, she dove into the sea. Her legs changed as the sea enveloped them.

Descending

She relished the change. She hated playing the part of a human, hated her exile. She was a mermaid. A mythical being with power humans could only dream of. The humans were rodents, soiling and polluting the land everywhere they went. They were lower than the lowest of creatures. But still, they served her purpose.

Aella surfaced at the side of a sleek, oceanic yacht, with a ladder hanging down. She pulled herself out of the water—her mermaid's tail changing to legs the moment they left the sea. She stepped her bare feet up the rungs and onto the deck. Her favorite blue dress clung to her wet body. The breeze had a refreshing bite to it.

A large, muscular human stepped up at her approach—his eyes lingering over her body. "Aella! Where did you come from? I thought you'd take your treasure and run."

"Oh Robert, you know me better than that."

"Do I?" he asked, frowning at her.

"Of course you do." She ran her fingertips over his chest as she smiled. "I'm going to need you to stay a while. I have another task for you."

"Sorry, babe. I've already spent too much time here. I've got a job to do, and it has nothing to do with looting and treasure hunting. There are a few pirates that need their throats slit."

Aella added just the right amount of singsong in her voice to gain his attention. "No. You're not going to kill pirates. You have someone much closer you need to kill."

His scowl melted away as he drew near her. "I do?"

She turned up the tone of her voice. "Yes, and you will do everything I ask."

Adoration filled his eyes as he repeated, "Yes, I'll do everything you ask." He reached out to touch her face.

She fisted his shirt in her hands and pulled him close. "I know you will."

And then their lips touched.

CHAPTER 8

Kyros watched the second hand of the clock twitch its way around the face. Sara's back was to him, but he could hear her fingers fly over the keyboard of her laptop. Her hand shot out, grabbed the mouse, and made a few clicks. "You know, Kyros, despite being on duty, you don't have to watch me every second. I'm sure you have other things you'd rather be doing."

Kyros jumped at her tone of voice. This was the first time she'd spoken harshly to him. Before, she had always used a sickeningly sweet tone. Maybe her true colors were emerging.

"I'm not watching you," he answered.

"Yes, you are. I can feel your eyes boring into my back."

He didn't respond. Xanthus made him swear not to upset her. Keeping silent was the only way to guarantee he wouldn't say something he would later regret.

Sara turned toward him, and he was taken back. She was livid. "Listen, I have no idea why you don't like me, but your glares are getting on my nerves. Now I know you're Xanthus's best friend, and I'd hoped to win you over by being nice, but it looks like that's not working."

"I've never said an unkind word to you," he said.

"You didn't need to. Your expressions say it all. I would like to know what I did to deserve this animosity."

Kyros narrowed his eyes and didn't say a word.

"See what I mean? You're doing it again."

"If you want to win me over so badly," Kyros said, "why don't you just sing a few lines? Use your mermaid charm, like you did on Xanthus."

"You think I…?"

Kyros pursed his lips. He knew he should stop talking. He was pushing his luck. She may just decide to take him up on his suggestion, but he couldn't stop himself from voicing his suspicions. They'd been festering and tormenting him since the moment he'd heard his best friend had married a mermaid.

"I would *never* do that to Xanthus."

"Right."

"I wouldn't! And even if I wanted to—which I don't—I couldn't. My father made him immune to my voice. Besides, the compulsion only works while I'm singing. And you haven't noticed me singing around here, have you?"

"It only works *while* you're singing?"

"Of course."

"But that's not right. The power lingers much longer."

"And how would you know?"

"I know."

"Right, because you've met a mermaid before," she said sarcastically. "Well, I happen to *be* a mermaid, and I think you're full of it."

Kyros clenched his fists. He'd never before hit a female, but right now, the temptation nearly overwhelmed him. Yeah, and the way Xanthus worshiped Sara, Kyros would probably find himself at the mercy of Triton the moment Xanthus saw a mark on her.

The doorbell rang, and the house fell silent. Kyros listened closely. No one moved, no one spoke, he doubted anyone even breathed—well, except for Sara.

"Isn't anyone going to get that?" she asked.

Kyros looked at her incredulously.

"What? Thanks to my father, you all speak English now. You are all perfectly capable of answering the door."

"Oh, forget it." She moved to step from the room, and Kyros put his arm out and braced it against the doorframe, stopping her. "Sara, one of *us* needs to answer it."

"Oh, good grief. It's probably only a salesman."

The bell rang again.

"Listen," Sara said, "it's rude to leave someone standing on the doorstep this long. Why don't you just come with me, and you can guard me while I answer the door."

Kyros sighed and gave a nod. "Okay, but I go first."

"Fine, let's go."

Kyros opened the door to find a human standing on the front step. He guessed it shouldn't have come as a surprise. Who did he think would be there? A Dagonian in a giant fish bowl? But what he didn't expect…this human was attractive. Not in a classic sense. She wouldn't be causing any frenzy, but her appeal was undeniable. She had brown, wavy hair cut just below the shoulders. And her eyes…big, brown, beautiful—and open wide. *Was she afraid of him?*

She shook her head, blinking. "I'm sorry. I don't mean to gawk. I'm just surprised at how tall you are. You must be a relative of Xanthus. Are all the men in Xanthus's family so tall?"

She didn't *sound* afraid.

"Who are you?" he asked, avoiding her question.

"I'm Gretchen, Sara's best friend."

He looked back. Sara was gone. Good. Sara couldn't be seen out of her wheelchair by anyone who knew her. How could she have explained her miraculous recovery?

"Can you tell her I'm here?" The human grinned sweetly.

Kyros nearly returned her charming smile. Instead, he scowled. This was a human. He couldn't forget that. He couldn't let his guard down.

"I'll see if she's here." He shut the door, leaving her on the step, and turned back. Sara raced in, wheeling through the hall, a blanket wrapped around her lower body.

"Why did you shut the door?" she asked.

"I was coming to get you," he said.

"It's rude to close the door in someone's face while they are standing on your doorstep."

Kyros shook his head. "I'm not here to play nice with the humans. I'm here to keep you safe."

Sara glared at him. "You need to play nice with *this* human. She's my best friend.

Sara opened the door, and her face immediately lit up. "Gretchen!" She squealed like a child as the human rushed in and wrapped her arms around her in a quick hug. "What a surprise. What are you doing here? I thought you had an internship."

"I did." She stepped back. "It's a long story. I'll tell you…" Her eyes drifted down at her blanket and widened. "You look different! Your legs…they look strange. What's going on?"

"Um, my dad…"

"You found your dad?"

Sara nodded.

"You're kidding me. Who is he? Where does he live? And what does he have to do with your legs?"

"My dad's name is Ty. Oddly enough, he lives near where Xanthus is from."

"Your dad is Greek?"

"Most definitely."

"Wow, what are the odds? So what about your legs…?"

This human was tenacious. Kyros sized Gretchen

up as he followed them down the hall. She was as small as a Dagonian child—about five feet. But her shape... absolutely *not* childlike, with curves in just the right places.

"My dad found a brilliant surgeon. He says he can fix my legs."

"You're kidding! Really?"

Sara's face turned bright red as she nodded. Kyros frowned at her. She was a terrible liar.

"That is so amazing!" Gretchen squealed. "I knew you shouldn't give up. Do you think you'll be able to learn to walk?"

"The doctors seem optimistic."

"Wow, I'm so happy for you." Gretchen leaned forward to give Sara another hug.

Sara sighed as Gretchen stood back up. "I've missed you."

"Me too," Gretchen answered.

Gretchen smiled, but there seemed to be a hint of sadness in her eyes. She glanced back to Kyros, and her eyes lightened. "And is this..."

"Xanthus's best friend, Kyros," Sara answered.

Gretchen raised an eyebrow. "I guess tall men like to stick together." As if to illustrate her point, Stanton, Drakōn, and Pallas were standing in the living room as they stepped through the door.

Gretchen's eyebrows rose. "Looks like I'm more right than I thought." A wide smile spread across her face. Her dimples were a bit distracting and made the human look even more adorable. She was nothing like he had imagined a human would be.

"Hello, boys," she said cheerfully.

The three Dagonians gaped at her; Kyros was shocked himself. Did she just call these Dagonian warriors boys? Was this not an insult? Her demeanor was friendly, even if her words were offensive.

"The hu...girl just said hello. Are you not going to greet her in return?" Kyros asked, his gaze as hard as granite. He didn't know why he stood up for the human, but he knew she'd meant no offense.

They gave a quick nod and grumbling hellos.

"Wow, I could use a sweater after that warm welcome," Gretchen said. Kyros caught the sarcasm in her statement and nearly smiled.

"Okay, out! All of you," Sara said, pointing to the door. "We have some catching up to do." Kyros pressed his lips together. They filed out obediently, making their way to the back door. The house Xanthus had bought had the most amazing view of the ocean. The scent of the sea breezed over the waves. Kyros decided not to join the others. Instead, he made his way to the library.

The book he wanted sat prominently on the desk: *The Mer—A Complete History*. He sank into a chair, opened the cover, and leafed through the pages. The first chapter was all about Triton. The next chapter was about Triton's children—when they were born, what each of their gifts and abilities were...*Gifts? Abilities?*

The first Mer listed in the book was Phiobe— born five thousand years ago. She spent much of her time among the reefs, playing with the sharks. She had the gift of speech. She could speak all the languages of sea—shark, dolphin, whale, even crab and bony fish. She loved her sea friends so much that she refused to eat them. Instead, she ate seaweed and kelp.

Kyros frowned. That mermaid was unlike any he'd heard of before.

Medon was next; he was a merman who had the ability to freeze water. Not only that, but he could form deadly weapons, freezing seawater in the form of a trident, sword, spear, and shield…With the raise of his hand or the flick of his wrist, he could send a blade straight at you, seemingly from nowhere. He didn't do much killing with his gift, however. Instead, he traveled to the far north, where he created a grand ice castle. Some say it was still standing, abandoned.

Delia's gift was one of healing. She could suffer horrific injuries and heal quickly from them. Boasting of her ability, she had her brother, Alexon, cut off her finger. After one short day, she'd grown another in its place. Claiming the new finger was better than her old one, she had Alexon cut off all her other fingers. When each of them regrew, they were far superior to her old ones. Painful though it was, she didn't stop there. Next, she had her brother cut off one arm, then the other, and lastly her tail. The amputated parts regrew—lovelier and more perfect. Enamored by the beauty of her new body, she thought if only she could get a more beautiful face, with luminous hair. Then, she'd be the most beautiful of all Triton's daughters. Emboldened by her previous successes, she had her brother cut off her head. Sadly, this was the end of Delia.

Kyros shook his head and cracked a smile.

Aella…Kyros scowled at the name. This mermaid he'd heard of.

She was the most powerful of all the Mer. Born four thousand years ago—with fair skin and dark hair— her beauty was admired throughout the sea. Kyros skimmed over the section.

Aella's voice was unmatched in its power. She could wield it with the utmost control—no one could resist. Not only that, but she could transform into a human easily—without the help of her father. Sara could have used that power to better mix with the humans. But Aella didn't mix with the humans—she terrorized them. Kyros turned back to reread one paragraph again; the horror of it was hard to fathom.

"When Aella tired of tormenting humans from afar, she rose from the depths to walk among them. She chose the Mycenaens as the first humans to visit. After she'd smiled and greeted them, she opened her mouth and unleashed a song filled with violence and warfare. Fathers killed sons, husband slaughtered wives, and mothers murdered their children. Every last man, woman, and child along the southern coast of Greece lay dead in her wake. Her laughter pealed across the mountains when she looked over what she'd done."

Kyros couldn't fathom such evil. This was brutal,

heartless treatment—even for vile humans. Aella was ultimately punished for her actions. Her father, Triton, banished her. She would live alone, forever without the company of her sisters and brothers—a hard punishment for a Mer.

This story, though it sickened him, did not surprise Kyros. He'd heard tales similar to this one. Aella was not the only Mer to wreak terror. The Mer had tormented Dagonians in much the same way as Aella did the humans. When Poseidon ordered the Dagonians to destroy the Mer, the Dagonians were understandably eager to carry out his command.

Kyros read on. He was surprised to discover each Mer had a unique gift and personality. There were no two alike. And although some were brutal and cruel, others were caring and compassionate. He considered the possibility Sara might not be as bad as he'd thought. He also wondered if she had a gift, and if she did, what it might be.

He continued to read on, filing away little facts in his brain. Triton fathered a total of seventy-two children. At the time of their destruction, he'd also had over a hundred grandchildren and a dozen great-grandchildren.

"Doing a little light reading?"

Kyros looked up. The human was smirking at him. He looked down at the book and tried to ignore her. Gretchen sauntered over and leaned against the desk—too close to ignore.

"Where's Sara?" Kyros shifted in his chair.

"Oh, she's talking to Xanthus. He called just a minute ago."

She furrowed her brows and narrowed her eyes. "What language is that?"

"Greek."

"No, it's not. I know Greek, and that's not Greek."

"It's ancient Greek."

She looked startled and leaned in for a better look. Kyros responded by closing the book and placing it in a drawer.

She sat back and eyed him curiously. "What's a guy like you doing reading ancient Greek?"

"A guy like me?"

"Tall, dark, with an attitude that says, piss me off and die.'"

Kyros almost smiled at that one. This human was not far off. She shrugged away from the desk and stepped toward him, each step deliberate, seductive. He could feel the warmth of her body radiating from her. The attraction he felt toward her hit him—immediate and powerful. He wanted nothing more than to drag her against him and take a taste of those full lips. The harsh reality of his desire for a human was a slap in the face.

He stood up, pushed her back, and snarled, "Keep your distance."

Gretchen stumbled back, nearly falling—catching herself against the doorframe.

He'd definitely caught her off guard. Her expression was a strange mixture of surprise, hurt, and anger. The surprise and hurt melted away, leaving the anger.

"Listen, jerk, I don't know what planet you come from, but you can't just push people when they get too close for comfort. I could have you arrested for assault."

Kyros continued to glare at her.

"But since you're Xanthus's best friend, I won't. Just don't ever touch me again, or I'll have you on the floor, screaming for mercy before you have time to pee your pants."

Hades, she was beautiful *and* had a sharp tongue. He cursed himself for noticing.

He stepped toward her, towering above her, and hissed, "Try it."

She slapped her hands against his chest, attempting to push him back. Her effort was pathetic. She had no strength to back up her threat. He might have been impressed with her courage if he wasn't so busy being ticked off at her.

"Kyros!" The sharpness of Sara's voice cut through the charged energy in the room. "Xanthus wants to talk to you."

He turned toward the mermaid. She thrust her cell phone at him. Oh yeah, here was another ticked-off female. She had nothing on him right now. Neither of them could possibly be as angry as he was.

He stepped out the door, putting the phone to his ear. "I sure hope you're on your way back home."

Xanthus chuckled. "Having a little problem on

the island? Are the locals giving you trouble?"

"The newest local human is."

"Yeah, Sara said Gretchen showed up."

Kyros grunted.

"What do you think of her?"

"What do you think?" Kyros snapped.

"Hey, I was just asking."

"I think she's as appealing as a harpoon in my backside."

"Really…?"

"What's that supposed to mean?"

"Nothing. Hades, you're touchy."

Kyros didn't say anything. He was tired of being baited.

"Listen," Xanthus said, "I invited Gretchen to stay a while."

"Wonderful," Kyros growled, glowering.

"I'm glad you think so. I want you to keep a close eye on her."

"On the human? Why under Olympus would this human need to be watched?"

"I have my reasons."

"You're getting dangerously close to overextending your favor. You only saved my life."

Xanthus chuckled. "Watching a human is worse than dying?"

"I said close."

CHAPTER 9

The wind whipped through Gretchen's hair as she pushed Sara in her wheelchair along the brightly colored shops in Hamilton. Gretchen smiled, thinking about her friend. She sure was funny about shopping. Sara now had enough money to buy anything and everything she wanted, but she still gravitated toward the sales and bargains. Even then, it was nearly impossible to convince her to actually buy anything. Once a cheapskate, always…

A sigh from behind interrupted her personal musing. Kyros obviously wasn't enjoying his shopping trip with two women. Well, he didn't need to come at all. Gretchen had no idea why he insisted. Every time she smiled, laughed, or made a joke, she could feel him glowering at her from behind her back, spoiling her good mood. If she could have just two minutes, she'd tell him exactly what she thought of him.

"Whoa, do you smell that?" Sara asked.

A tempting aroma wafted from a quaint restaurant with small, outdoor tables.

"Please tell me they have fresh sushi," Kyros said.

Gretchen turned, surprised. *Kyros spoke a coherent*

sentence? This entire trip the closest he'd gotten to speaking to them were his grunts, frowns, and low mumblings.

"I don't think so," Sara answered. "Let's look for a sushi house."

Gretchen frowned. She had no idea why Sara catered to the ornery gorilla. As if she could read her thoughts, Sara whispered to her, "Kyros has a sensitive stomach. Sushi seems to be the only thing he can keep down."

Gretchen looked back at him. He did seem a bit pale. Maybe even green. She caught herself before she asked him if he felt sick. The way he scowled at her, he wouldn't appreciate her concern. She didn't know why she was worried about him anyway. He obviously didn't care about *her.*

They made their way onto Front Street and found a sushi restaurant. The sophisticated elegance of the place screamed expensive. But Sara must have figured it was worth spending the money to feed Kyros. His rumbling stomach was beginning to drown out his sighs.

They stepped up to the door, and a man in a crisp suit greeted them. "Welcome to Orchid. Do you have a reservation?"

"No, we don't," Gretchen said.

"I'm sorry; we can't seat you without one."

Kyros stepped forward and looked around. "There seems to be a lot of tables available."

"Yes sir, but it's our policy. We only serve those

with reservations."

Kyros narrowed his eyes. "What's a reservation?"

"What? You don't know..."

Sara whispered to him. "It's when you call ahead and reserve a table."

"Couldn't I just make a reservation now?" he asked the host.

The host cleared his throat. "Now?"

"Yes, I would like to make it now, for now."

"You want a reservation for now?"

"I am speaking English. Do you not understand?"

"I understand. How many in your party?"

Kyros looked back to Gretchen and Sara. "Obviously, there are three of us."

"Three it is. And what name should I list this under?"

"Dionysius."

"Okay, I have a reservation for Dionysius party of three at..." he glanced at his watch, "four fifty-five pm."

"Would you like to be seated now?"

"What an amazing idea," Kyros said dryly.

Gretchen bit back a laugh.

They were seated and served a few minutes later.

Gretchen didn't even touch her food for a full fifteen minutes after it was set in front of her. She just couldn't take her eyes off Kyros. He had the strangest eating habits. He asked for only raw fish—dismissing the suggestion he might like his sushi with rice and seaweed.

He demanded and got thick slices of assorted, raw fish fillets, which he practically inhaled. *Where the heck did he put twenty pounds of fish?*

"What ever happened with Hal?" Sara asked.

Gretchen sighed. "He turned out to be no different than any other man I've dated."

"Really? I thought he *was* different. You know… sensitive, caring, a good listener."

"Yeah, well, apparently I wasn't the only one he was sensitive and caring toward."

"How did you find out?"

"I came home early from work."

"And they were…" Sara let that statement fall away. "In *your* apartment?"

"Oh yeah, in my *bed*."

Gretchen could feel Kyros's eyes on her. She shifted in her seat.

"I'm so sorry," Sara said.

"Yeah, well. I'm just glad I found out what kind of man he was before I made any commitments to him." Gretchen pushed herself away from the table. "I don't know about you, but I'm stuffed."

"Me too," Sara said.

Kyros didn't say anything, but he *had* to be full. Didn't he?

The breeze blew through Gretchen's hair as they left the restaurant, and it had a chill that cut through her—raising goose bumps on her skin. She moved several feet behind Kyros, letting his bulk block the wind.

Perhaps he was useful for *something* on the shopping trip.

The sun hung low in the sky, and the orange and purple clouds dripped color over the **waves**. The scent of the sea filled her nose. It was interesting how the salty ocean breeze could smell different, unique from the Hawaiian scent she was used to. Yet the familiarity of it tugged at her consciousness and twisted her insides. She narrowed her eyes and peered out to the harbor. Boats nestled among the waves, preparing to rest for the night. Everything seemed calm.

Sara stretched her arms, as if working out stiffness from too much exercise.

"Are your arms sore?" Gretchen asked.

"Oh, um yeah. I haven't wheeled around so much in a long time."

"Do you—?" Sara's gasp interrupted her. Her friend bolted out of her wheelchair and raced toward Gretchen. Sara slammed into her, sending her flying back. Gretchen wasn't sure what surprised her most, seeing her best friend running on legs, or Sara pushing her hard into a wall. A loud crack pierced Gretchen's ear as her head hit the wooden slats. Gretchen staggered away from the wall. Pain pounded against her skull as the image of the restaurant and sidewalk swam in her vision. When everything finally settled into place, she honed in on Sara's face—a mixture of shock and pain darkened her blue eyes. Crimson red bloomed like a flower under her right breast, soaking Sara's white blouse. Then her legs—the legs Gretchen had never seen before—

collapsed under her. Kyros caught Sara before she hit the pavement.

Shouts thundered in Gretchen's ear as the whole area erupted in chaos. Giant men rushed in from all sides. Gretchen recognized them—they were Xanthus's friends. All of them, it seemed. Gretchen lost sight of Sara behind the wall of men.

"Sara," she shouted, searching for her. When she didn't answer, Gretchen shouted again, her heart pounding against her chest.

Strong arms surrounded her, dragging her inside the building. She fought against them, desperate to reach her friend. "Let go," she screamed. "She needs me!"

"Gretchen," a deep, warm voice spoke in her ear—Kyros's voice. "You can't see her now. She's hurt. Straton is taking care of her. He's a doctor of sorts. She's in good hands."

"Did someone shoot her? Was that what the sound was?"

"Yes."

"But they weren't trying to shoot *her*, were they?" she asked, sagging back against his chest. "She pushed me out of the way. How did she know?" Gretchen sobbed, tears streaming down her cheeks. "If anything happens to her, if she dies because of me..." She couldn't finish the thought. Her mind couldn't even go there.

Kyros turned her to face him and pulled her into his chest. "Straton is doing everything he can." She didn't resist, but wrapped her arms around him, accepting the comfort he offered.

"Did someone call 911?" she asked.

Sirens in the background answered the question for her.

The next hour passed in a blur. Gretchen sat cold and shaking in a hospital waiting room. Her mind was filled so thick with emotion that individual thoughts found it difficult to penetrate. She looked down at her hands. Someone must have given her coffee. She held an empty Styrofoam cup.

Gretchen could hear thundering steps approaching the door just before Xanthus exploded through it.

"Hades," Kyros whispered, lifting his arm from around her shoulders. "This is not going to be pretty."

Gretchen looked over to him in a daze. She hadn't even realized his arm had been around her. The anger radiating off Xanthus was impossible to miss. Kyros stood to meet his angry glare.

Xanthus made a beeline for Kyros, grabbed him by his shirt, and slammed him up against the wall. "Tell me she's going to live!"

Gretchen could hear a nurse call for security. One of Xanthus's friends responded to the nurse's concern and seemed to be trying to calm her.

Kyros absorbed the blow and the anger. "She is," Kyros said. "The doctors say she'll be fine. Nothing vital was hit. She's expected to make a full recovery."

Xanthus loosened his grip, and his shoulders

sagged. "What happened?"

"Someone tried to shoot Gretchen. Sara pushed her out of the way and caught the bullet. As far as we could figure, the shooter came from a boat in the harbor."

"But Sara's going to be all right? She'll sustain no permanent damage?" Xanthus asked.

"She's going to be fine."

Xanthus sighed, his breathing haggard. "How much longer until I can see her?"

"They said it will be at least another hour," Kyros said.

Xanthus sank into a chair. "She was shot," he said again, as if trying to wrap his mind around the situation. "Someone shot her. Who could have done this?"

Gretchen stood. Her legs wobbled a bit. She felt weak. "Xanthus, I'm sorry. This is my fault…" Her voice caught, thick with emotion.

"Do you know who did this?" Xanthus asked, his voice laced with anger.

Kyros put out his hand to hold her back. She could feel the warmth of his body as he stepped behind her.

She shook her head. "No."

"What about Hal?" Xanthus asked.

She blew out a quick breath. "No way. He hates guns. This doesn't make sense. Who would want to kill me?"

"Could it be she was just in the wrong place at the wrong time?" Kyros asked Xanthus.

Xanthus pursed his lips. "Could be."

"Until we find out for sure," Xanthus said, "I want Sara guarded at all times. I'm having trouble getting a hold of her father. I've a feeling when he finds out, he'll want her close to him and I'll need to stay with my wife."

"What about Gretchen?" Kyros asked.

Xanthus looked at her. "Until we know any different, we'll assume she was the target. You and the others will take turns guarding her, and I'll have Drakōn hunt down the shooter."

"Just make sure he doesn't kill him too quickly," Kyros said. "We need information."

Gretchen's eyes widened as she turned back to Kyros. "Nobody's going to be killing anybody."

Kyros raised his eyebrow as his eyes darted between Gretchen and Xanthus. "Right."

She turned to face him straight on. "No. Really. No one is killing anyone. What kind of people are you?"

He gave her a hard look that chilled her to the bone. "You don't want to know."

She believed him.

CHAPTER 10

Sara had sacrificed herself for someone she cared about, and she'd nearly lost her life doing it. The thought made Kyros's head hurt. He padded down the hallway, through the darkness. The entire house slept. Well, except for Drakōn. Who knows where his investigation would take him? But Kyros knew his friend wouldn't rest until he found the person responsible.

Stepping into the library, he switched on the light and sat down at the desk. He pulled the ancient book out of the drawer he'd placed it in.

He flipped open the pages, reading the headings. He paused when he came to "The Mer: Myths and Fallacies." Maybe he could find some answers there.

"Myth #1: The song of the Mer proceeds death.

"The Truth: While this is often true, death is not necessarily imminent. The song of the Mer is used to control its victims. Oft times the hearer is not killed immediately. If motives of Mer are benign, the song may be used merely to entertain. The Mer may influence the hearer to perform various acts, depending on his or her whims. If the motives are more sinister, the Mer may convince the hearer to drown or kill themselves in various ways. Some Mer have been known to create elaborate plots to kill and/or injure others (see the story of Aella).

"Myth #2: The Mer are born of the sea.

"The Truth: While the Mer are descended from Triton and thusly sea creatures, they are almost always also descended from humans. At birth, Triton would erase the memories of the humans, and take the babe to live with him in his kingdom. Other descendants of Mer may come from unions between Triton's offspring and other creatures, including humans. This has been known to lead to unwanted births. Humans giving birth to children born from these unions were quick to kill them—driven by superstition. The Mer were often as eager to rid themselves of any baby born too human—ones born with legs or without gills."

Kyros skimmed over a few pages until he came to the subject he'd been searching for.

"Myth #7: The Mer are not capable of compassion.

"The Truth: This is perhaps one of the greatest fallacies among Dagonians. The Mer are just as capable of showing empathy and kindness as any Dagonian. But, because of the power they wield when they are cruel or vicious, they can wreak much more damage than other creatures, including a Dagonian. Thus, the cruel acts of the Mer overshadow any kind acts they may perform."

Kyros frowned. Was he wrong? Was his thinking based on ignorant stereotypes?

Perhaps.

Descending

He continued to read on for a couple of hours before his back protested. The hours of reading were mind changing and enlightening, but his body wasn't adapting to the toll gravity took on it. Standing, he stretched. He could use a good swim before he returned to bed.

He strolled into the pool room and stripped. Diving into the salty water never felt better. It slicked over his body like a lover's caress. He braced himself for the pain of the transformation from human to Dagonian. He growled as his skin tore open, his muscles morphing and tying his legs together, forming his fin. It always hurt like Hades, but it was worth it. When the pain subsided, he began his swim. He circled around, his powerful tail driving him forward. He swam as fast as he could in such a tight space. Diving down and skirting the bottom of the deep end. He swam back up, leaping out of the water, only to dive back down into the surface.

When he had swam enough to satisfy himself, he slowed his pace and circled leisurely. At last he surfaced, finding himself face to face with Gretchen. She raised an eyebrow. "Out for a late-night dip?"

Kyros plastered his tail against the side of the pool. Had she seen it? He searched her face for surprise or shock. She looked tired, her eyes shadowed. Her brown eyes stood out, dark against her pale face. But she seemed composed.

"I couldn't sleep," Kyros said smoothly, regardless of his racing heart.

"I know what you mean. Listen, I'm sorry for, you know, before. I shouldn't have come on to you. I didn't even know if you had a girlfriend, were married, or whatever. My behavior was uncalled for."

Kyros frowned. "No." He sighed and shook his head. "You have nothing to apologize for. I may have overreacted."

"So why did you?" she asked.

Kyros was surprised by her boldness. How should he answer? He couldn't very well say he didn't want to get mixed up with a human. He also couldn't say she wasn't attractive enough. Not only was that an outright lie, but he couldn't bring himself to say anything that might crush that fiery spirit of hers.

"You know, I *can* handle the truth," she said. "I'm no stranger to criticism."

"It's not you…"

"Oh please!" She chuckled. "Don't tell me you're going to give me the it's-not-you-it's-me line."

Kyros pressed his lips into a fine line. He wasn't used to females handling rejection as easily as Gretchen, and it bothered him. Probably more than it should.

"Listen," she said, "let's just forget it happened. But, just to make things clear, are you opposed to a friendship with me, or would you rather I kept my distance?"

He'd rather close the distance and pull her into his arms—that was the problem. He should break off all contact with her. Yeah, right. How could he protect her if he stayed away from her?

"I'm not opposed to a friendship," he finally said.

"Good." Gretchen crossed her legs and sat down near the pool's edge.

"As friends," she said, "would you answer a few questions for me?"

Kyros shrugged. "Sure."

"How long have you known Xanthus?"

Kyros had to stop himself before he answered truthfully. He doubted she'd believe that they'd known each other for nearly eighty years. "A long time."

"Well, I've only known Sara for a little over a year."

He blinked and held his silence. *Only a year?*

"I know. It doesn't feel like only a year. I can't explain it, but when I met Sara, I felt like I'd known her forever. It's like we had some kind of cosmic connection."

Kyros cocked his eyebrow and looked her over from head to toe.

"No! Not that kind of cosmic connection." Gretchen brushed her hair behind her ear as color rose in her cheeks. "It was more like sisters, only closer. We were like twin sisters. At least, I thought we were. But now…"

"You're wondering about her legs."

"Yes! I just don't know what to think. Did *you* know she was lying?"

Kyros knew she'd ask this question sooner or later. "I didn't know," he lied. Telling the truth would just lead to more questions, questions he couldn't answer.

"At least I wasn't the only one. I just can't believe it. Sara has legs, perfectly workable, normal legs. The whole thing with her being crippled and in a wheelchair, it was a lie. If she weren't lying in a hospital, if she hadn't nearly died to save me, I'd be pretty ticked off right now. I just don't know what to think."

"I don't know what to say about her lying," Kyros said, "but I do know this. She didn't hesitate to put herself between you and a shooter's bullet. That kind of sacrifice is not insignificant."

"I know. And I've already forgiven her for the lie. I just don't know *why* she lied."

Kyros didn't know what to say. Telling her the truth was completely out of the question.

Gretchen sighed and uncrossed her legs. He couldn't bring himself to look away. Her legs were surprisingly appealing. She turned to lie on her stomach and propped her head on her hands. "How's the water?"

"Um, it's a bit cold. I don't think you'd like it." *Great! That was all he needed, Gretchen getting in the pool.* He doubted she'd miss seeing a four and a half-foot-long, grey tailfin.

He prepared to have to push her back. He didn't care if she started hating him again for being rude. There was no way he could let her see his body.

She furrowed her eyebrows. "Oh really?" She reached out and dipped her finger into the water, yanking her hand away like she'd touched burning acid.

Scrambling back, she stood up.

"That's seawater," she said accusingly.

"Yes, it is." Kyros's eyes flew open wide before he narrowed them.

Gretchen took careful breaths and looked around, studying the pool. He could sense her trembling.

"Why would Xanthus have a pool filled with ocean water?" she asked.

Kyros didn't skip a beat when he answered. "He's health conscious. Seawater has many benefits."

She still seemed startled. Her eyes searched her surroundings; they lingered over a puddle inches away from her.

"Are you okay?" he asked. "You look a bit pale."

She started to shake her head, but changed to nodding. "Um, oh yes. I'm fine. I'm just still in shock, what with Sara getting shot and having legs. Uh…it's late. I should get back to bed." She hesitated a moment before she turned and stepped out the door, but not before glancing back one last time.

What in Hades was that all about?

CHAPTER 11

The moment Aella saw Robert, she knew he'd failed. He stood before her—his shoulders hunched and his face downcast. She nearly ordered him to slit his own throat at that moment, but stopped herself. He might still be of use to her.

"I'm so sorry." His voice hitched. She frowned at his show of emotion. With Robert's physique and his military training, he shouldn't be blubbering. She much preferred the less-enamored Robert—the one who battled pirates and gave her attitude. This was an unfortunate side effect. Her voice may put men under her control, but it also made them emotional, needy, and desperate to please her. Not one of those traits was appealing.

She sauntered up to him and caressed his face. "Robert, you disappoint me."

"I know. I don't know how I could have missed. I had her in my sight."

Aella frowned. "Yet, you did miss."

"It wasn't my fault." He shook his head. "The girl in the wheelchair, she seemed to know what was going to happen. And then those men rushed in, and I couldn't get in another shot."

Aella pursed her lips. "She was in a wheelchair?"

He nodded and wiped his nose with his muscled arm.

"What did this *girl* look like?"

"She had dark hair, slim build—pretty."

Aella narrowed her eyes.

"Oh, not as beautiful as you." He reached out.

She slapped his hand away. "Don't touch me."

"Forgive me." He cowered away.

"You're so pathetic." She strolled to the railing and looked out over the waters. Closing her eyes, she breathed in the ocean air. She opened her eyes and frowned.

She could feel the human staring longingly at her back. "Tell me," she said, "why I should let you live." She spoke without looking at him.

She could hear his quick intake of breath. "There's a man—rough, big, intimidating. He was asking questions. I'll bet he could lead me back to her."

"No, you've done enough damage. Find this man and lead him to *me*. I'll deal with him myself."

"Yes. Yes, Aella."

CHAPTER 12

If Gretchen was going to stay at Xanthus's house while Sara recovered, she'd better try and make nice with the local giants. She bustled around the spacious kitchen cooking as she went—admiring all the features. There was not one, but two ovens, marble countertops, a double-wide copper fridge—which had been practically empty until her quick trip to the store.

This kitchen had everything a domesticated person could want. Gretchen remembered Sara's previous apartment, the stained sink, the chipped, laminate countertop, the square footage that allowed you to cook, wash dishes, and eat all in the same place. Sara had to *love* her new house.

Gretchen lifted the lid of the frying pan. Bacon and sausage sizzled and popped. They were crispy, brown—perfect. The waffle iron beeped as she placed the meat in the oven. Gretchen carefully removed the waffle and placed it on top of the giant pile in the warm oven. Given the size of Xanthus's friends, she thought she'd better make a lot of food. She didn't want any of them walking away hungry.

"What is that smell?" a deep voice rumbled. A

sandy-haired, brown-eyed man stepped into the kitchen. Six-six, she guessed. She'd decided to play a little game and guess how tall each of these men were. For each one she got right, she'd have to give herself a little reward.

"Come on in. I've made enough breakfast for everyone." Gretchen smiled.

His eyes widened in surprise. At least she thought it was surprise, but it almost looked like horror. That didn't make sense, though. Why would bacon, sausage, and waffles horrify anyone? She'd even made her mother's buttery syrup.

He hesitated a moment before stepping next to the table.

"Go ahead. Sit down," Gretchen urged. "Now, I'm sorry we weren't introduced properly yesterday. My name is Gretchen, and you are…?"

"Pallas," he croaked as he continued to stand there in a stupor.

"Nice to meet you, Pallas. Do have a seat." She pulled him over to a chair. He hesitated before he sat.

"Would you like orange juice or milk with your breakfast?" she asked.

"Milk?" He briefly glanced down at her chest. He turned away, blushing. Wow. Gretchen had never seen a man that size blush.

"Milk it is."

At those words, he jerked and looked like he was thinking of springing from the chair and bolting out the door. Gretchen tried to think of something to say to put him at ease.

"How long have you known Xanthus?"

"Um, I haven't known him long."

"How did you two meet?"

"You don't want to know." The answer didn't come from Pallas, but from another man standing in the door. Six-seven, no maybe six-eight—about the same height as Kyros.

"Hello there, I'm Gretchen."

"Straton," he answered, hesitantly.

Gretchen's smile widened. "Welcome to the party."

Straton raised an eyebrow. "Party?" He looked genuinely confused.

"Breakfast," Gretchen clarified as she dropped two plates filled with hot food in front of Pallas.

"Oh no. I'm not hungry." Straton shook his head.

"Oh, don't be silly. A man your size has to eat a lot of food. Sit down. I didn't slave over a hot stove all morning for nothing."

He bit down on his lip and glanced longingly at the door, but did as she told him and took a seat.

What was wrong with these men? Perhaps, being Greek, they weren't used to American food. "Look, just try it," she urged.

The next of Xanthus's friends passed by the kitchen with barely a glance. Six-seven. "Hello?" she called out. He didn't acknowledge her at all, but continued on.

"Who was that?" she asked as she placed two plates piled with food in front of Straton.

"That's Amar," Straton answered, eyeing his food dubiously. "He's not social. It's probably best to let him be."

Gretchen shrugged and sat down to her own plate. She'd just raised a bite of waffle to her lips when she noticed Kyros in the doorway. Her heart fluttered in her chest. She immediately set her fork down and stood. "Kyros, you're just in time for breakfast."

"Gretchen," he said, looking around at the scene, "I need to talk to you for a minute."

"Now?"

He frowned. "Yes."

"Don't you want to eat?"

He didn't say anything, just shook his head and crooked his finger at her.

She followed him out of the kitchen. He strolled down the hall, through the billiard room, and finally out the back door onto the terrace. Where in the world was he taking her?

He finally turned around to face her. She opened her mouth to protest his bizarre behavior when he pulled her to him and covered her mouth with his.

Kissing Kyros was unlike anything she'd ever experienced. It was hot, it was mind-bending, and it would have knocked her socks off if she'd been wearing any. His body surrounded her, his heat, his spicy, masculine scent. Gretchen took hold of his shirt and dragged him closer.

He lifted her off the ground, and she wrapped her legs around his waist.

Too soon, Kyros tore his mouth from hers. His breath was ragged as he shook his head. He looked her directly in the eyes and growled. His expression hit her like a jolt. He looked like an animal—raw, primal. It both frightened and excited her.

"I shouldn't have done that," he said, half to himself as he sat her back down on her own two feet. She swayed a bit before righting herself.

"I agree," she smirked, feeling a bit drunk from the kiss. "You shouldn't have stopped kissing me. Why did you?"

"I shouldn't have kissed you in the first place."

"Why not?"

He didn't answer.

She stood, confused and still a bit muddled, and then a thought washed over her like ice water. "Oh no. You're not!"

"Not what?" he asked, surprised.

"You're married, aren't you?" She pushed him in the chest.

His brows furrowed. "No, I'm not married."

"You have a girlfriend?"

"No girlfriend."

"Then why? Why shouldn't you kiss me?"

"It's complicated."

"Well, then…why *did* you kiss me?"

Kyros thought for a moment. "It's like you people

say, desperate times call for desperate measures."

"I have *no* idea what you're talking about."

He cracked a smile. "I know."

"But you're not cheating on anyone?"

"No."

She frowned and shrugged. "There's that."

When Gretchen left Kyros and returned to the kitchen, Pallas and Straton's plates were sitting empty on the table. The men themselves were nowhere to be seen. There went her attempt to get to know them.

She sank into a chair, ate her breakfast, and tried not think about the kiss.

※ ❧

Kyros waited patiently for the others to return from their hunt. He desperately needed a dip in the cool Caribbean waters. That kiss, Hades, he hadn't expected it to be so…intense. He blew out a breath of air. That little human packed a punch.

He licked his lips, closed his eyes, and moaned. He could still taste her. What under Olympus was he to do? Well, he couldn't kiss her again—*ever* again. That was their first kiss. First kisses with a woman were supposed to be tentative, shy. His first kiss with Gretchen was the equivalent of a volcanic eruption. Pallas and Straton didn't know how much peril Kyros had put himself in to save them from eating human food. They'd better not expect him to do it again.

He could hear Straton's voice on the ocean breeze. "I didn't think I'd be able to stomach eating anything after smelling that."

"Oh, yeah," Pallas said. "How can humans stomach eating old, dead, burnt animals?"

"And what were those brown disks with holes in them?" Straton asked. "And that yellow liquid didn't smell right."

"I don't know how you could smell that with the scent of burning flesh permeating the air," Pallas said.

"Pallas, Straton," Kyros called out. "You *do* realize there is a human in the vicinity. It might be prudent to hold your tongue. She might hear. What would she think about this conversation?"

The two stepped out from the rocky cave and came into view.

"And why would you bring her here?" Pallas asked.

"She goes where she wants," Kyros answered. "She might decide to take a walk along the beach."

"These humans need to keep a tighter line on their females," Straton said. "By the gods, Xanthus's wife nearly died. I wasn't sure I could stop the blood flow. And all that happened because she decided to take a shopping trip. Why he *allows* her to shop is beyond me. Xanthus could provide her with all the apparel she'd need."

"Human women are used to more freedom than Dagonian women," Kyros said. "They don't have to ask permission to travel anywhere."

"If you ask me," Pallas said, "they should. It's not safe for them, wandering about on their own." He shook his head.

Kyros raised an eyebrow. "Somehow, I don't think that would go over well in this culture."

Pallas frowned. "Yeah, well, look how badly the humans have messed up their world. Maybe they should reevaluate their system. And then there's their moral system. Talk about loose. Did you know Gretchen offered me her breast?"

Kyros clenched his fists at his sudden rage. Was she offering affection to others? He knew he himself couldn't have her, but he'd be run through with a spear before he'd allow anyone else to. Rushing up to Pallas, Kyros grabbed his arms and jerked him close. "Did you accept her offer?" he snarled.

Pallas's eyes widened in shock. "What in Hades is wrong with you? Of course I didn't. She's a human!" He spat out the last words.

"Tell me about this offer," Kyros said.

"She asked if I wanted milk."

Kyros loosened his grip. "Milk? Tell me exactly what she said."

"She asked if I wanted orange juice or milk."

"Like offering you a…drink?" He relaxed, confused at the strange offer.

Pallas nodded.

"Oh no, you haven't." Straton gasped. His wide eyes stared at Kyros. "She's sunk you."

Kyros turned to Straton. "I haven't been sunk by anyone. Only a fool would love a human."

"I know what my eyes are telling me."

Kyros shook his head.

"You'd better stay away from her." Straton jabbed his finger at Kyros.

Oh yeah. Easier said than done. "I have no intention of getting involved with a human."

Straton frowned. "You'd better not. Just stay away from her."

Kyros turned away. He didn't need a keeper.

Straton and Pallas returned to the house as Kyros went to hunt.

Kyros entered the cave and dove into the water. His troubled mind embraced the sea eagerly. Things had been getting so confusing, so muddled on the surface. His life was much clearer down below. Here he knew who he was, what he believed.

Kyros snaked his way through the rocky tunnel. The sea opened before him, welcoming him back among the seaweed and coral. Searching the stalks, he looked for prey. He scented the water, his tongue savoring and seeking out just the right taste. His muscles tensed, and his instincts took over the moment he scented a predator—a shark. Diving deeper, he kept his eyes up, probing the sea for the source of the tantalizing smell. Prey was best attacked from beneath. And then he spotted them—Caribbean reef sharks. Kyros had never tasted the Caribbean variety before, but it sure smelled good. His stomach clenched in anticipation.

The presence of other sharks didn't worry him

at all. They wouldn't dare interfere with an attacking Dagonian, not unless they wanted to be added to the menu. Kyros honed in on a small male. It looked to be just the right size. Big enough to satisfy his appetite, without too much food left over.

Hovering below, he watched the juvenile shark. Kyros floated in stillness until the shark swam into position, and then exploded like a rushing torpedo. He slammed full speed into the creature's abdomen, stunning and injuring it in the collision. Without missing a beat, he slashed his blade across the shark's throat, spilling its blood.

His canine teeth elongated in anticipation of tearing into the flesh. And a moment later, he did—ripping away chunks of meat and devouring them. His mind briefly wandered to Gretchen. How would she react to seeing this? Would she be disgusted with his behavior? Of course she would. He remembered her reaction at the restaurant, when he'd eaten fish fillets laid out neatly on a plate. He'd even used a knife and fork to eat the stale flesh. But still, she'd been shocked, disgusted.

When Kyros had his fill of the shark meat, he left the carcass for the other sharks waiting in line for their opportunity to eat. His stomach was no longer hungry, but it felt a bit sick—like it was twisting into knots. Gretchen was not part of this world. She never would be. She was a human. He couldn't forget that. Just a few days ago, he'd hated all humans. They'd killed his sister. They'd killed thousands of Dagonians. But now…? Gretchen wasn't all humans.

He surfaced in the darkness of the cave.

"Oh man, I love reef shark." Xanthus stood at the water's edge. He sucked air through his nose, breathing long and deep. "You didn't bring any back with you to share, did you?" He stripped off his clothes, obviously preparing for his own hunt.

"There are others, you know," Kyros said. "A lot of them actually."

"I know. But I promised Sara I wouldn't eat shark anymore. She's become quite fond of the beasts."

"You've given up shark meat? I don't know if I could do that. Doesn't she know how good they taste?"

"Yeah, right. She'll never eat one to find out. And you better hope she doesn't notice any of her favorites missing. She'd have a fit."

"Her favorites?"

"Yeah." Xanthus shook his head. "She's even naming them."

"By the gods." Kyros frowned. "Now I feel guilty."

"Don't worry about it. Sharks come and go all the time. She'll just think it moved on."

"So, is she getting the hang of hunting?" Kyros asked, genuinely curious about her.

"She hasn't gotten a chance to try. The sharks keep bringing her offerings."

"Oh man."

"I know. I'm surprised she hasn't gained about fifty pounds. She feels obligated to eat some of everything they bring her."

Xanthus stretched and stepped toward the water. He looked tired, forlorn.

"How is she doing? Is she healing well?"

"She's recovering just fine. She should be home in a few days, but she's hesitant to come back."

"Let me guess. She's not ready to face Gretchen."

"Neither of us can figure out how to explain her miraculous growth of legs."

"Gretchen is struggling with that too. She doesn't know why Sara lied. Perhaps you can claim Sara has some sort of mental disorder."

"Adding lie upon lie will only make things worse. What I'm hoping is Sara's father will erase Gretchen's memories about the shooting."

"Would he be willing to do that?"

"I've no doubt he would, but I can't get a hold of him. No one seems to know where he is. Until he comes, we'll just have to deal with the situation as it is."

"Good luck. Oh, and could you give a message to Sara from me?"

Xanthus raised his eyebrows. "Sure."

"Tell her I'm sorry…about what I said."

Xanthus furrowed his brows and nodded.

CHAPTER 13

Aella awoke to male voices coming from the deck. "She'll tell you everything you need to know."

Lying in the soft, king-sized bed, she stretched her limbs and sat up. She got up and stepped over the blanket lying on the hardwood floor—the human soldier's temporary bed.

A loud crash was followed by angry words. "If I don't get some real answers, I swear I'll separate your head from your body and feed them both to the sharks."

Aella stepped out on the deck to see a monster of a man holding Robert by the throat, his feet dangling a foot above the floor. "Ooo, sounds like a tasty option—for the sharks. Personally, I prefer seafood." She used just the right amount of lyrical voice to capture the stranger's full attention.

He dropped Robert and staggered around to face her. She sauntered up to the big man and smiled seductively. Danger radiated from him like heat radiated from fire. Closing her eyes, she dragged his scent through her nostrils. Recognition hit her immediately. She opened her eyes, and her smile widened. "I know what you are,

Dagonian."

His eyes widened. "What is your name?"

"My name is Aella."

His eyes widened. He tensed, ready to attack, but her voice caused him to pause.

"What is yours?" She amplified the tenor of her voice to increase her control—careful not to overdo it. She needed him able to answer a few questions. He still knew who and what she was. And from his reaction, he'd also heard of her. Her spirits lightened knowing her reputation was still intact, even after two thousand years of hiding.

"My name is Drakōn."

"Drakōn, I have a question. Why would a Dagonian guard a mermaid?"

"We either guard the mermaid, or we return to prison."

"And who would send you back to prison if you didn't do this?"

"Xanthus Dimitriou."

"Who is Xanthus?"

"He is the mermaid's husband."

"A merman?" She could hear the surprise in her voice.

"No, a Dagonian."

Her laughter pealed, causing him to jump. "That *is* surprising. But it makes things easier for me."

She circled him, tracing her fingers over his impressive muscles. "So who is the girl in the wheelchair?"

He looked confused. "The mermaid, of course."

Aella was caught off guard for a moment. They hadn't been talking about the same girl. "And who is the *other* girl. The one the mermaid was with."

"She is the mermaid's human friend."

"A *human* friend, huh?" This situation was better than she'd thought. "Does this human know her friend is a mermaid?"

"Of course not."

"I'm assuming all the men surrounding the mermaid are Dagonians. Am I right?"

"Yes."

"And who is this human to each of you? Do you know her well?"

"She's nothing to me."

"What about the others…?"

"The others feel the same, except…"

"Except who?"

"I'm not sure, but Kyros seems to be taking an interest in the human. He's extremely protective of her."

She smiled. A plan began forming in her head. She could rectify this situation easily *and* teach the mermaid a lesson. Aella unleashed the full power of her voice to give her next instructions. "When you leave me, you'll remember nothing of me, this conversation, or the directions I give you. Regardless of that, you will follow my instructions exactly. I want you to return to your Dagonian friends. You will bring Kyros to me. Make sure no one else accompanies you. Make sure no one else follows. Kyros and the others must suspect nothing. Once you bring Kyros to me, I may let you follow through on your threat to separate Robert's head from his body and feed him to the sharks." She smiled and smirked at the human who stood, swaying on his feet. Drool dripped from the side of his mouth—disgusting.

She turned back to the Dagonian. "I'll be waiting here for you to return. If for any reason, you cannot complete this mission, you will kill the mermaid and her human friend immediately, and then kill yourself. Do you understand?"

"Yes."

"Do you have any questions for me?"

"No."

"Well then, you are free to leave," she said in a normal voice.

He stood for a moment, in a daze. Then he shook himself. "What in Hades am I doing here?"

"You were just leaving," she said, surprised at how quickly he returned to himself.

"I came here for answers." He stepped toward her and stared her down.

Aella narrowed her eyes. "No." She unleashed her voice, long and shrill. "You are leaving."

He stiffened—immediately overcome, and proceeded to leave without another word.

As he got into his skiff and headed back to shore, Aella wondered if her plan could yet have a flaw. Drakōn was a little too hard to control. She hoped the one called Kyros would give her no trouble.

CHAPTER 14

Gretchen lay across the sofa and flipped through the channels. There was absolutely nothing worth watching on. Maybe if she were interested in screeching idiots fighting over who was the father of whose baby, or perhaps if she cared about how to clean up spills with no residue, but barring those things, there was nothing on TV.

Kyros stepped into the doorframe. He took one look at her, turned around, and strode away. He hadn't said two words to her in the last two days—ever since they'd shared that kiss. Gretchen sat up to adjust the pillow. On a whim, she punched it. But once she got started, she couldn't seem to stop. An image of Kyros's face flashed in her mind—his handsome, rugged, face with the stupid scowl. "Idiot, jerk, butt wipe..." She punched with each insult, each one getting progressively fouler, until she finally ran out of names to call him.

Kicking her feet up on the couch, she slammed her head back onto the pummeled pillow and glared at the ceiling. Maybe she should check Facebook. Perhaps she could squeeze some enjoyment from social media.

She turned on her phone and opened the app.

Descending

It looks like Carrie—her old high school cheerleading captain—just had her second kid. Whoopee for her. Oh and Hal…*click* unfriend. Who cared who—*oh, excuse me*—what Hal was doing? Her brother, Matt, just pulled the biggest prank of the century. He put bras and tutus on Tim Tebow, Danny Wuerffel, and Steve Spurrier—well, on their Heisman statues at Griffin Stadium at least. He even gave them wigs and a makeover. He posted pictures to prove it—and got fined two hundred dollars. If he hadn't posted the evidence on Facebook, he might have gotten away with it. If he called, she wouldn't answer. He just hit her up for a hundred bucks two weeks ago. There was no way she'd spot him two hundred for stupidity.

Gretchen stood and turned off her phone. Stepping toward the window, she wanted nothing more than to pull up the blinds and look out. Pallas caught her last time she'd done that and gave her a thirty-minute lecture about safety. She frowned, considering whether or not it was worth another reprimand.

Gretchen seriously needed to get out of this funk. Cabin fever had never agreed with her. She was a free spirit, a social being. She was not meant to be kept cooped up in a house for days at a time.

If only she had some work she could do, but losing your job meant no work.

The doorbell rang.

Pausing in surprise for just a moment, she sprinted for the door. She had every intention of beating her jailers to it before they could hide her away from the threat of an Avon lady.

"Gretchen," Kyros shouted from down the hall. "Get away from that door." He strode toward her, his expression livid.

She glared right back. "I was going to look through peephole before answering. I'm not stupid, Kyros."

"Go back and watch TV. I'll handle this."

"Listen, I don't know what kind of backward culture you come from, but no one gives me orders. I'm getting sick——"

"Do you have a death hope?"

"A what?"

"Do you want to die?"

"Oh, you mean death wish. And yes, I'm on the verge right now, I'll have you know. One more day cooped up in this house, and I'll shoot myself and save the gunman the trouble."

Kyros frowned at her.

The doorbell rang again.

Gretchen stepped past Kyros and looked through the lens. A short, dark woman stood on the doorstep. A small child squirmed in her arms. Gretchen pulled the door open. Kyros yanked her back and pushed her behind him.

"I, uh…am here to clean," the woman said, her eyes darting between Gretchen and Kyros. "Do you want me to come back later?"

"Yes."

"No."

They answered simultaneously.

Gretchen stepped around Kyros. "Come on in." She pulled the woman inside and smiled at the little boy who was attempting to wriggle free.

"Hello there, little guy," Gretchen greeted.

He stopped squirming and shoved his thumb in his mouth. His brown eyes searched Gretchen's face. "Do you have any toys?"

"No, they don't have toys," the woman answered. "You'll have to color in the coloring books you brought."

Gretchen thought about how this house must look to a five-year-old boy. Pretty darn boring. Except for the pool, that is. But there was no way she could take him swimming. Still, she knew exactly what little boys liked to do these days. She stooped down to speak to him.

"Do you want to play video games?"

His eyes widened as a smile of anticipation spread across his face. His head bobbed up and down in a nod.

Gretchen looked up to the mother's relieved face. "Is it okay with you?"

The woman nodded. "Nothing violent."

"Of course not," Gretchen answered, taking the boy's hand in hers.

She straightened up, and her eyes met Kyros. He was frowning—of course. He was *always* frowning. He turned on his heels and left to go down the hallway.

"I'll get started," the woman said. "Let me know if he gives you any trouble."

"I'm sure he'll be a perfect angel," Gretchen said

as she led him to the living room.

"So, little man," Gretchen said, "what's your name?"

"Charles."

"Well, Charles. Do you like racing cars?"

"My mom won't let me drive."

"She won't?" Gretchen raised her eyebrows in mock surprise.

He shook his head.

"I have a game that lets you race cars. Do you want to play it?"

He nodded, cracking a smile.

She led him into the living room and hooked up the game system. They chose a two-player game, pitting themselves against each other. She'd make sure he won, but she'd be careful to not let on she was letting him.

They'd only been playing for a few minutes when she saw movement in her peripheral vision. She glanced over to see Pallas watching them in wonder. She smiled at him; he smiled back, his eyes darting over to the boy with the most peculiar, confused look—as if he'd never seen a child before. She looked back to the game to see she'd driven off a bridge into the ocean. Thank heavens the game was more forgiving than real life. A moment later, her car was dropped back onto the road. Pallas left as she was swerving to miss a banana.

Straton stopped in the doorway a few minutes later. He looked just as surprised by the presence of a child as Pallas had been. Gretchen did her best to ignore the strange men who stopped by one by one to gawk. Charles didn't seem to notice, but chatted on about how well he was doing, and how his friend, Stefano, had the same game. These men acted like a celebrity was in their presence. Even Amar—the man who never even looked at her, never even paused at her presence—stopped at the sight of this child.

Gretchen lost miserably, and she hadn't even let Charles win on purpose. The men in this house had so thoroughly distracted her that she was easy prey.

"Charles," his mother called. "It's time to go." She stepped into the room.

"Perfect timing," Gretchen said. "Your son just won the game."

"Thank you," his mother said, smiling. "I appreciate you taking time to play with him."

"It was my pleasure," Gretchen answered. "He's a nice boy. You should be proud."

"I am," she said, but her eyes kept looking around.

"They're a strange bunch, aren't they?" Gretchen whispered.

The woman gave a sigh of relief. "Yes. They watched me like I was a criminal. I promise you I've never stolen anything in my life."

"I'm sure you haven't. These men are an odd lot, but I assure you, they mean you no harm."

"I didn't feel threatened. They just seemed… suspicious."

"I know what you mean." Gretchen frowned.

"How often do you come here to clean?"

"This is my first time, but the owner, Mr. Dimitriou, wants me to come in once a week. I must be honest, I'm not sure I'll be back."

"Oh now, don't let them worry you. They are actually quite nice once you get to know them. And I'd love an excuse to play video games with your son. I've been going out of my mind with boredom since my best friend was admitted to the hospital."

"Oh no. What happened?"

"Um, well, she was…shot."

The color drained from the woman's face as she looked back into the hall. "I…I've got to be going." She scooped her son into her arms and rushed to the front door.

"I didn't mean to alarm you." Gretchen rushed to follow her.

The woman ignored her and continued on. "Tell Mr. Dimitriou he can send me my check." She said the last words just before she pulled the door shut behind her.

Pallas, Straton, and Kyros trickled into the hallway.

"I've a feeling we won't be seeing them again," Gretchen said.

"Why not?" Pallas asked. "We didn't threaten her."

"No, you only did your prison warden thing on her."

"Prison warden?" Pallas asked.

"Yeah, you made her feel like a criminal."

Pallas looked appalled. "I didn't mean to treat her like a criminal."

"Yeah, well, you did. And it unnerved her."

"I guess we could have been friendlier," Straton said.

Gretchen rolled her eyes and returned to play more of the game.

CHAPTER 15

Gretchen stomped up to the front door with the annoying giant on her heels.

"I'm sorry, but I'm not just going to sit around the house hiding." Gretchen stopped at the front door and turned to glare up at Kyros. He was returning her glare and then some.

"Gretchen," he growled, bracing his hand against the door. "Until we find the man trying to kill you, you shouldn't be putting yourself out there."

"And what if we never find him? What then?"

"I think you should give it more time before you assume we're never going to find him."

"I don't want to give that creep even one more moment of my life. Listen, I'm sorry if you don't like it, but I *have* to see Sara. If you want to come with me, I'd like that. But either way, I'm going with or without you."

"You would die to see your friend?"

"I would die rather than give up my freedom," Gretchen clarified. "Now, let me pass."

She could feel his emotions simmering, the heat of them radiating off his skin. She narrowed her eyes and stared him down.

After a long couple of minutes, his shoulders loosened. "Okay, you can go. But not until you do a few things."

He dragged her to a chair and sat her down. "Wait here."

The minutes ticked by. Where in the world did he go? Finally, she could hear him stomping down the stairs. He appeared with an armful of stuff. There was a blonde wig, a wide-brimmed hat, dark sunglasses, a bulky sweater, and various scarves.

"You've got to be kidding me." She chuckled.

Kyros frowned, obviously not appreciating her laughter.

"Oh fine. Give me those," she said, gathering the bundle in her arms and tromping down the hallway to the bathroom.

A few minutes later, she emerged—a wannabe spy. Or maybe she was a bag lady. It was hard to tell which look she'd achieved.

"There," Kyros said, satisfied. "Now no one could possibly recognize you."

"Oh yeah, and no one could possibly suspect I'm wearing a disguise either."

Kyros's brows pinched together. "Is that sarcasm?"

"Oh no. Not at all."

He frowned at her, looking her up and down. "Let's get this over with."

They only had to walk from the parking lot, through the hospital, and up the elevator to the third floor. And truly, there were not many people about, but with everyone gawking, it felt like a thousand eyes were on her.

"Why is everyone looking at you?" Kyros whispered.

"Because I'm dressed like an idiot," she whispered back harshly.

As they approached room 391, they were headed off by a hefty nurse. "Can I help you?"

"Is Xanthus here?" Kyros asked. "I'd like to talk to him for a moment."

The woman's eyes kept darting to Gretchen. She could understand why. Who would be wearing a getup like hers?

"Let me see if he's available." The nurse slipped through the door, closing it behind her. A moment later, she returned with Xanthus. His face was drawn with concern. Then he saw her. His eyes widened in surprise. Oh yeah, even *he* could see how ridiculous she looked. The corners of his mouth pinched down, suppressing a smile.

"Hello, Kyros," he said. "Who is that with you?"

"See," Kyros whispered to Gretchen. "I told you the disguise would work."

This man needed to learn how to recognize sarcasm. Especially when it was so obvious that it practically slapped you in the face.

"This is Gretchen," Kyros answered. "I thought it best if she were to disguise herself."

"Good thinking. But I'm sorry; your timing is terrible. Sara has been taken to the lab."

"Is it anything serious?" Gretchen ripped off the sunglasses.

Xanthus sighed. "No. Just routine tests."

Gretchen nodded—her stomach like lead in her gut. "Will you tell her I came? And let her know I miss her, and I want to see her again."

"Sure. I know she misses you too. I'm sorry this had to happen on your visit. You are welcome to stay as long as you'd like. Just let Kyros know if you need anything. I'm sure he'll be happy to help you." Xanthus turned to Kyros. "Won't you?"

"Oh yeah," Kyros grumbled.

"I do have a favor to ask." Gretchen kept her eyes on Xanthus.

"Oh?" Xanthus said.

"I'd like nothing better than to go get some lunch, like in a restaurant, in public."

"There is this quiet, out-of-the-way sushi place I found recently," Xanthus said.

Gretchen smirked. "You and your sushi."

"We Mediterranean men love fresh fish. How about I walk you out and give you directions?"

Kyros was glowering as they stepped outside. The three of them were quite a draw for curious eyes—a short, skinny "bag lady", walking between two nearly seven-foot-tall, muscular men. Minds were spinning.

"Have you heard from Drakōn?" Kyros asked.

"Not yet," Xanthus said. "He'll let us know if there's any news."

Xanthus turned to Gretchen. "Have you thought of anything else that might be helpful? Did you think of anyone who might want you dead?"

These men knew nothing about being subtle. "Um, not anyone *recently*."

"Recently?" Kyros stopped walking and whipped around to face her.

She tugged him across the parking lot crosswalk before the elderly man approaching in the large sedan ran them over.

"What do you mean, recently?" Kyros asked.

"My birth mother was not exactly happy when I left her. She had a bit of a temper, hurt a lot of people. But it's been *ages* since I've seen her."

"How long?"

"About fifteen years."

"How old were you when you left her?"

"I'm not sure."

"You don't know?"

"No. The social worker thought I looked to be about eight years old."

"And this mother wanted to kill you?"

"She threatened me."

"What exactly did she say?"

Gretchen frowned and took a deep breath. "She said if I ever left her, she'd hunt me down and rip my heart out."

Xanthus and Kyros seemed to share a 'look.'

"What?" she asked.

Kyros shook his head. "It's nothing. You left her anyway," Kyros continued, "regardless of her threat to your life. Did you not believe her?"

"Oh no, I believed her. I left because I knew she was capable of that and more."

"Where did all this take place?" Xanthus asked. "In Hawaii?"

"No, um, it was Florida…Miami."

"Isn't Miami nearby?" Kyros asked Xanthus.

"It's about a thousand miles away—southwest of here."

Kyros nodded.

Squealing tires marked a car coming at them fast. Kyros pushed Gretchen back out of the path just as the car braked, stopping inches from them.

Drakōn rose from the rumbling car. "Kyros, I need you to come with me."

"What's wrong with you, Drakōn?" Xanthus growled. "Are you trying to run us down?"

"I need Kyros to come with me," Drakōn repeated as he turned to Xanthus. "And you'll need to take the girl back to the house. I've found the would-be killer."

Xanthus narrowed his eyes. He looked suspicious. Kyros turned to her. "Go with Xanthus."

"What?" Gretchen squeaked. "You're not going with him. We need to call the police. Now is no time to play hero."

"I have to go."

"No, you don't *have* to go. You can just pull out your phone and dial 9-1-1 or whatever number they use here to call the police."

"Gretchen, I'm not debating this right now."

She pulled Kyros toward her. "I need to talk to you."

"But we're already…"

"In private," she snapped and turned to lead the way. She heard him sigh at her back as they walked. They passed a couple of cars and ended up standing behind a minivan. Gretchen stopped and turned toward him. She tried to ignore how close he was standing, or how much she wanted to reach out to him. The way he'd been acting since their kiss, he'd probably just push her away.

"I don't know how they do things where you come from," Gretchen said, "but here there are laws, laws you are not exempt from. You can't just go chasing after criminals. You can't."

"Mm hmm," he hummed in agreement as he took a step toward her.

"You need to let go of your anger. Let go of your need for revenge. Let go of…"

"Gretchen?" He took another step in.

"Yes?"

"Stop talking and kiss me." He moved toward her.

She stiffened. A flame ignited at his words. She wasn't sure if it was fueled by anger or desire, but she sure wasn't going to kiss him after he avoided her at every turn the last few days. "Take one more step toward me, and I'll make you wish you were dead."

His eyes widened, and a slow smile spread across his face. "You are not like any other woman I've ever met."

She narrowed her eyes.

"I shouldn't want you," Kyros said, his voice as smooth as silk, "but I do."

"You can *want* all you wish. You won't be getting anything more from me."

"Gretchen…?" He paused. What he was waiting for, she had no idea.

"What?"

He traced his fingers over her jaw and down her neck. She trembled at his touch. "Your body betrays you."

Stiffening, she clenched her fists. She'd like to see how well he could kiss with a fat, bloody lip. Instead of giving in to her violent impulse, she turned on her heels and walked away. Before she reached Xanthus and Drakōn, she shot Kyros one more message over her shoulder. "Do what you want. I hope he shoots you through your black heart."

CHAPTER 16

The sound of the surf outside penetrated Gretchen's consciousness as she lay in bed. Worry assaulted her. Worry for Kyros, worry for Sara, and worry about her world coming to an end. But finally a troubled sleep found her, and unbidden, another reality thrust itself upon her. Another life, another girl, another place, a place that held memories that only served to torment her.

"It's okay; you're safe," Ambrosia said. Her voice was the sweet voice of a child. It was the type of voice that loosened tongues, emanated kindness, and made you want to pour your heart out.

"What's your name?" Ambrosia asked.

There was no response from the young girl at her side—only a blank stare. She was shaking. Her teeth chattered in her mouth.

"Don't you have a name?"

Still no answer.

"Are you hungry? I could catch you a fish or a sea urchin."

Still nothing.

"Why are you shaking?"

Silence.

"Here, maybe you just need to sit and rest." Ambrosia

tugged the girl, pulling her to the back of the cave. Pointing to a pile of seaweed, she said. "This is my bed. It's softer than it looks."

Despite the friendly overtures, the girl stood, unblinking.

"Let me show you." Ambrosia pulled her down to sit on the weeds.

"See? Nice and soft."

Ambrosia frowned at the girl. She didn't seem happy. Perhaps a little song would help. Ambrosia sang a simple tune, a song about rainbows and jellyfish. It was light, and it was soothing. A song one would sing to a friend. When her song was through, she tried again. "What is your name?"

"Gretchen," she finally answered. Ambrosia smiled, pleased she was now speaking to her.

"Do you like being human?"

"Um, I guess so."

"What is your favorite game?"

"Mario Party."

"It's a party? Do you play it on the beach?" Ambrosia asked.

"It's a video game."

"What's a video game?"

"It's a game you play on a TV."

The questions poured from Ambrosia's lips, but the answers seemed to only multiply the questions in her head.

"Do you live with other humans?"

"I live with my mom, dad, and brother," Gretchen answered.

"Do you love them?"

"Yes."

"Really?"

"Yes."

"Do they love you?"

"Yes."

"How do you know?"

"They tell me."

Ambrosia noticed tears leaking from the girl's eyes. "Are you sad?"

"Yes."

"Why? I haven't hurt you. Aren't I being nice to you?"

"I miss my family."

Ambrosia didn't ask any more questions. The answers only made her heart ache.

Ambrosia laid Gretchen down to sleep. She couldn't ignore the tears streaming down the girl's cheeks.

Tears of her own began to fall when she realized she couldn't keep her human. She had to take her back. But it was night. She'd wait until morning. She would absolutely take her to shore later. For now, she would spend a little more time with her. She curled up next to the girl, relishing the contact, drifting to sleep with a smile on her face.

Hours later, Ambrosia awoke to an ear-piercing scream. She blinked her eyes open and sat up. Her mother was dragging Gretchen toward the water.

"Where are you taking her?" Ambrosia screamed.

"The humans have about twenty boats and divers out there. They're looking for her."

"But, I'm not ready to give her back yet."

"Ambrosia, you will not argue with me. I have to let them

find her."

"How will you return her without them seeing you?"

"I'm not going to stay out there with her."

"But…can she swim? Some humans can't swim. I've seen it. The small ones often can't."

Her mother laughed. *"I don't care. You think I care about a human?"*

"But she could die."

Her mother smirked at her. *"Oh, she'll die. I'll make sure of it. We can't have her blabbing to the humans about us."*

"No!" Ambrosia screamed as she raced toward her mother. *"I won't let you kill her."*

She met her mother's fist, while running full on. The pain was blinding just before everything went black.

The next thing she was aware of was the throbbing pain in her head. It was excruciating. She opened one eye; the other one seemed glued shut. She gingerly touched it. Her face felt all puffy.

Pain slammed into her heart when she remembered what happened. Her mom was going to kill Gretchen.

She dove into the water. Her legs tingled as they changed into a fin. A moment later, she raced out, swimming toward the shore. Surfacing, she looked around. Her mother had said there were humans searching for the girl. The moon shone above the empty beach. There was no sign of her friend. No sign of the humans. Tears sprang to her eyes. She was too late.

Her mother had proven her cruelty again. She didn't care about the girl. She didn't care about anyone. She didn't even care about her own daughter. Ambrosia swam aimlessly through the water, sobbing. She should have taken the girl back last night. If she had, she would still be alive.

Guilt crushed down on her, making it hard for her to breathe. Her mother was a monster. Ambrosia hated everything about her life. Why couldn't she have been born a human? Why couldn't she have a mother and father who loved her, who would search for her if she'd gone missing?

Finding herself back at the cave, she swam in and kept swimming. She didn't go back to her sleeping area, but wandered through the endless maze of tunnels.

Looking up, she was surprised to find herself in a place unfamiliar to her. She continued to swim, uncaring where she was. She just wanted to escape the reality of her life. The darkness deepened. She could have turned on her lighted necklace, but she found the blackness comforting. She could pretend she didn't exist… pretend the world didn't exist.

As she swam, she was assaulted with a smell. It wasn't horrible, but it wasn't a pleasant smell either—just strange, ancient. She'd never smelled anything like it. Swimming into the room, she could feel seaweed brushing her skin. How seaweed grew in such a dark place, she didn't know. But it would help to keep her hidden from the world—hidden from her mother. She settled in among the weeds and fell fast asleep.

She didn't know how long she slept, but eventually, consciousness returned. Her head didn't hurt nearly as much, and her mind was clearer as she awoke. She needed to make a plan. She dreaded going back to her mother, but where else could she go?

A thought struck her. What if she went to shore? What would the humans do to her? Would they hurt her? Would they accept her? She'd never seen humans hurt or mistreat each other the *way her mother did. Could life on shore be any worse than the life she had?*

Ambrosia finally turned on her orbed necklace.

Her scream echoed off the cave walls. She'd found herself face to face with a white skull haloed with long wisps of hair. She continued to shriek as she turned and swam into a tiny skeleton. It floated in front of the bones of a small tailfin. She turned around again only to find countless more skeletons floating above a pile of bones. She knew at once who they were—these were her brothers and sisters.

She swam through them on her way to the exit. Their skeletons floated like specters—their eyes gaping wide, their jaws grinning at her. She frantically swam through the caves, the scent of her own cavern leading the way. But she didn't stop there. She kept swimming—leaving the cave system and heading into open sea.

She swam with no destination in mind. She only wanted away from the island, away from the nightmare, away from her cruel mother. How far she swam, she had no idea. She only knew the sun arched over the sky many times on her journey.

Sleep was a torment, and wakefulness a nightmare. She didn't eat much on her journey. Sharks would give her food along the way, but she could barely choke it down. The sickness afflicting her mind also affected her stomach. Just the thought of food turned it sour.

When she finally spotted land, she wasn't sure whether or not she was dreaming. The sound of laughter and the soft roar of human voices seemed to penetrate her consciousness. Finally, she snapped out of her stupor.

Popping her head above the surface, she took in the

view before her. There were humans, hundreds of them. Giant, rectangular rocks with shiny, square holes in them stood behind the humans. Ambrosia looked closely to see whether the people looked angry, mean, or threatening in any way. She was relieved to see they looked pleasant, many of them smiling.

It took hours of coaxing herself to go ashore. She had to. She could leave the sea. Leave the horror. She could make a life for herself among the humans. She could be human—forget what she was.

She found an area of the beach that seemed to be free of people. Surfacing was the hardest thing she'd ever done—even scarier than talking back to her mother.

Pulling herself from the water, her fin turned to legs. No one shouted, and no one looked shocked. She'd done it without a single witness. Her legs felt weak, wobbling as she walked. Going days with little food had sapped her strength. But, she was more concerned with the humans than her empty stomach. As she walked toward them, their eyes shot open wide and their jaws dropped. She wondered if they could tell she was a mermaid after all. She'd thought she looked human. Was there something she'd missed? Something they could see that let them know she wasn't one of them? She backed slowly away.

"Mommy, that girl's naked," said a small child to a woman, who snatched her up in her arms. All the humans were gawking at her.

Naked? Then she noticed it. The humans were all wearing clothing. A plump woman with white hair approached her with a wide, rectangular piece of cloth. "Are you okay, sweetie? She walked right up to Ambrosia. "Here, let's get you covered." She wrapped the scratchy material around her, and all the humans seemed to relax. Okay, humans did not like to see people naked.

"Where's your mother?" the woman asked.

Ambrosia didn't answer. She didn't know how she should answer.

"What's your name?"

Ambrosia thought about how to answer that question. She wanted to start a new life, wanted to escape her past. She needed a new name. But she didn't know any human names. Well, actually, she did know one.

She looked up into blue eyes framed with worried creases and answered. "My name is Gretchen."

CHAPTER 17

Gretchen awoke to a dark room, with tears streaming down her face. She remembered everything with crystal clarity. She'd pushed her memories back so many times she'd actually convinced herself they were not real—that they were false memories.

But coming out of that dream, she knew it was real. Her past was real. She wasn't crazy. Still, doubt tickled her mind. She had to prove something to herself.

After fifteen years, it was time.

Gretchen walked across the dark room, pulling out a nail file from her makeup kit. Stepping over to the window, she carefully shoved it under the sensor. It easily popped off. She kept it close to the other half of the sensor to prevent the alarm from tripping. She stuck the freed one directly on top of the other. The adhesive stuck tight.

Ah ha! Now she could open the window without alerting her overprotective guards. She slid the windowpane up and was greeted with a cool Caribbean breeze.

Looking down, she searched to see how far it was to the ground. She was on the first floor, but this house was huge. Its first-floor windows were surprisingly high. Still, she'd probably be fine getting down. Climbing back up might be an issue. She'd just have to find a ladder or something. Maybe the garden shed held one.

She shimmied her body backwards out the window. Holding on to the sill, she dropped down and stumbled before falling on her butt in the soft grass. That wasn't too bad. Standing up and brushing herself off, she looked toward the beach. It looked amazing. The moon shone through the cresting waves before they crashed into the sandy surf. She breathed the salty air deep, allowing the scent to fill her mind and comfort her.

Gretchen approached the shore. Looking around, she tried to locate any late-night beach goers, or crazed killers. She seemed to be alone. Then she saw it—the twinkling of lights coming from a ship offshore.

Her heart pounded. Why it did, she wasn't sure. But something didn't seem right. She jogged behind an outcropping of boulders and pressed her back against its rocky surface. Through the thundering surf, she could hear something squeak. She turned her head toward the sound and saw only more rocks with deep, black crevasses. It quieted for a moment before growing louder. A black, flailing shadow covered her vision as she squeaked out a cry. Her heart pounded in her ears, and she sank to the sand.

A bat. A stupid bat.

She stood and brushed the sand off. More squeaking. *Where's it coming from?*

She stepped toward the boulders and began to climb. She scrambled up and slid down, scuffing her skin against the rocks as she drew nearer to the noise. Then she saw it—the mouth of a cave. As she scooted down a u-shaped crevice toward the opening, some rocks jostled loose and tumbled down. The sounds of leathery wings beat in her ear, and a cloud of shadows flew up and over her. When they were gone, she stood. Stepping through the cave door, she could see the lapping water of a sea cave. A vice clamped around her heart. This place looked all-too familiar. But no, it wasn't the same. Deep in the repressed memories of her mind, she remembered the other one. And it didn't have a land-based entrance. The only way in and out of that cave was through the water.

Gretchen's legs were shaking as she approached the water's edge and looked down. She half expected to see the empty sockets of a skull looking up at her.

Gretchen wanted to run away, but she forced herself to stay. She'd been running for fifteen years—running from the horror, running from the memories. But her mother was not here. With her heart in her throat, she stripped out of her clothes. She'd been fighting since the day she'd left her birth mother—fighting for her independence, for her happiness. But there was one fight left to wage, one she'd been too afraid to confront—the sea itself.

It had been a long time. Would it still work? Had she been human too long? She sure felt like a human. She'd gone to public school, all the way from elementary to high school—she had the emotional scars to prove it. She'd gone to college, joined a sorority, and kissed more boys than she could remember. She'd talked to her mom—her real mom, the one who adopted her—on the phone every weekend since leaving for college. She'd practically forgotten who she used to be, where she'd come from. But here, standing on the tiny shore of this dark sea cave, she was ready to confront it.

Inching her way forward, her toes were nearly touching the ocean water. She pressed her lips tightly together and decided to take a leap. Well, her leap was actually only a small step. But, with fear pulsing through her veins, she slipped one foot into the cool water, and then the other.

The world rose around her as her body changed, plunging her into the salty sea. She sat in water a foot deep. It had been fifteen years since she took her first, terrifying steps on an open shore, leaving her previous life behind. Fifteen years since she'd touched the sea, but regardless of her heartless abandonment of the ocean those many years ago, it seemed to welcome her back in its soft, lapping arms.

Gretchen lifted her tail from beneath the rippling water and examined it in the dim, moonlit cave. It was pale, flesh colored—not like the ridiculous, scaled fins of mermaid legends. Did the humans really believe mermaids were descended from lowly fish? *No way.* Mermaids were daughters of the sea—daughters of Triton. Gretchen had never actually met her grandfather, but she had always dreamed he would come and rescue her. She didn't know a lot about him, but her birth mother was angry with him. Angry he had banished her. So he couldn't be too bad, could he? When he took too long to save her, she had simply rescued herself.

As she reminisced, she fingered her flipper, remembering every jagged edge, every fold, even the scar she got from playing with a young shark. She marveled at the fin that hadn't seen the light of day in so long. She slapped it playfully against the water's surface. Excitement mingled with apprehension as she sat in the shallow water. She'd promised herself she'd never return. She feared if she did, her mother would find her. And her life would be over.

But she wasn't a child anymore. She couldn't, she *wouldn't*, let fear rule her life or steal her happiness. She needed to put her fear where it belonged— in her past.

Pulling herself forward, she slipped in deeper, heading out into the water. Her head dipped under the surface, and she took her first, cleansing breath of fresh sea. She relished the flavor of the sea. It had been so long. She hadn't even known she'd miss it so much, but down here, she remembered all the good things she'd forgotten—the feel of the sea caressing her, the briny scent of the seawater, and the variety of tastes that assaulted her with flavors of all kinds.

Swimming down, she looked around. A silvery light shone off the rocky walls—it was brighter deep down. Curiosity pulled her to that glow. There was a

tunnel. She swam through it, twisting and turning. The
farther she went, the more she worried it would narrow
too much to let her through. Then she'd have to back
slowly out of it. But it went on until she was finally bathed
in a sea of moonlight. She'd made it to the outside.

She looked through the glowing water, crisscrossed
with moonbeams. The light danced through the water
and across her skin. Stretching her fin, she swam—timid
at first. She took in her surroundings. Seaweed rose
around her, brushing her body as she snaked through the
stalks. Several small fish darted away.

Looking up, she spotted dark shapes silhouetted
against the bright, rippling surface. Sharks circled above.
They seemed to catch her scent and turned toward her,
coming at her from all sides.

A large female with sharp, glimmering teeth
reached her first. Gretchen giggled as she playfully
swept past her. Then there were more, circling her like a
celebrity surrounded by adoring fans. "Well, hello," she
greeted impishly.

She continued her one-sided conversation. "What
are you all doing here?" A small bull shark swam up and
turned over, his belly facing up. Gretchen rubbed it until
his eyes rolled over. Feeling a bit giddy, Gretchen took off,
swimming in circles around and through the coral reefs.
The sharks followed her like a line of follow the leader.
Gretchen hadn't swum like this in years, but it was just
like a bicycle—you never forgot.

She played in wanton abandon for hours—

laughing harder than she'd done in a long time. She could almost forget her troubles on the surface, but soon enough, it encroached on her dream. She gasped when she looked above. The light of the sun was touching the waves. *Holy crap!*

If she didn't get back, Straton and Pallas would miss her and come looking for her. She bid her new friends goodbye and headed back through the tunnel. Breaking through the surface, she heard voices. They were coming! Should she go back? No, the voices were still faint. If she moved fast, she'd have plenty of time. She pulled up to the shore and dragged her body from the water. As her body left, she could feel the familiar tingle as her human legs returned, inch by inch.

"This is where the footsteps lead." She could hear Straton's voice clearly.

Gretchen found her nightgown and slipped it over her head.

"Hades! Straton, Pallas, I leave for a day and you lose her." Kyros's voice rumbled in anger. "If anything has happened to her, I'll tear your head off."

"By the gods, it's not my fault. She tampered with the window alarm."

"What was she doing coming here anyway?" Straton asked.

"Do you realize how dangerous this makes it for us?" Pallas asked.

What the heck does that mean? She saw their shadows in the entrance. Gretchen focused on trying to not look guilty. Then they walked in.

"Gretchen," Kyros said. "What are you doing here?"

"I got bored." Brilliant answer. Why couldn't she have thought of a better one?

"Well, Gretchen, you are one lucky woman. Your killer has been caught and will not be giving you any more trouble."

"Really?" She stumbled forward, tripping over a rock.

Kyros reached out to steady her and smiled. "Yes. So you're a free woman. How would you like to get out and have some fun?" he asked.

Straton and Pallas frowned. She didn't know what their problem was now. Since the criminal had been caught, there shouldn't be anything keeping her in.

"You want to do something with me?" she asked, unsure. She didn't trust the change in him. His personality seemed as unpredictable as the sea. Still, she was simply sick of staying indoors. "Okay, but if you start grumbling at me, I'll slap that frown right off your face. Today, I want to have fun. Got it?"

"Fun it is then." He smiled and offered her his arm.

An hour later, they were walking out to the car. "Look," Kyros said. "I know I can be a bit hard to take, and I realize I've been a tad controlling."

A tad? Gretchen nearly laughed at the understatement.

"To show you I can be reasonable, I'll let you drive."

She did laugh then. "Oh. You'll *let* me drive."

"That's not what I meant," he said, backpedaling.

"No, I'm sorry. I know what you meant. And since I'm such a wonderful, forgiving soul, I'll *let* you ride up front while I drive."

He raised an eyebrow, but didn't say more.

"Where to?" Gretchen asked as they sat in her car.

"Since you've had your swim, how about we find other things to do on the island?"

She couldn't have said it better herself. "Sure."

"There's a place called Gib's Hill Lighthouse. It's supposed to have a great view of the island."

"Okay, sounds like a good start." She entered it in the GPS. "Soooo," she said as she pulled onto the road. "What happened while you were gone?"

His brows immediately pinched together. "We got him."

"Yeah, that much I'd heard."

"That's all you need to know."

Great, she was probably aiding and abetting a criminal. "The less I know, the better, huh?"

He looked relieved she understood. "Exactly."

Oh brother.

Perhaps spending the day with Kyros was a bad idea, but she'd been known to exercise poor judgment before. She snuck a glance at him. Man, *he* was gorgeous.

Descending

And despite his wide mood swings and ability to make her want to murder him, she liked him. She loved being with him when he was being nice. She loved debating with him when he was being unreasonable. She liked spending time with him—period. Oh, and that man sure could kiss. Yeah, she'd never been smart when it came to men.

The lighthouse came into view, towering high above the island. Kyros thought they should take a walk from Horseshoe Bay, up to the lighthouse. It looked like she should have gone with tennis shoes instead of her white, strappy sandals. How was she to know they'd be hiking up a giant hill?

By the time they reached the top, Gretchen was sucking air through her lungs. Maybe she should work out more often.

She looked over at Kyros. She could barely even see him breathing at all, much less hard. It wasn't fair. She hadn't seen him work out at all in the time she'd been here on the island. Narrowing her eyes, she came to the realization. He *had* to work out. No one had that kind of physique naturally. He just probably exercised before eight AM.

"What?" Kyros was watching her.

"Huh?"

"Why are you glaring at me?"

"Oh. No reason."

"Do you want to rest before we head up to the top of the lighthouse?"

"No! Of course not. Why should I need to rest?"

He shrugged. "Okay, lead the way."

She stomped up each step. Her lungs burned, her heart was thumping profanities at her, and she was dripping with sweat. Finally, she took the last tortured step. "Here…we are."

"Are you okay, Gretchen?"

She answered him with the hardest glare her tired body could muster. She really needed to work out. It hadn't been that long since she'd trained, had it? Her schooling and internship had severely cut into her workouts. As soon as she got back to Honolulu, she was going back to the gym.

"Sorry I asked." The way he smirked as he held up his hands in surrender, made her smile. "How about we see what all this was for." He led the way onto the balcony.

The view was spectacular. Pockets of seawater sparkled between lush little islands hugging the coast. Inside each of those pockets were hundreds of boats. Several boats had masts pointing up like little raised hands saying 'look at me!' The ocean horizon spread in an expansive circle around them. The water looked so far below.

"If I were to be able to dive into the ocean from this height, do you think I'd survive?"

Kyros shook his head. "Not a chance. Even falling thirty feet to the water makes you feel like you're going to die."

"You've dove from thirty feet?"

"I've never actually measured it. But, yeah. I'm sure it was at least that."

"Cool."

Kyros raised an eyebrow. "You are? We probably should have brought you a jacket."

"What?" Gretchen shook her head. "Not cool as in cold. It's cool as in awesome, great…you know."

"Oh, so you're not cool?" He stepped toward her and cracked a smile.

She swallowed as she looked at his lips. "No, I'm not."

"I'm going to have to disagree." His lips were inches from hers. His warm breath tickled her face.

"Please don't tell me you're going to kiss me again."

His head jerked back. "You don't want me to?"

"I do. I just don't want to deal with the aftermath. You know…the avoidance, cold shoulder, regret…"

"I do regret kissing you," he said, resigned.

Sometimes, Gretchen was impressed when people were brutally honest. This was not one of those times. "Well then, just don't," she snapped.

"I hurt you." He sounded surprised.

Well, duh!

"I'm sorry." He stepped closer.

Gretchen stepped back. "Me too. I'm sorry I ever *let* you kiss me."

He took another step. "I'm sorry I ever stopped."

"How can you regret kissing me, but wish you'd never stopped?" she asked as she took another step back.

He stepped forward again. "Ever since I kissed you, I can scarcely think of anything else. You haunt my thoughts every moment of the day and my dreams at night. I can't seem to get you out of my head."

She took another step back, and her body pressed against the railing. "Really?"

He slipped his arms around her. "Yes, really." His mouth lowered to hers. Their lips touched, lighting a fire in her belly. She wrapped her arms around him and kissed him with a ferocity she'd only ever felt with him. She'd never wanted a man more than she wanted this one. He lifted her up on the high railing and sat her down. She had to lower her head to continue kissing him. He stepped into her, and she wrapped her legs around his chest.

Giggles in the background brought her back to the land of reality. The children's laughter must have had the same effect on Kyros, because he immediately pulled his lips away from hers. Gretchen glanced behind him. There was a little family with three young children. The girl who looked to be about six was smiling at them, her eyes sparkling.

"Perhaps this is not the best place for this." Kyros's voice was rough, and his breathing heavy. Gretchen smiled. It looked like kissing her was more exhausting than a hike up a mountain. She glanced behind her back and gasped. She sat perched on a narrow railing with nothing but a hundred-foot drop at her back. If she fell from here, she'd be dead. She tightened her grip around Kyros's neck.

He smiled and seemed to take her action as an invitation to nibble on the flesh below her ear. She was immediately distracted by the sensation of his lips moving down her neck. The hundred-foot death drop and gawking family seemed less and less important to her.

"Why don't we go somewhere more private?" she whispered.

His breath hitched. "Now that would be a bad idea. If we do that I can't…" His voice trailed off as he straightened up, his eyes widening.

He narrowed his eyes and said, "You know exactly what would happen."

She smiled at his apparent naivety. "Not *exactly*, but I have a pretty good idea."

He roughly lifted her off the railing, dropped her to her feet, and stepped back. "You've done it before? With other men?"

Gretchen could hear a tiny gasp. "Of course I have," she whispered. Her eyes caught the frightened look of the girl. Her father snatched the child up and led his children back through the door. She could hear him mutter something about a public place.

"Way to go. You just scared away that family," she said.

"Good. We need to talk alone."

"No, our conversation is over." Gretchen tried to push her way past him, but he pinned his arms on either side of her.

"Do you not know how that cheapens you?" he asked. "To be…"

Gretchen could feel the heat rise in her cheeks at his words. She couldn't believe he was talking to her like this. Like she was a…a…

"Why would you give away that which is most precious to a woman?" he asked.

She jabbed her finger at her own chest. "Me! I'm what's most precious. Not…*that*. Me!"

He looked her up and down. "*This* is you, Gretchen. Your body, it's you. You give away a piece of yourself every time you let other men have you without a commitment, without marriage, and everything that entails. Your body is not a gift you give someone on a whim, or when you feel an urge, or even if you care about him. It's a treasure that should be earned, that should be fought for. It's not something *anyone* should get easily."

"Well, *you* don't want to fight for me. You're attracted to me, sure, but you don't care about me. Not in the way you described. You don't even like me. So what *do* you want?"

He looked like she struck him. Well, she was just being honest. "That's not true," he said. "I care about you. If I *didn't*, I'd take what you offered. And I certainly wouldn't be lecturing you about morality."

"So if you *didn't* care about me, you'd take what

I offered? Now that sounds like a double standard to me. Wouldn't that be giving a part of *yourself* away?"

He looked shocked at her reasoning. "It's not the same."

"Oh really? Why not?"

He stood, the wheels turning in his head so loudly, she could almost hear them grinding. "Well, that's not important now," he said. "What's important is I do care about you, Gretchen. I do. On every level. You're funny, intelligent, and beautiful. You are definitely worth fighting for, worth waiting for."

Her heart warmed at his words. "You are such a confusing man."

"I've been told that before."

Gretchen straightened herself up. "We seem to have difficulty getting through a conversation without arguing. I'm sorry. How about I take you home?"

"No way. I promised you a day of fun, and I'm determined to give it to you."

Gretchen gave a small smile and shrugged. "Okay, where to next?"

CHAPTER 18

Kyros's muscles tensed when he heard a low growl. He turned to the passenger side of the car. Gretchen's head lolled back, her mouth slightly open. Another growl rumbled. The sound vibrated from her throat. She was asleep. He smiled at the sight. This human didn't sleep like a goddess, more like a humpback whale with a sinus condition.

His heart rate picked up with approaching headlights on the highway. He hadn't had much experience driving, and it made him anxious every time he had to pass other cars traveling at such a high speed. If Gretchen hadn't been falling asleep on her feet, he would have insisted she drive.

Gretchen gave a loud snort, her head turned toward him, and her eyes remained closed as she mumbled, "...such a jerk." He looked over at her and smiled. She was so refreshingly different from any other woman he'd met. And she was such a pretty thing. Why had he been so determined to stay away from her? And why did he decide to break down his self-made barrier and let her in? A sudden, sharp pain pierced his skull. Hades, what a headache. As fast as it came, it left just as quickly.

He passed by the exit that would have taken them back to the house. Instead, he drove on to the east side of the island. Regardless of the fact he'd never traveled this way, he knew exactly where he was going. Winding its way around the island, the road hugged the shore. He drove on, turning off onto a small road lined with trees. The darkness deepened with the towering foliage. He had only one thing on his mind—the destination.

As he came around a bend, the trees thinned and he slowed. Turning off, he drove onto a dirt road that was actually little more than a path. The car rocked up and over bumps on the road.

"What's going on? Kyros, where are we?" Gretchen said, having obviously been jostled awake.

"I've got someplace special to take you." he said smoothly, the words playing from his lips like lines from a script.

"It'd better be special. You're going to ruin this car's alignment driving over this. Is this even a road?"

The moon peeked out over the trees. Kyros pulled up next to several big boulders and turned off the car.

Gretchen chuckled. "This is…something."

They both stepped out of the car. Kyros strode to the left of the boulders. "Come on, Gretchen. It's just over this way."

"Another hike?"

Kyros turned back. She had her hand propped on her hip as she smiled.

"It's over this way," he answered.

"Yeah, so you said." Gretchen frowned.

Kyros stepped toward her and pressed his lips gently against hers. Gretchen melted into him. Desire and fear jolted through his body. Again, pain plunged like a knife into his skull. And again, the pain was gone.

"Are you okay?" Gretchen squatted next to him.

He must have dropped to his knees. "Yeah, just a headache."

"Maybe I should drive you home."

Kyros smiled as he staggered back onto his feet, "No way. This place is awesome. Besides, my head is feeling much better now." He took her hand and tugged her forward. "Come on."

She frowned, but relented. "Okay, but if your head starts to hurt again, we'll call it a night."

"Sure."

He took her around the rocks, and into a jungle. The foliage was so thick that it was difficult to tell where they were going. The trees opened up to a wonderful view. The ocean shore spread out before them.

"We're not going swimming, are we?" she asked, the color draining from her face.

"Don't you like to swim?" he asked. His voice didn't sound like his own, didn't feel like his own.

Gretchen slowly backed away. "Kyros?" He thrust his hand into his pocket and found what he needed—two balls of wax. He shoved them into his ears and turned to Gretchen. She looked stunned by what he'd just done.

Descending

"What's going on, Kyros?" He could still hear her, but the sound was faint, muted.

"What's wrong, baby?" he asked as he smiled.

Gretchen's eyes grew wide.

Kyros could sense her fear. It was sweet on his lips—sinfully delectable. He chuckled.

And then she was running into the woods. Kyros was impressed with how fast she could move. Despite her short legs, she flew over the ground. He tore after her. His legs felt awkward, cumbersome. But because of his long stride, he was able to keep her in his sights.

She scrambled up and over logs, under low branches, and sloshed through muddy puddles. He nearly caught up to her as she tripped and fell over a thick vine. But she was immediately on her feet again. He remembered how difficult she found climbing the stairs at the lighthouse. She sure seemed to have energy now.

He wondered for a fleeting moment why he was chasing her in the first place. Pain exploded behind his eyes as he stumbled into a tree. Why was he being plagued by headaches? He'd never had so much as a twinge of a headache in the entire 116 years of his life, but now they seemed to afflict him at every turn.

The hurt subsided, and he pushed himself away from the tree. Getting back to the task at hand, he scented the air. Gretchen's sweet perfume was like a beacon showing which direction she was headed. Kyros took off running. His legs felt more natural, more a part of him with each step. Soon, he could hear something.

It was faint at first, but then became clearer. Stumbling footsteps, gasps of air—breathing in and out, in and out...

"Gretchen, you don't need to run from me," he said. "I would never hurt you. I love you." At the expression of love, it happened again. Pain, like he'd never felt before, slammed into his head. He staggered and pressed his hands against his temples. It felt like someone had opened his skull and put an angry viperfish inside. It seemed to be trying to bite its way out with its long, razor teeth. He roared, the sound echoing across the treetops.

Understanding dawned on him. Someone had taken over his mind. Who could have done this? This was a power born of the gods. But what god would have even an errant thought for a human, much less want to harm one. A demigod? A mermaid? No, mermaids were extinct, all except for Sara, and Sara certainly wouldn't have done this.

Pain continued to slice through his head. Regardless of who did this, he had to make the agony stop. He could give in and just go along. But he didn't know what would happen. Whoever had done this had Gretchen in their sights. A surge of protectiveness filled him. He had to protect her. An explosion a thousand times greater erupted in his skull. Crying out in agony, he sank down to his knees. He had to make it stop. Any way he could.

His hand shook as it inched closer to the knife

in his belt. A vision of plunging it into Gretchen's body accompanied a significant lessening of the pain. If he killed her, it would stop. He was certain of that. His flesh leapt at that thought, eager to complete the deed, but his mind fought it. Like a tsunami, pain once again slammed into him. He finally touched the knife, his fingers tapping the handle as his hand shook. Making one last effort, he made a grab for it. If he had to, he'd thrust it into his own skull. That would surely stop the torture.

"Kyros?" Gretchen's faint voice shook.

He looked toward her, and there she was—trembling, her legs looking as if they would give out at any moment. Why did she come back for him? She should have kept running. Snarling, he hurled himself up and leapt at her. He grabbed her by the throat and slammed her to the ground.

The pain was gone. He nearly shouted with joy.

A whistling sound turned his attention to the task. Gretchen looked up at him, tears springing from her eyes. Her terrified face shone pale in the moonlight, her full lips staining blue. This woman was beautiful, witty, and kind-hearted...and Kyros had never in his life wanted to kill anyone as much as he wanted to kill her.

"You thought you could escape me?" The voice once again came from his lips. His laughter rang out. "You're a fool, Ambrosia."

Gretchen's mouth gaped open, over and over. A small squeak escaped each time she attempted to draw breath. When her eyes started to dim, Kyros loosened his grip and she greedily sucked in a breath of air. "I would have killed you quickly," he continued, "painlessly, when it was time. But you left me. You turned your back on me. Now you'll suffer. I'll make you suffer at the hands of the man who loves you." A wicked smile spread across his face.

"You see how much power I have? You are nothing but a shadow of me. My father was a god, a powerful king. Your father was a lowly human, a pathetic creature worth nothing. I killed him the day you were conceived, slit open his belly. You should have heard him beg me, cry for me to finish him, to end his suffering. Now you'll suffer your father's fate."

Kyros kept her throat tight in his fist as he stood up and stepped into the forest, dragging her behind. Her legs snagged thorny branches and scraped jagged stones. He could smell her blood as images swirled in his mind—Gretchen bleeding, broken, dying…The images were alluring, appealing beyond belief. The rumbling roar of the sea increased in volume as they neared the shore.

A tall, thick tree stood out alone in the sand, its jagged branches slashing toward the sky and across the bloated moon. Kyros strode toward the tree and slammed Gretchen against the trunk, cracking her head against the bark. Her whimpering cry caused him to pause. He shrunk back from the cresting pain his pause brought. Snatching her wrist, he yanked it up and pressed it against the tree. He was immediately rewarded with relief. He let go of her throat and pulled out his dagger. Gretchen took a whooping breath and eagerly sucked in air.

"Kyros, please," she cried. "Don't do this."

"Kyros can't help you," the voice said, coming from his lips. "No one can." At those words, he raised his blade and thrust forward, piercing flesh, muscle, and bone in her hand—pinning it to the tree. Gretchen screamed, high and loud.

Kyros, horrified at what he'd done, was hit immediately with blinding agony. He collapsed, writhing on the ground. He lay there in misery, not wanting to give into the voice, not wanting to cause Gretchen more pain. He peeled his eyes open, forcing himself to look at her. She sobbed loudly—attempting to hold completely still. The blade was so sharp that it would take little pressure to slice it cleanly through her hand. Blood dripped down her arm as her body trembled violently. "Please," she said with a sob. "Please, Kyros. You're strong. You can resist her." Her shaky voice was barely audible over the earplugs, but the fear and pain written across her face was clear.

The pain grew a thousand times worse as he briefly considered freeing her. "No." The word tore from his lips in a desperate cry. He knew what he had to do. The image burned clearly in his mind. If he ever wanted the pain to stop, he had to slice her open. It subsided as he accepted her fate and climbed back up to his feet. He pulled out a long, curved blade and stepped up to her. He stood, heaving breaths into his oxygen-deprived lungs.

He allowed the other entity free reign of his mind

as he cowered mindlessly in a dark corner of his brain. What other choice did he have? He approached her, and her eyes widened in pure, unadulterated horror. She knew he'd given in. She shook her head in denial of what her eyes were telling her. Her lips formed words. He couldn't hear the words, but he knew she was pleading for mercy. Those lips, the lips that he so recently kissed, were now asking him to spare her. Another growl escaped him as he brushed away the memory and the pain. He couldn't fight it any longer. The agony of resistance was too great. This was a fight to the death, her death or his.

He lifted his knife and honed in on the target, centered just below her ribs, at the top of her abdomen. He would cut her down to her pubic bone—opening her stomach.

The knife sliced down as Gretchen screamed his name. "Kyros!"

Just before blade met flesh, his consciousness leapt out to the forefront of his mind and forced his arm to take a different path. He grazed Gretchen's belly and pierced himself through his thigh.

The explosion of pain was unbearable. Collapsing to the ground, he clutched his head in his hands, pressing hard, desperate to stop the agony. Regardless of having a knife pierce his leg, he didn't feel it at all. The pain in his skull was so great, that being stabbed in the leg was a caress, a mother's kiss in comparison.

Why was he awake? Suffering this great was just not possible. He should have passed out by now. But here he was, wishing he could die rather than have to endure a moment more. Tears flowed from his eyes. He'd never cried before, not even when Kassi was murdered. These tears that came were beyond his control. The pain had grown too great to fight.

Somewhere in his head, he heard Gretchen cry out. Slick hands pulled on his fingers, attempting to pry them off his head. "Kyros, let me help." Gretchen's voice was soft—seemingly coming from far off.

Kyros attempted to crawl away from her. "No!" he roared fighting her off with his elbows. "Get…away from me." He bit off the words between jagged, pain-filled breaths.

"I can help you," she cried out, while continuing to try and approach him.

She was making it impossible for him resist murdering her. "Kill…me," Kyros urged her. "Please," he begged. The idea of the sweet relief death would bring was his only comfort in that moment.

"I can make the pain go away," Gretchen said. "But I have to get the ear plugs out. You need to move your hands."

Kyros desperately wanted to believe she could do what she claimed. It took a tremendous amount of courage to even move his hands at all. He felt as if they were holding back the sea and if he moved them, he would release a tidal wave of pain, causing his skull to explode. But somehow, he did it. He moved his hands away.

Her fingers brushed his ears.

And then the angel came, releasing the pressure in a sea of sweet bliss. She came by way of a heavenly song. The song was as sweet as his pain had been sour. Kyros again cried, but this time, he was crying for joy. His suffering was over.

How long he lay there sobbing, he had no idea, but he came to himself at the close of the angel's tune. He was lying with his head cushioned in softness, gentle fingers stroking his head. His eyes opened to the loveliest sight he'd ever seen—Gretchen smiling down on him, his head in her lap.

"You had me worried," she said, her voice ragged. He could feel her shaking.

Kyros pushed his body up. "Gretchen, by the gods, you're hurt. I hurt you." His voice was thick with regret as he lifted his shaking hand and examined her injury. The first thing he noticed was the blood dripping off her fingers. Then he saw the gaping wound.

"What did you do? My blade's not that thick."

"The blade isn't, but the handle is."

Kyros's eyes widened in horror. "You pulled your hand…"

"I did what I had to do. I couldn't pull the knife from the tree, so——" Her voice caught, tears sparkling on her cheeks.

"Oh baby. That must hurt."

She gave a shaky nod. "Yeah. Probably about as much as your leg."

Kyros looked down. He'd forgotten his injury. The knife was impaled in his leg so deep, only the handle was showing. He reached for it. Just as he pulled, Gretchen screamed, "Don't pull it out."

It made a wet sucking sound as he slid the blade out of his leg.

"Kyros!"

He examined the wound for a short moment. It was oozing blood, but it was nothing serious.

"You should have let a doctor pull that out," she said. "What if you had pierced an artery?"

Kyros shook his head. "The knife was nowhere near the artery."

"How do you know?"

"I know."

He stood and, despite feeling weak and injured, scooped her up off her feet. "I need to take you to a hospital."

She shook her head at him. "No, no hospital. They'll ask too many questions."

"Gretchen, you need your wound tended."

"And you don't? Straton. He could do it."

Kyros pressed his lips together.

"He's a doctor, isn't he?" she asked.

"Of sorts." Or rather—of Dagonians. Humans were…A thought struck him, followed by many others— memories of what had transpired that night.

"You're not human," he blurted, jolting to a stop midstride.

Gretchen's cheeks drained of color. "What are you talking about? Of course, I'm human. What do you think? That I come from another planet?"

"No. You're a daughter of the sea a mermaid."

"Kyros, do you know how crazy you sound? Do I look like I have a fish tail?"

"Of course you don't have a fish tail. That would be crazy." He looked toward the sea.

"Kyros, you're an intelligent man. You can't believe mermaids exist. You've had a hard time tonight, with your headaches and all. And you blacked out for a while."

"I did not."

"Yes, you…you were unconscious. After we got out of the car, you passed out. You looked like you were having vivid nightmares."

"And how did you get your hand injured, and my leg. What happened there?"

"Oh, uh…well, you kind of went a little nuts before you passed out, which is why we should be getting you to a hospital."

Kyros ignored her blatant lies. "While we're there, we can have them look at your hand."

"What? No. I'm fine. Do you have any idea how much trouble you'd be in if I told a doctor what happened?"

"Perhaps I should tell them I was mind-controlled by one mermaid and saved by another. She was your mother, wasn't she?"

"You remember her?"

"No, but I remember you. Your voice saved me."

"That doesn't make me a mermaid."

"Okay, so you're not a mermaid." Kyros shifted his weight off his injured leg. It was throbbing, but compared to the other pain he'd felt tonight, it was literally nothing. Still, perhaps he could use that excuse. "Listen, my leg is killing me. I just need to wash it out in the cool surf."

"No way. You don't want to get sand in it. Besides, the ocean water is filled with microscopic creatures. They could cause an infection."

"I've never had that problem before."

"Do you get injured near the ocean often?"

"Baby, I've only ever gotten injured in the ocean." He looked down at his blood-soaked leg. "Until tonight. Your hand could use some fresh seawater to clean it out as well."

"No way. Where did you get this ridiculous thinking?"

With Gretchen in his arms, he hobbled toward the water.

"Kyros, I don't want to get in. I changed my mind. A trip to the hospital is exactly what I need."

"Come on, just a quick dip. But…" He narrowed his eyes and looked her over. "This won't work." He sat her down and slipped his t-shirt over his head.

"You'll need to put this on," he said.

Gretchen's eyes darted from the shirt, to his face, lingering on his bare chest, which he tightened to improve the view for her. She looked down at her own shirt.

"Why do I need your shirt?"

"For modesty. You'll need to take off those shorts. You can't be wearing them when we get into the water."

"What? You think…? I told you—I'm not getting in the water, and I'm not a mermaid!"

Without asking permission, he shoved his shirt over her head. When her head popped out the top, she was cursing. "You are crazy—certifiably insane."

His shirt was so long on her, the bottom of it touched her knees—perfect. When he reached to pull off her shorts, she screeched, "You are not taking off my pants!" He ignored her and attempted to slip them off. She pounded on his chest with her good hand and shouted. "I'll do it myself!"

Smirking, he stepped away. Holding her injured hand against her chest, she used her other hand to unbutton and yank down her shorts. "You know, after all you put me through, you'd think you'd be a little more sympathetic. Here I am, hurt and bleeding, and it's all your fault." When her shorts were off, she stood and jabbed her finger at him. "I am not getting in the water."

"You'll need to remove your sandals too."

She scowled, yanking them off.

He strode forward and made a swipe for her. She dodged him and stumbled away. He caught her before she fell down and made her injury worse.

His heart broke when he saw how white she was. He lifted her into his arms and cradled her against his chest. He could feel her tremble. She had to be in tremendous pain.

"I don't feel so good," she whispered. "Can't you please just take me home?" She sounded on the verge of tears. He wanted to give in to her pleas, but that was not what she needed right now. She needed to get her focus off her injured and broken self and put it where it needed to go—on him.

"No," he answered firmly.

"You know you're heartless, cruel, and——"

"Gretchen," he interrupted, "we're going in the water."

"I'm not a mermaid," she said, each word clipped and colored with anger. He much preferred her angry than crying and broken, so he continued to egg her on.

"There's no denying what you are."

"Okay, so what if I am? What then?"

"If you are what I think you are, I won't waste any more time. You'll be my wife at tomorrow's daybreak." The words slipped from his lips, surprising himself as much as it likely surprised her. Yet as he spoke them, his resolve set the words in stone. She would be his wife.

"You're crazy!" Her voice rose. "Do you have some kind of mermaid fetish? Well, forget it. I wouldn't marry you if you were the last man alive, as handsome as Matthew McConaughey, and as rich as Bill Gates! What happened to fighting for a woman? Or did your long-winded lecture mean nothing?"

"Baby, tonight I fought harder for you than all the

other people I've known in my entire life—combined. And your mother's right. I'm the man who loves you. I love you, Gretchen."

"You don't love me." She choked on her words. "You don't even like me."

"I thought I already explained myself. Is the problem that I'm human? Would you marry me if I were born of the sea like you?"

Her eyes flickered in surprise. She didn't speak, but simply shook her head slowly.

"We'll see, little mermaid." He paused for a moment before he carried her into the surf and strode out into deeper water.

CHAPTER 19

Gretchen's heart pounded and stomach churned as Kyros stepped into the surf. Could it be? Was he like her?

No, it couldn't. This man was about to have the shock of his life.

The ocean water brought the change, like a thousand tiny fins brushing over her body. The water covered their heads as they plunged down into the moonlit sea. Her throbbing hand felt immediate relief. It still hurt like crazy, but it was much better.

She could hear Kyros growl. It sounded like he was in pain. She could feel his arms trembling around her. A moment later, he relaxed.

Cradled in his arms, she couldn't see his legs. Were they still there? Of course they were. What had she been thinking? There was no way to hide her secret now.

What could she say? She wanted to say, *Close your eyes so I can disappear.* Or maybe she could say, *I know what it looks like, but this isn't what you think.* Perhaps she could convince him he was dreaming.

That was it, darn it! How could she be such an idiot? She could make him forget. And then his arms were gone, and she was floating. She looked up, expecting him to be surfacing for a breath. But he wasn't there.

A dark shape rose from below. Gretchen screamed. The figure slapped its hands against its ears. Her scream turned to a breath of relief when she saw it was Kyros.

"Hades, Gretchen! Watch the volume." He had his hands firmly against his ears. He rose higher. She caught a glimpse of his entire body and nearly screamed again. He had a tailfin. A grey tailfin!

"You…you're a merman?"

He narrowed his eyes as if to gage her reaction to his next statement. She could see his tail curled, and his muscles tensed. He looked as if he were ready to chase her down. "No, I'm not. I'm a Dagonian."

"A what?" She was taken aback. Her mother never said anything about any creature called a Dagonian.

"You've never heard of us?" He immediately relaxed.

Gretchen shook her head. "No. Are you a descendant of Triton too?"

"No, Dagonians descend from Calypso and Dagon."

"I'm familiar with Calypso, but I've never heard of Dagon. Is he Greek?"

"No, he's a Sumerian sea god. Their union caused quite a stir in both pantheons."

Gretchen circled him, slowly swimming round, enraptured by the sight. She'd never seen a male creature like him. He looked even larger as a Dagonian than he did as a six-foot-eight-inch human. His arms and chest were well muscled, and so was his tailfin. It was sleek, grey, and his whole body radiated power.

She reached a tentative hand out to touch his fin. It felt like course-grit sandpaper to her fingertips—not unlike shark's skin. She looked down at her own tailfin. It was soft, smooth, skin-colored, and…she was about to show too much! Kyros's shirt billowed up. She immediately pulled it down and tied it into a hard knot.

"I have one question I must ask you," he said gravely. "How old are you?"

She frowned. "I'm twenty-three."

He blew out a breath and relaxed. "And your mother…?"

"How old is she?" she asked, confused at why he felt the need to know their ages.

"Yes."

"I'm not certain, but she's been around a long time—several thousand years."

"More than two?"

"Yes, at least three or four. Why?"

He pressed his lips together and frowned. "Because two thousand years ago, we were ordered by Poseidon to kill all the Mer. And that order is still in effect."

Gretchen felt a bit faint. "You're supposed to kill me?"

His expression softened, and he pulled her closer.

"No, gods no. You were not even born when the Mer committed the unthinkable act."

"What unthinkable act?"

"They mocked Poseidon."

"What? Mocking someone is a capital offense?"

"Mocking a god is one—especially a god as powerful as Poseidon."

"That's...horrible. For the other Mer, I mean."

"It is what it is."

"Good luck in trying to kill my mother. She's not easily entrapped—which is probably why she's survived as long as she has."

"Tell me about this mother of yours."

The sea seemed to darken as she thought of the past. "I don't remember a whole lot. I was eight years old when I left. Today was the first time I'd ever been back in the sea."

"You could stay away?"

"Oh, yeah. That was easy. I didn't want to remember anything from my life before. Although, I do still feel the ocean's pull. I guess that's why I've always chosen to live near it."

"I can't imagine wanting to leave the sea for good," Kyros said. "Just these last few weeks have been torture. I hate living on land."

"Why do you do it?"

"I..." He hesitated. "I'm a soldier. It's my job to guard and protect."

"You're guarding..." Gretchen's eyes widened as

she realized what he was implying. She looked him up and down. Kyros was about six foot eight inches tall on land, Xanthus about seven feet, and each of the others no less than six-six. "Xanthus is a Dagonian too, isn't he? And the others? Straton, Pallas, Drakōn, and Amar?"

"Yes."

"Oh man. Xanthus is sooo overprotective. He brings Dagonians out of the water just to protect his wife. But..." The wheels were turning in her head. Sara confined to a wheelchair, but now she was miraculously not. "Is Xanthus a god?"

Kyros' eyes widened in surprise, like she'd overlooked the obvious. "No. He's a Dagonian, although thanks to Triton, he is immune to the mermaid's voice."

Gretchen scowled. What was she missing—something about Sara? What was she missing about her best friend? The friend she'd thought she'd known. The friend who'd been like a sister to her from the moment they'd met. Then it hit her.

"Sara's like me," Gretchen blurted.

"Yes."

"But why was she in a wheelchair?"

"Not all mermaids have legs on land. In fact, it's a rare gift."

"My mother has that gift."

"Which is probably why you do too. You inherited it from her."

"But Sara didn't? And she lived on land anyway. Oh my gosh. She was terrified of the water. What happened to her?"

"I truly have no idea."

"I need to go to her. I have to talk to her." Gretchen started to swim back toward shore.

"Hold on." Kyros snatched her hand and pulled her back. "Before we leave, I have to take care of your wound."

"What? Here?"

He chuckled. "Where else?"

He closed his eyes and drew deep breath in through his nose. His eyes snapped open. "Stay here. I'll be right back." He darted off like a rocket. And then he was gone.

A dark shape moved in from behind and brushed her back —a lemon shark. It gave her a jagged-toothed grin. A sleek blue shark came in on her right and swept past her. It took only minutes for sharks to come in on every side.

"Have you guys been hiding?"

She'd barely asked the question when they scattered. Kyros emerged from out of the dark water with seaweed clutched in his hands. "Here." He pressed it down on her wound, packing it in and around on both sides. Surprisingly, it didn't hurt too much. "This should speed up the healing."

"Sharks don't like you very much, do they?"

"What?" he asked, looking around.

"You *like* sharks, don't you?"

Kyros frowned. "I'll have you know, sharks are

one of my favorite sea creatures."

"Hmm. How come I don't believe you?"

"I promise you, I love shark."

"Good." She smiled.

He wrapped a long, flat leaf around her hand and tied it in place. He let go of the extra weed—they drifted, floating away.

Gretchen frowned. "What about *your* wound?"

Kyros shrugged. "It's not that serious."

"Not that serious? You had a huge knife go clear through your leg."

Kyros shrugged. "I've had worse."

"We still need to take care of it." Gretchen swam around, snatching the weed from the ocean water. "Men," she grumbled under her breath. She looked down at his fin and searched for the cut. When she saw it, she gasped. When his legs formed into a fin, it must have warped and stretched the skin around his injury; it was now long, jagged, open flesh. *Not serious, my butt.*

"There's not enough seaweed to cover this," Gretchen said.

"This is not a weed. It's called Nori."

"Whatever it is, there's not enough."

"Gretchen, anything you put on it will get messed up when I get the horrid legs back."

Exasperated at not being able to help Kyros, she exclaimed, "Well, forget it. When we get back, I'll pour alcohol on it and call it good."

"You're angry," Kyros said, surprised.

"I'm not angry; I'm frustrated." She blew out a breath. "I'm sorry; it's not your fault. I just hate not being able to fix things."

"You don't need to fix me, Gretchen. I'm perfectly capable of taking care of myself. I've done it for a hundred years."

"A hundred...! Oh yeah, you're immortal too, huh?"

"Too?"

"Like my birth mom."

"Why do you call her your *birth* mom?"

"Because she's not my real mom. A real mom is someone who loves you, takes care of you, and sacrifices for you. I *have* a real mom—a mom who loves and cares for me. She lives in Miami."

"She's human."

"The best human alive."

"Does she know what you are?"

"If you're talking about me being a mermaid, then no. When I turned my back on the sea, I never looked back. I did everything I could to forget what I was. But my mom knows what's inside of me. She knows my heart, through and through, and that's the most important part."

"She sounds like a special woman."

"She is; she's the polar opposite of my birth mother."

"What do you know about your birth mother?"

"I know her name is Aella."

Descending

Kyros jerked to a stop. His eyes were wide pools of darkness.

"You've heard of her?"

"Yes." His voice was hard and cold.

Gretchen swallowed.

"What else do you know?" Kyros asked.

"I only know what happened to me personally. I don't know what she did while she was away. She kept me hidden in a cave. I spent most of my time in a large, air-filled pocket with a rocky shore. My only entertainment was playing up and around the boulders and swimming in and around the cave. What she didn't know is, while she was gone I would watch the humans on the beach. I would dream I was human, that I was part of a human family. That was, until she caught me."

Kyros's eyes darkened. "What did she do?"

Even now, Gretchen didn't like to talk about it. "She…"

"Go on."

"She got me a playmate."

Kyros scowled. "A human?"

Gretchen nodded. "She brought a little girl into the cave to live with me. The girl was about my age, seven or eight years old. At first, I thought it was the most wonderful thing my mother had ever done for me. But the girl wouldn't play with me. She spent all her time crying. I did everything I could to try to comfort her, coax her into being my friend. I offered her gifts of seashells, pearls, and the most succulent fish…Nothing seemed to help."

"Looking back, I should have returned her to the shore. I was just so starved for attention. I desperately wanted a friend."

"What happened to her?"

"My mother happened."

"What did your mother do?"

Gretchen shook her head as her lip trembled. "The humans came searching for her. So my mother gave her back to them, but not before…"

"Before what, baby?"

"Before she drowned her." She choked on the words, tears leaking into the seawater.

Understanding mixed with pity passed across Kyros's face. He pulled her into his arms and said, "I'm sorry."

Gretchen wrapped her arms around his chest and wept. These tears were long overdue. The events of that day were so horrendous that she'd repeatedly pushed them from her mind. But now they came back fresh — her heart breaking at the memories. "I wish I could go back and change the past. I wish I hadn't been so selfish."

Gretchen held tight to Kyros's chest. His warmth filled her, surrounded her body and penetrated her heart. She cried until her tears were spent. Finally, she pulled away from Kyros and sighed.

"I'm sorry. I'm not usually a crier."

He caressed the side of her face. "You have nothing to apologize for. It was a terrible thing your mother did."

"I could have saved her."

"Gretchen, you were a child yourself. You didn't know what your mother would do. It's not your fault."

"I know. My head understands perfectly, but my heart can't seem to accept it. I guess that's why I've tried to devote my life to protecting others."

"Yeah, you do tend to rush to take care of people, but I think the child you once were is still in you—wanting love, acceptance, and someone to take care of _you_."

She looked into his eyes, wanting so much for that someone to be him, but her track record was against him. When it came to men, no one ever stayed.

"So," Gretchen said. "You know all about my mother. She's a heartless witch with a special place in hell waiting for her. I'll bet you don't want to marry me now."

He shook his head. "Gretchen, you are not your mother."

"Sometimes I worry I am."

Kyros frowned. "You are nothing like your mother."

Gretchen cracked a weak smile.

"She kills without hesitation or remorse," he said.

"Don't I know it," she mumbled. The images of the past clouded her mind.

"You have more compassion than anyone I've ever met," Kyros told her.

Gretchen could hear his words, but her mind was elsewhere—deep in the recesses of a cave.

"Gretchen?"

She swallowed the lump in her throat. "Hm?"

"What's wrong?"

She gave a sad laugh. "You're asking that question while we talk about my birth mom?"

"There's something you haven't told me."

"I don't know how talking about it will help."

"Ignoring things rarely makes them better."

She looked up into Kyros's face. He looked forlorn. "Tell me about it," he said.

"Aella has a cave—hidden deep in a maze of tunnels. I discovered it just before I left."

"That cave is the reason you left, isn't it?" he asked. "It wasn't the human girl."

Gretchen nodded.

"What's in that cave?"

"Bones."

"Bones? Of who? Of what?"

"Mermaids—young ones."

"How young?"

"Children. Babies."

Kyros shook his head in disbelief. "They could only be her own children."

"That's why I left," Gretchen said. "I knew it was only a matter of time before I joined them."

"I've never heard of such wickedness," Kyros said. "Makes sense, though, in a twisted, evil kind of way. She's got to be paranoid about being discovered. Offspring might eventually leave her. And if they were discovered, it would only be a matter of time before they were traced back to her—which is exactly what happened with you. You left her, and now we've found her. And this gives us the reason why she wants you dead. But there's something I don't understand. Why would she keep having children?"

She sighed, struggling to remember. "She was cruel and indifferent, but she was also needy. One day, she would be mean and spiteful; the next, she'd be crying on my shoulder."

"What would she cry about?"

"She never told me."

"That *is* a mystery."

CHAPTER 20

K yros had Gretchen on his arm as they staggered into the office of a tiny, sky-blue, clapboard motel in Somerset Village. Gretchen leaned heavily on his arm, with dark circles shadowing her eyes. She looked exhausted. Still, she gave a friendly smile to the man at the desk.

A hefty, middle-aged man with a shiny, bare head stood as they walked in. Curly, grey fluff stuck out from his collar. Kyros was never so glad he didn't have to worry about the effects of aging.

"Good evening," the human greeted.

"Good evening," Kyros answered. "I would like a room with two beds."

The man smiled. Kyros was taken aback at the gaping spaces between the man's teeth. "Now why you be needing two beds with a girl as pretty as that one on your arm?" He gave an exaggerated wink.

"Are you always this rude to your guests?" Kyros scowled.

The man blinked back in surprise. "I, uh…No, sir. I'm sorry. I didn't mean anything by it."

Gretchen ran her hand down Kyros's arm and

smiled at the uncouth human. "Don't mind Kyros. He's had a *really* bad night."

The man avoided Kyros's gaze as he spoke to Gretchen. "Yeah, he needs to lighten up."

"Don't I know it," she said. "Listen, do you have a room with two beds? Or two adjoining rooms would be fine too."

"Yeah, I got adjoining rooms." He kept his eyes on Gretchen. "You paying with card or cash?"

It looked like this man didn't want to deal with him anymore. "Cash," Kyros said, forcing the man's attention.

The man looked at him briefly while completing the transaction. "Okay, sure. Follow me."

The rooms were much smaller than the rooms in Xanthus's home, but they looked clean, well tended, and each had a wide window. Through the dark pane, he could see a few yellow flowers lighted by the glow from the room's lamp.

"This is perfect. Thank you," Gretchen said.

"Well, pretty lady, just dial 3 if you need anything."

Pretty lady? Kyros scowled. Finally, the human left. "Is that normal behavior?" Kyros asked.

"What behavior?" Gretchen looked baffled.

"Human men calling you nicknames when they don't know you?"

Gretchen shrugged and sank into the bed. "I guess. But not every man is that friendly."

"Friendly? That was friendly?" Kyros stood, too

angry to sit.

Gretchen smiled and nodded.

"When would you say they've crossed the line?" he asked.

"Oh, I don't know." She lay back on the bed and turned toward him on her side. "It depends on the culture."

Kyros raised his eyebrow.

"Oh, all right." She sat up. "I guess if he touches me too much, or in an inappropriate way. Or if he starts calling me baby, honey, or 'ooh la la woman.'" Gretchen's smile broadened as his frown deepened. "Or if he looks me over like he's undressing me with his mind. And a guy looking at me like that while licking his lips…" She gave an exaggerated shudder. "Then there's pinching my butt, grabbing my—"

"I get it," Kyros snapped, interrupting her. He had the insane urge to crush his fist through the human's face.

Gretchen smiled innocently, but the gleam in her eye told him she knew exactly what she was doing to him.

"Okay," Gretchen said, "so tell me again why you're determined to lock me away in here while you leave and go talk to Xanthus."

Kyros paced the floor, his leg shooting daggers of pain with each step. "Drakōn can't track you here. He's the one that took me to your mother—"

"Birth mother."

"Right. Anyway, I think it's safe to assume he will

kill you if he gets the chance."

"Probably. You know he'll most likely kill you too."

"I'm much harder to kill than you are."

"I'm not a weakling."

"No, you're not. But you *are* injured and exhausted."

"So are you." She crossed her arms over her chest.

Kyros sighed and dropped onto the bed beside her. "All right. I give up. I'll call Xanthus and have him meet us here."

"Sara too?"

"Okay."

"We might want to wait 'til morning," she said. "It's pretty late."

Kyros frowned and nodded. Lifting her chin, he examined her face. "You look worn out."

Gretchen cracked a smile. "Let's see. What did I do today? I escaped from prison, took an early morning swim, played a game of tag with the sharks, hiked a mountain, explored caves, ran for my life while being chased down by a murdering lunatic, got choked near to death, stabbed in the hand, and yanked my own hand out from said knife." He internally cringed at the memory, regret still fresh in his mind. "Can't wait to see what tomorrow brings."

"Get some sleep," he said. "You need your rest. I'll...I'll keep watch until you fall asleep."

"You don't need to. I'm sure I'll be asleep as soon as my eyes close."

He sat, not moving. She was right. Obviously, she wasn't afraid to be left alone. He should just go to bed himself. After all, he was honest enough to admit he was also dead on his feet.

Pulling back the blankets, she slid under the sheets. She punched her pillow a few times, lay her head down, gingerly placed her injured hand across her chest, and closed her eyes. Still, he didn't move. He looked to the door of the adjoining room. He should go to bed. But he didn't. He just sat there, watching her—unwilling to leave her alone.

"Are you just going sit there and stare at me all night?" She spoke without opening her eyes.

Kyros grunted.

She sat up and ran her fingers through her hair. "Look. If you're scared—"

"I'm not scared," he snapped, angry at the mere suggestion.

Gretchen cracked a smile. "I know."

He continued to glower at her. What was wrong with him? Why couldn't he bring himself to do something as simple as go to bed? Because, in order to do that, he'd have to leave her alone in this room. That was just not something he could do right now. Gretchen had nearly died today. He came close to spilling her guts on the sand—the woman he loved!

Drakōn had no such feelings stopping him. If

Aella compelled him to, he would slice Gretchen to ribbons without a second thought.

Gretchen scooted next to him. She looked deep in his eyes. "Why are you so angry?"

"I came so close to killing you." He dropped his head and closed his eyes, too ashamed to look at her. "And I wouldn't blame you if you don't believe me, but I love you, Gretchen. I truly do. I don't know how it happened so quickly, but it did. I don't deserve you. You have no idea how much I wanted to kill you, even *while* I loved you. I wanted to see you broken, bleeding, and dead."

"That wasn't you, Kyros. That was her. I don't blame you at all. And I'm the last one to judge you. You're less of a murderer than I am."

Kyros jerked his head up, shocked at what she was implying. "What do you mean? It's not your fault your mother killed that girl."

"That's not what I'm talking about." There was a glimmer of a tear on her cheek.

He tugged her to lean against him. "Tell me."

She took in a ragged breath. "It's why I came here in the first place. I killed a man—back in Hawaii."

Kyros forced back his reaction. He needed to hear the whole story before making any judgments.

"Who was he?"

She looked down and took in another shaky breath. "He was the father of a client—a five-year-old girl he nearly beat to death. The state took her away from him and placed her with a good, loving family.

They were trying to adopt her. But somehow, the father convinced the judge he'd changed. They gave him back his daughter. He almost killed her, and they gave her back to him! She was terrified. She didn't want to go back. And I...I was angry. I wasn't thinking straight. I walked straight up to him and told him if he ever hurt her again..." She couldn't finish; she couldn't say it. "I didn't realize I'd used compulsion. I was just so angry."

"You compelled him without singing?" Kyros asked.

She nodded. "It's not so much the song that holds power, it's the emotion. Singing emits much more emotion than speaking, and it's easier to control. But that day, I guess my voice was emotionally charged. Regretfully, it was enough to compel him to kill himself."

"You and I share a similar past, Gretchen, but at least you didn't know what you were doing. I was fully aware of what I did."

"What happened?"

"That's a story for another time. You need your sleep." He lay down, keeping her in his arms.

"Isn't this against your moral code? Sleeping with me in my bed?"

"Not if all we do is sleep. And to tell you the truth, I'm too exhausted to do anything but sleep."

"Me too." Her voice trailed off and within seconds, her breathing deepened. Minutes later, he joined her in his dreams.

CHAPTER 21

Aella paced back and forth across the deck. She picked up a chair and smashed it through the nearest window as she screamed. Glass shards flew everywhere. "I knew it! Why didn't I listen to my doubts? I knew Ambrosia would give me trouble. Kyros should have delivered me her body by now." She turned to Drakōn and snarled. "Why isn't he here?"

She knew he wouldn't answer her. Being entranced—he didn't embrace a conscious thought. "Come here, Drakōn." He responded at once and strode over to her.

She softened her voice, allowing him to speak. "What do you think happened with Kyros?"

His eyes lightened. "I think he defied your commands."

"Impossible!" Aella glowered at him. "How could he?"

"He loves her."

"I only told him to *say* he loved her. I didn't compel him to actually feel anything for her. Besides, love's a myth."

She waited for him to contradict her, but he

remained silent. "Do you believe in love?"

"Yes."

"Have you ever felt love?" She circled him as she spoke.

"Yes."

"Can you give me more than a one-word answer?"

"Yes."

"Well…" She stopped to face him "Tell me more. Who do *you* love?"

"My…" He collapsed to the floor, writhing in pain.

Aella frowned at his resistance. "Your wife?"

Still thrashing around, he growled.

"Your son?"

He slammed his fist into the deck, cracking the floor.

"Your daughter?"

At those words, he bellowed out a roar and snarled, "Leave me alone, witch!"

"Ah ha! You have a daughter."

"I'll kill you. I swear I will." He slammed his head against the deck, breaking the wood. Blood dripped down his forehead.

"Stop hurting yourself. You don't want to damage that handsome face."

"Release me!" he shouted.

"I'll release you under one condition."

"What?" he growled.

"Kiss me."

Descending

He pushed up from the deck, taking labored breaths, still recovering from the pain.

"Kiss me like you want me," she said. "Kiss me like you...love me."

He staggered to his feet as the fire of passion lit in his eyes.

Aella had learned a lot about this Dagonian. Drakōn was a killer, an assassin. He could end a life without a second thought. What she didn't know surprised her—surprised a woman who had lived four thousand years. A woman who'd witnessed countless men rise and fall over the ages. This killer's heart had tenderness in it. His touch was gentle, his caresses like silk. And for a brief time, she pretended he loved her. For a brief moment, she pretended she loved him in return.

But love was a fallacy. It was a lie. Hours later, cradled in the arms of her fantasy, Aella awoke to reality. She'd been weak. She'd made her heart vulnerable. She'd entertained a dangerous fantasy—the dream that someone could ever learn to love her. That she could ever learn to love him in return. And with that realization, her indignation began to rise. She was above this. Love was weakness; love was pathetic. And she needed a healthy dose of reality to atone for her momentary lapse.

"Drakōn, wake up," she snapped. His eyes immediately opened. They were more glazed than usual. He looked exhausted. She pushed his arms away and stood.

She was *power*.

She was *control*.

And she was curious about how enamored her love slave had become. Most men gave easy adoration after making love to her. Robert no longer needed a siren's song to compel him. He gave his devotion willingly.

She eliminated the tenor in her voice, testing the Dagonian who had touched her so gently, who spoke so tenderly in the night. "I need a champion. Will you fight for me?"

He staggered to his feet and growled, anger surfacing as hot, molten lava. "I'll fight *you*, witch!" She recognized her mistake immediately and rang out a powerful, "Stop," just as he leapt at her. With his momentum springing forward, he wasn't able to obey. He plowed her over, knocking her to the floor and cracking her head against the baseboard. His body went limp in reaction to her command. She gasped for breath and pushed with all her might. "Get off me," she ordered, remembering to put a generous amount of power behind her voice. He rolled off, and she whooped in a breath. That Dagonian weighed as much as a whale did.

Anger boiled in her. He didn't love her. They never did.

"This is how *I* fight, Dagonian," she sang. "Hit yourself in the groin as hard as you can."

He snarled, clutched his head, and collapsed to the ground. "Go to Tartarus!"

"Do it," she said, despite knowing she didn't need to repeat herself. Her voice would continue to inflict pain as long as he defied her. Drakōn finally fisted his hand and slammed it into his groin. He grunted, but seemed relieved not to feel the agony in his head.

"That was disappointing," she said.

She sauntered up to him and spoke, her voice syrupy sweet. "You *will* fight for me. I want you and Robert to fight to the death. Not only that, but I want you to tear him limb from limb with your bare hands. Will you do this for me?"

"Yes," he answered clearly, all hints of venom gone. He'd given in completely.

"And then I want you to return to Kyros and Gretchen and kill them both in the most painful way possible. Do you understand?"

Pain flashed in his eyes, and then he relaxed again. "Yes," he answered.

Aella led Drakōn down to the lower deck. Opening a door, she found Robert inside a storage room.

"Aella," Robert said with tears in his eyes. "I thought you'd never come back! I thought you were tossing me aside, now that you have him." He glared at Drakōn. Drakōn stood indifferent.

"You can have me," Aella said, caressing the side of Robert's face, "if you want me."

"Oh, I do." He turned to her and took her hand.

"Are you ready to fight for me?" she asked him.

"Yes," he answered.

"Okay." She looked from Robert to Drakōn. "Whichever of you survives gets to have me." She was about to explain to Robert the part about ripping limbs apart, but it wasn't worth her breath. This man might be a mighty warrior among humans, but he was no match for this Dagonian.

"I only ask that neither of you brings the fight close to me. You wouldn't want me to get hurt, would you?"

"Oh no. Baby, I would never let you get hurt," Robert exclaimed vehemently. Aella frowned at Drakōn's lack of response and rubbed the throbbing lump on the back of her head.

"All right, let the fight begin," she said. Drakōn leapt forward and snapped Robert's neck in less time than it took her to blink. Aella looked down at Robert's broken body. He died with an adoring expression on his face. The fool must have been looking at her instead of his opponent.

"When you're done, clean up the mess," she ordered as she opened the door to leave. "Oh, and make sure you shower and put on clean clothing before returning to bed. You can have all of Robert's clothes. *He* sure won't need them."

She turned and left without a backward glance.

CHAPTER 22

Gretchen awoke with her back pressed against Kyros's stomach. His arms wrapped around her. She'd never felt so loved, so protected…*Wait a minute.* Someone was knocking.

Gretchen sat up. "Did you call Xanthus?"

"Yeah, about half an hour ago."

"Kyros, it's me, Xanthus. I'm here with Sara." Xanthus's voice came from outside.

Kyros stood and stepped to the door.

Gretchen's heart pounded. Darn it. She hadn't had time to run through what she was going to say to Sara—how she'd break the news to her. Not only that, but she was probably a mess. Her hair, most mornings, looked like hedgehog had parked himself on her head.

"Are you alone?" Kyros asked.

"Yes."

"I've got to go shower first," she whispered at Kyros and ran for the bathroom. "I'll just be a minute."

She'd just shut the door when she heard talking in the next room. Turning on the shower, she began to collect her thoughts. Needing to cleanse her mind as well as body, she ran the water cool. It was probably a mermaid thing, but she preferred a nice cool shower to a hot one.

She washed out the salt, applied conditioner, and scrubbed her body. Luckily, she didn't have to shave. Her favorite mermaid perk—no leg hair. She was careful to keep her injured hand out of the stream of water. Still, she was in and out in five minutes. She did have one problem though; she had nothing to wear. Hopefully, the motel had laundry service.

She heard a soft knock on the door. "Gretchen, I brought you some clothes from the house." It was Sara.

Gretchen cracked the door and snatched the bag. "Thanks, sweetie."

Minutes later, Gretchen had fresh clothes on and her hair combed out. She stepped out of the bathroom and found Kyros, Xanthus, and Sara all sitting at a table, talking.

Sara immediately stood. Gretchen's heart skipped a beat at the sight. The only other time she'd seen her on her feet was the day she was shot. Should she be walking around?

Gretchen didn't know what to say. Sara looked to be feeling about the same. They both stood, not moving. Gretchen decided she needed to make the first move. She stepped across the room and wrapped her arms around her best friend. "You're walking. I still can't believe it."

"I'm sorry I lied. I just didn't know how to tell you." Her eyes went to the seaweed wrap around Gretchen's hand. "What's up with your hand?"

"Oh, it's just a scratch. Kyros overreacted and put some herbal seaweed stuff on it."

She could see Kyros shaking his head in her peripheral vision.

"I don't know how to explain…" Sara said, looking over at Xanthus.

Gretchen glanced at Kyros and asked, "How much have you told them?"

"I thought you should be the one to tell her. We'll just be outside," he said, gesturing Xanthus to the door. Xanthus hesitated a moment before he followed, pulling the door closed behind him.

"Tell me what?" Sara asked, turning back to her.

"Why don't you sit down?" Gretchen tugged her down on the couch. "Well, you know how well we hit things off when we met. We both felt like we were long-lost sisters."

"Yeah…"

"Come to find out, that's not far from the truth."

Sara's eyes widened. "You. Can't. Mean."

"That we're related? Yes, we are."

Sara swayed, obviously stunned by the news. "What are we? Distant cousins?"

"Not cousins, and we're not distantly related. I think it might be easier for you to understand if I tell you a little about my background. You already know I'm adopted."

"Yes," Sara said. "You have an amazing mom."

"My birth mom is not so great."

"I thought you didn't remember her." Sara lifted a shaky hand and brushed her hair behind her ear.

"Oh no. I remember her. I just didn't want to. She was a monster. She killed a lot of people or rather, she convinced people to kill each other." Gretchen's voice shook as she spoke. She'd never imagined she'd be having this conversation with another living soul—least of all, Sara. Just talking about it caused Gretchen's chest to tighten and her heart to tremble.

Gretchen could tell exactly when the truth hit Sara. Her eyes widened, and she visibly paled. "Are we related on my mom's side or my dad's?"

Gretchen hesitated a moment before she quietly said, "Your dad's."

"You know who my dad is?"

Gretchen nodded. "Your father is my grandfather." Gretchen looked at Sara and realized for the first time where Sara must have gotten her striking blue eyes. Gretchen's own brown eyes were like brown mud puddles next to Sara's eyes, which were as blue as the clear Caribbean Sea.

"Then your mom is…" Sara stammered, wringing her hands. "You are…"

"A mermaid."

"But…" Sara's brows pinched together as she looked at Gretchen's legs. "You don't have a tail."

"Not on land."

"You mean, you can change?"

Gretchen nodded.

"Did my dad give you that gift?"

"I was born with it."

"Really? You can change?" Sara reached out as if she might touch Gretchen's knee, but jerked her hand back before she could. "Good grief. I guess I wasn't the lucky one."

"I'm sorry," Gretchen said. "I wish you had been."

"Oh." Sara shook herself out of a stupor as she looked at her friend. "Don't listen to me. Here I am feeling sorry for myself when it's your story that's important. Is your birth mom still alive?"

"Unfortunately. By the way, how's your injury? Did it heal all right?"

Sara rubbed her side. "Oh, I've been fine for days."

"I'm really sorry you got shot. It should have been me." Gretchen frowned at the regret that clenched her heart.

"Don't be ridiculous," Sara said, smiling. "I couldn't let my niece get shot."

Gretchen cracked a smile. "Thank you, Aunt Sara."

Sara giggled and shook her head. "Please don't call me that. Coming from you, it makes me feel like an old woman."

"Sure thing, Auntie Sara."

"Oh." Sara gave a tortured moan and a half smile. "That sounds even worse."

Gretchen smiled back and put her arm around Sara's shoulders. "I wish we'd known about each other from the start."

"Me too." They leaned against one another for a few minutes, comforted by each other's presence.

Sara shrugged away from Gretchen. "Well, I think it's time we invite Xanthus and Kyros back. We have to figure out what to do about this killer."

Kyros stepped through the door and searched Gretchen's face. She gave him a reassuring smile. Xanthus followed and looked Gretchen up and down. He looked stunned that he hadn't figured out what she was from the start.

"So," Sara said, "someone is out to kill Gretchen?"

"Um, yeah," Gretchen answered. "That would be my birth mother."

"What? Why would any mother want to kill her own daughter?"

"If she's found, she's dead." Gretchen shrugged, acting as if the fact her own mother was trying to kill her was no big deal. Deep down, it was a very big deal. But she couldn't change who her birth mother was. She just had to deal with it, no matter how much it sucked.

"She's been around since Poseidon made his decree," Kyros said. "Her death is long overdue."

Gretchen nodded. "She was trying to cover her tracks."

"...by killing you?" Sara gasped out the question.

"Yeah."

"I'm so sorry," Sara's eyes showed the depth of her sympathy. Gretchen's own heart lightened with the fact that she was not alone. Sara would always be by her side. She glanced over at Kyros. The depth of his sympathy and regret were apparent on his face. It looked like she had his undying support also.

"So, what's happened so far?" Sara asked.

"Well, after the shooting, Drakōn went looking for the killer. He came back and told Kyros he'd caught the killer and needed Kyros to come with him. When Kyros came back, he tried to kill me."

"You what?" Sara turned to Kyros.

He frowned. "I did all I could to resist."

"And he did," Gretchen rushed to defend him. "He stabbed himself in the leg instead of stabbing me."

"Drakōn has yet to return," Kyros said. "My guess is, when he sees I didn't succeed, he'll try to kill both of us."

"Oh boy," Sara said. "How do we stop him?"

"You don't." Xanthus said, looking from Sara to Gretchen. "Either of you. This is our fight. Dagonians are charged with eliminating the mermaids, and Drakōn is our responsibility."

"You *do* know that since he's been compelled," Gretchen said, "he'll not stop until my birth mom releases him, or he's been compelled to stop. And the only ones capable of compelling are Sara and me. And since it's *my* mother who is at the root of all this trouble, *I'm* the one who should do it."

"I don't think you know how dangerous Drakōn is," Xanthus said. "He can be vicious and heartless. When it comes to criminals, he has no mercy."

"That doesn't change a thing," Gretchen said. "You still won't be able to stop him without me."

"Killing him would stop him," Kyros said.

"No!" Gretchen turned to Kyros. "You are not killing him. He's an innocent man."

"You don't know him like I do," Kyros said. "He's far from innocent."

"You could say that about me too."

Kyros stepped toward her, towering above. "No, I could not. Compared to Drakōn, you, Gretchen, are an angel."

Gretchen looked up defiantly. "I'm still going."

"No. You're not," Kyros said.

"Did you just tell me I *can't* go?" Gretchen asked

"Did I not speak clearly?" Kyros asked.

"Kyros," Sara said. "I understand that you're worried about her, but you have to understand——"

"She's not going."

"I can go anyplace I please," Gretchen said. "I don't need, nor will I *ever* ask your permission."

"In this case you do," Xanthus said. "This is now an official Dagonian hunt. Only soldiers are allowed to participate."

"Xanthus dear," Sara said. "You can't be serious."

"Sara, you need to understand, we've been trained for this."

"I've had training of my own," Gretchen said to Xanthus. "You could make me a soldier."

"You're a woman," Kyros said, his expression incredulous.

"Oh?" She turned a glaring eye at him. "I hadn't noticed."

"Xanthus wouldn't do anything so ridiculous," Kyros said.

"Kyros is right," Xanthus said. "Neither of you know Drakōn the way we do. He's lethal. You stand no chance against him. He'll kill you before you even know he's there, much less before you get a chance to sing to him."

"We've wasted enough time arguing," Kyros said. "Xanthus and I have planning to do."

Gretchen narrowed her eyes, fuming. *Oh, so that's how they are going to play it?* Well, she could show these Dagonians a thing or two. She knew she'd sworn to never use compulsion again, but desperate times…Darn it. Xanthus couldn't be compelled, could he?

No, but Kyros could. All she needed to do was get him alone. "Kyros, can I speak to you please?"

He didn't even look at her. "No."

Her jaw dropped. She was about to spit out an angry retort, but snapped her mouth shut. Raising her temper would not help her cause. "Please, Kyros. I just need a moment."

"Gretchen. You are not getting me alone. I know how your mind works. You just keep your siren's song to yourself."

"I would never…"

He turned to her and smiled. "Oh yes you would."

She stood, fuming, as he turned his back to her. How dare he dismiss her like that? She was about to delve into a debate when she noticed his phone sitting on the table near the door. "Fine, you two do your planning. Sara and I have important things to do too. You know, like painting our nails, doing each other's hair, watching chick flicks, boy talk…" Gretchen tugged Sara to the door and discretely snatched Kyros's phone.

Xanthus and Kyros were deep in conversation, but Kyros managed to grunt a response to her.

As soon as they were outside, Sara spoke. "We're going to do all those things out here?"

"Of course we are," Gretchen responded sarcastically.

"Right. So what's the plan?"

Gretchen simply raised Kyros's phone.

Sara's eyes widened. "Listen. I don't know if I completely disagree with them. This sounds dangerous. And I know nothing about fighting, stealth, or killing mermaids."

"You have your voice, don't you?"

"Yes, but it's not nearly as powerful as this mother of yours. Mine only lasts a couple of minutes after I stop singing."

Gretchen was taken aback. "Really?"

Sara's face flushed red. "Yeah. I guess I'm not

that great a mermaid, huh?"

"I don't know about that. How did you know I was going to get shot?"

"I…don't know. I just knew."

"Precognition is a pretty good gift if you ask me. It saved my life."

"Precognition? I don't see the future I just…"

"…know when bad things are going to happen?" Gretchen said.

"I wouldn't go so far as that. I just…sense things."

"Right. Precognition."

Sara shrugged. "What are we going to do?"

"Call Drakōn."

"Can you sing to him over the phone?"

"I wish. No, it has to be in person. But we can find out where he is."

"You aren't going to meet him alone, are you?"

"I just need to be within hearing distance."

"I don't like this."

"Look, I'll just hide out someplace secluded and call him to meet me there. Then I'll start singing. I'll sing all night if I have to. That way, he can't catch me by surprise."

"Sounds foolproof."

"Exactly."

"But from what I'm hearing, Drakōn is no fool. What if he has ear plugs?"

"I'll have to go in armed."

Sara frowned.

"I'll admit. It's not without risk, but I have to try. Drakōn didn't ask to be compelled any more than Kyros did. I can't just let him die. Once I have him out from under my mom's spell, he can help Xanthus find her."

Sara nodded. "It sounds like a good plan. I am worried though. How dangerous is your birth mom?"

"Her only power is what she exerts through her compulsion. Personally, she's a weakling."

"Okay. I just, I'd be crushed if anything happened to you."

"I'll be fine," Gretchen said, but her eyes betrayed her, showing a hint of fear.

"You'd better be," Sara said, pulling her into a crushing hug.

CHAPTER 23

Kyros stood and watched Xanthus pace the floor. "We've got to figure out how to get Drakōn to lead us back to the mermaid," Xanthus said.

"That may be harder than it seems," Kyros said. "I have no recollection of ever seeing Aella."

Xanthus gasped. "Aella?"

"I know. I could scarcely believe it myself."

"But I thought she was dead."

"I guess the reports were wrong."

"Is Gretchen sure——"

"Of who her own mother is? Of course she is."

"It's just. Hades, she's the worst of them all."

"Nobody knows that more than Gretchen. You might be interested to know Gretchen is not the first of Aella's children to be born."

"There are more of them?"

"Not anymore. She's killed them. Slaughtered them while they were still young."

Xanthus blew out a breath. "Just when you think you've seen the worst of evil."

"Yeah."

"Okay, so how do we proceed?"

"We should simply kill Drakōn," Kyros said. "He's too dangerous to toy with."

"Killing him will not help us find her."

"Forget Drakōn; we can pull the knowledge out of *my* brain. It has to be there, hidden somewhere. Gretchen should be the one to do it. Her compulsion is as powerful as her mother's."

"Do you think she'll cooperate?"

"If we approach it right."

"Like we approached her this morning?"

Kyros shook his head. "I know. I admit I was over the line. But by the gods, just the thought of her in Drakōn's hands…"

"Have you admitted it?"

"Admitted what?"

"That you love her?"

Kyros frowned. "Yes, but I'm not happy about it."

Xanthus smiled. "She's a handful, that's for sure."

"More so than Sara."

Xanthus's smile widened. "Sara's plenty enough for me to handle. Good luck with Gretchen. Have you asked to marry her?"

Kyros's eyes widened. "Asked?"

"Yes. It's customary for human men to ask their woman to marry them."

"I should have known. I didn't ask her; I *told* her I would marry her at today's daybreak, which was a bit unrealistic. I first have to find a priest to do it, but I have every intension of marrying her."

"How did she respond to being *told* you would marry her?"

Kyros smiled. "She told me she wouldn't marry me if I were the last man on earth, as handsome as some guy named Matthew, and as rich as Bill's gate—whatever that means."

Xanthus laughed. "It's Bill Gates. He's a billionaire."

"Oh well, I'm sure I can convince her to cooperate."

"I don't know. It sounds like a challenge to me."

"I'm never one to back away from a challenge."

"Do you think she'll be happy with you?"

"What? Why wouldn't she?"

"She's spent a lot of time being human. She seems happy living on land. What if she doesn't want to return to the sea?"

Kyros gaped at Xanthus. The thought had never entered his mind. She was a mermaid. Her place was in the sea. How could she possibly be happy to stay on land? Sure, she might dwell on land for a while, but she couldn't want to remain there forever. "Once we're married, it won't matter. She'll live where I do."

Xanthus shook his head. "You might want think more about Gretchen's needs. Is your happiness worth her misery? Do you think either of you would end up happy?"

Kyros shook his head. "Land dwellers are so

confusing. I don't understand their thinking. I mean, I know Gretchen has spunk and attitude—it's what attracts me most. But…gods, there has to be an order to things. Husbands direct, wives follow. Tell me that's not how you and Sara live."

"It's not. We work together to make decisions."

Kyros shook his head. "And it works?"

"Better than you'd think. I've a feeling there are a large number of unhappy Dagonian wives."

"At least the husbands are happy."

"You're a fool if you think husbands can be happy with a miserable wife. Do you think you could truly be happy knowing Gretchen was unhappy?"

Kyros frowned. Why did Xanthus have to make so much sense? "I'll think about what you said. I won't promise I'll ever agree, but I'll consider it."

There was a soft rapping on the door Kyros opened to Sara on the doorstep. "I…" She choked on her word the moment their eyes met.

Xanthus stepped around Kyros. "What is it, moro mou? What's wrong?"

"I'm not supposed to say…"

Kyros's blood froze in his veins at those words.

"But," she continued, "I'm afraid she's going to get herself killed."

Kyros roared in anger.

Xanthus slammed him back. "Keep your distance from my wife while you rage," he snarled at Kyros.

"Where is she?" he growled at her.

Xanthus fisted Kyros's shirt in his hand. "Stop posturing toward my wife, soldier, or you'll have a battle on your hands."

Kyros snarled at Xanthus. "Bring it on."

"Do you want to waste time?" Xanthus asked. "The more we fight amongst ourselves, the more time we lose. Now calm yourself or *I'll* do it for you, and Sara and I will go after her without you."

Kyros clenched his jaw and attempted to cool his fury. He took several breaths and turned to Sara. Her eyes were wide, her face white. "I'm sorry, Sara. I shouldn't have taken my anger out on you. Can you forgive me?"

"Of course. I'm just as upset as you are. I just… Kyros, you have to find her. She's gone after Drakōn."

"How does she even know where to look?" Kyros asked.

"She took your cell phone. She's going to call him and tell him where to meet her. She thinks if she just sings and keeps singing, that he'll hear her before he reaches her. And if he can't hear her, she's brought a gun to shoot him."

"That's not a bad plan," Xanthus said. "If only she'd brought me with her to protect her."

"If he puts a mark on her," Kyros said. "I'll kill him with my bare hands."

Xanthus pulled out his cell phone. "I'll call her. Perhaps she'll be willing to tell us where she is if we agree to help her."

"Gah!" Kyros roared. "I hate this. She was not

supposed to be a part of this."

"She's already part of this," Sara said.

"Yes, but she shouldn't be at risk."

Xanthus stood with the phone at his ear. "It's gone to voice mail." He waited a moment, and then spoke into the phone. "Gretchen, I know you're upset. I'm sorry we didn't listen to you. But I can help you with your plan. Just let me stay with you and protect you."

Kyros hated that he couldn't offer to go himself. He couldn't listen to her siren's voice without it affecting him. But Xanthus could. He knew he had no reason to be jealous, but Hades, he was. He hated being left out.

"Please call me back," Xanthus said before ending the call.

"*Now* what do we do?" Sara challenged. Kyros looked up, surprised at her anger. He might have scared her into a corner, but she'd come back baring teeth.

"She didn't tell you where she was going?" Xanthus asked.

She shook her head, frowning.

"Then there's not much we *can* do, moro mou."

"Actually, Sara," Kyros said. "There might be something you can do. We were going to use Gretchen to tap into my forgotten memories. Do you think you could do it?"

"I can try."

"I don't think it'll work. Gretchen's voice is much more powerful than yours," Xanthus said to her.

"Why, thank you for pointing that out, dear. And

while you're at it, I'm sure you'd like to point out how the extra five pounds I've put on since we've married disgusts you."

"Sara, I have no idea what you're talking about. And if you've put on five pounds, you probably needed to. You look more beautiful than ever."

Her face lightened up. "Really?"

"Look," Kyros said, "I hate to interrupt this pointless exchange, but I think it's worth a try."

Xanthus shrugged. "I don't see how it could hurt."

Sara sat Kyros down. He prepared to open his mind to her influence.

The song started low, uncertain, but it hit him hard. His heart rate spiked, and a smile spread across his face. All thoughts flew from his mind. Was there something he was supposed to do? He tried to search his thoughts, but the sweet melody had him mesmerized. He had to touch this angel. He looked into her eyes and saw the most beautiful creature he'd ever seen, since… Gretchen. This angel wasn't as compelling as Gretchen was, but she was close, within reach. But then there was another angel. Where had that thought come from? Why should he care for that one when this one was close enough to touch, close enough to taste?

Steel arms like a vice clamped around him. A gruff voice growled in his ear, "Keep your hands off my wife." *Xanthus?*

The third mermaid surfaced again in his mind.

She too was beautiful, but chilling. Her eyes sparkled like diamonds—clear, lifeless, cruel. She wielded her voice like a caress, like a whip. She stood on the deck of a ship, her dress hugging her lush features. She had Drakōn and another man on her arms, worshipping her, stroking her.

The memories of her words rose in his mind. "Kyros, make Gretchen love you, sweep her off her feet, declare your love for her, and then I want you to gut her like a bloated fish…"

"She told me I have to kill Gretchen," he growled—his own voice like sandpaper against the silkiness of the other. His heart pounded, his anger rising. One angel wanted him to kill another. Sweet, comforting words caressed his ears. The voice said he didn't have to kill her.

Like a waterfall gone dry, the voice dropped away, trickling into nothingness. Kyros awoke to find Xanthus sitting on his chest, his hands pinning Kyros's wrists against the floor. "What are you doing?" Kyros growled, barely able to take a breath.

"Saving your life."

"Why? Who threatened me?"

"I did. If you had made one more grab for my wife, I would have ripped your head off."

"What? I tried to touch Sara?"

"You tried to grope her, kiss her. You know there are easier ways to commit suicide."

"I'm sorry. I didn't know what I was doing."

"Obviously."

Descending

"Did it work?" Kyros asked.

"You expect me to know?" Xanthus asked. "You're the one with the memories."

"I..." The memories were there—filling his mind, sickening his stomach. Two days of torture, bliss, and everything in between. "I remember. I remember it all." Red filled his vision. Aella was worse than they had all imagined. Kyros wished more than anything he could be the one to rip out her heart—if she had one.

CHAPTER 24

Gretchen sat on a bolder with her back pressed against the rocky wall of a crevasse. There was only one way in and one way out of here. Drakōn would not be sneaking up on her. If she could not save him, she'd have to kill him.

The phone vibrated in her pocket. She pulled it out. *Xanthus.* She briefly considered answering. There was still time to ask him to help her. No. He'd made it perfectly clear she was not equipped to handle a soldier like Drakōn. Well, she could and she would.

She hit the call reject button and scrolled to find Drakōn's number. She pushed dial, before she could lose her nerve. The phone rang several times before it picked up.

"Hello?" Gretchen's knees nearly buckled. The voice speaking in her ear was one that used to be more familiar than her own. It was the one she remembered longing to hear after days left alone.

It was her mother.

She straightened her shoulders, determined not to give her birth mom the satisfaction of frightening her. "Hello, Mother." Gretchen's voice was smooth, confident, and reflected none of the anxiety that twisted her insides like the tangled tentacles of a dead octopus.

"Ambrosia, my dear. How good of you to call." Her voice sounded sweet, affectionate…like any other mother would sound to their daughter. The only difference was, this woman wanted to murder her daughter.

"You know how it is," Gretchen said, playing along. "I've been busy with school and all. I'd love to come home for dinner. Maybe we could catch a movie, make cookies together, and have a nice chitchat…You know, reminisce the old days. Oh, and I met a boy. I simply *have* to tell you all about him."

"Oh yes, Kyros. I've met him, dear. Quite the catch, isn't he? Although, I heard he could be quite dangerous. You know, the love 'em and kill 'em type."

"Oh, no. He's been a perfect gentleman. I don't know *where* you could have heard such a rumor."

"Well, the love 'em part, I experienced firsthand."

Gretchen could feel her temperature rise. "If there's one thing you excel at, it's getting men who couldn't care less about you to think they do."

"Oh, that's a low blow, child. They care. They just might need some coaxing at first, but once they've had me, they're like putty in my hands."

"That didn't work out so well with Kyros, did it? He didn't kill me, after all."

"Nobody's perfect—although the situation was. The man you love spills your guts on the——"

"You are one sick woman," Gretchen interrupted.

"Mermaid, dear. Or have you forgotten? You've been living among slime for so long, you're slick with it."

"I'm through talking with you. Put Drakōn on."

"Oh, you mean my newest——"

Gretchen pounded her fist against the stone wall and shouted, "Just put him on!"

"Fine," her mother huffed.

Gretchen had to wait several minutes before she heard his voice. "Gretchen."

"Drakōn? Are you all right?" She knew it was pointless, but she just had to ask.

"You'd better run, mermaid." His voice was forced and thick with effort.

"I can help you."

"Help yourself." His cry nearly blew out her eardrum.

"Drakōn," she yelled, hoping he could hear her. "I'm at the Witch's Cove. Take the trail into the hills and turn left at the second turnoff. I'll be waiting. Have your ears open to me. However you can do it, open your ears and I can help you."

The phone clicked off. She sat looking at it for several minutes. She had no idea if he actually heard her. All she could do was wait. She placed her pistol on her lap and began to sing.

Two hours later, her voice wavered. Maybe he hadn't heard her, maybe he wasn't coming. Another hour after that, she was almost sure he wasn't. Her voice cracked. She stopped singing to take a sip of water. She tried to sing again, but her throat was swollen, making her hoarse. *This won't do.* She couldn't compel anyone with a scratchy voice. Her plan wasn't going anything like she thought it would. Perhaps she was wrong for trying to go about this on her own. She pulled out the phone and dialed Xanthus's number.

"Gretchen?" Kyros answered.

"Kyros." She breathed his name.

"Thank the gods you called. Are you all right?"

"I'm fine. Drakōn didn't show."

"Thank the gods," Kyros said. "Listen, I'm sorry. I was wrong to dismiss you like I did."

She sighed, unable to hold the anger that had gripped her heart before. "I'm sorry too. I shouldn't have tried taking him on all by myself. I was just so angry."

"Where are you?"

After giving him directions, she ended the call and sipped her water. It was warm, but it soothed her dry throat. After several minutes, she stood to walk back to the car. It would be safer waiting there.

She heard something. Rustling. Coming from above.

She looked up to the top of the rocky cliff wall in time to see a figure drop down. The body slammed to the ground in front of her. His face was chalky white and smeared with blood—the face of a stranger. Gretchen screamed, scrambling away from him and dropping the gun in the process. She turned to see a rock tumbling down, bouncing over boulders. No, not a rock—a head.

The long, blonde hair of a woman trailed behind as it bumped down the cliff and landed with a thud. *Oh, please no!* Gretchen's mind screamed the denial. *This cannot be happening.* She turned to run, but stopped as a headless body landed in her path. Her mother's laughter rang out.

"You thought you could outsmart me?" Her mother's voice seemed to surround her as Gretchen's legs threatened to collapse underneath her. "I've been playing these games for four thousand years!"

Gretchen flinched away as a long, narrow knife speared toward her, impaling itself into the ground at her feet. "You may as well just slit your own throat, daughter. Here's a knife to do it. Just get it over with, and no one else has to die."

"No," Gretchen shrieked. She dropped to her knees, slammed her hands over her ears, and squeezed her eyes shut. She tried to block out the nightmare unfolding in front of her. How could she have been such a fool? She should have known her mother wouldn't allow her pet to leave without a fight. Tears poured down Gretchen's cheeks as a sob shook her chest.

"It's up to you." Her mother's siren voice penetrated through her hands, driving like a knife into her mind. Gretchen felt, more than heard the thumping of bodies hitting the ground. "The blood of thousands will be on your hands if you don't do it. You know me well enough to know I speak the truth. Look around, Ambrosia. See the destruction? Watch your precious humans die, and you can decide. Is it them, or is it you?"

Gretchen's heart iced over. Her mother was right. Aella didn't care who she hurt, how many people suffered, or who died. But she knew Gretchen did. Aella had all the power here. Gretchen had to get out of there. If she left, Aella would stop. Her mother needed an audience.

Gretchen opened her eyes, and bile rose in her throat. Bodies were piled up around her. Most of the people had died on impact, but some were still groaning, moving…The man nearest her had a broken neck. His head lay against his back at an unnatural angle. Gretchen leaned forward and slapped her hand over her mouth as she willed her stomach not to heave.

Another body came down. She dove away as it nearly hit her, brushing her leg. She scrambled onto her feet and raced toward the exit.

"Gretchen!" It was Kyros's voice coming from down the path.

"Kyros! Oh, please help me," she sobbed.

She stumbled and fell, landing on a lifeless woman. Strong arms lifted her up, pulled her off the poor woman, and into his arms. "It's okay. I've got you." Kyros spoke in her ear. She tried to run, but as fast as Kyros was moving, her feet barely brushed the ground.

Gretchen could see Xanthus scaling the rocks, to reach the top. Sara ran to her, intercepting them at the mouth of the cavern. "Oh Gretchen, are you hurt?" Sara took her hand. Gretchen was too stunned to answer. The horrific images consumed her mind. "Let's get her out of here." She heard Sara say. "She's in shock."

A voice like a tsunami rang out, filling the air as loud and full as a Roman Cathedral's church bells. Kyros dropped to his knees, spilling Gretchen onto the hard ground. "Oh gods, no," he gasped. The impact of hitting the ground seemed to knock some sense into Gretchen. She looked up and saw Kyros on his knees writhing in agony. *Please, not again!* There was only so much pain one man could take. She crawled forward and reached for him, grasping his arm. She looked up at Sara. "You need to sing."

"I'm no match for that," Sara said, blinking.

"Then we'll sing together," Gretchen said.

"Okay, together."

Sara's voice was soft, sweet, and pure as a summer's rain. It was not as loud or as strong as Aella's, but it was filled with power. Gretchen opened her mouth to join her, but her voice came out crackled, dry. She was not much help.

Gretchen looked up at her best friend. Sara was singing words of comfort. Her face brightened, glowing. Then her voice swelled, in volume and in power.

The harsh clash of steel reverberated off the rocks above. A battle was ensuing. "Sara, you need to sing louder—so Drakōn can hear. You don't want Xanthus to have to kill him."

Sara's voice rose like the crest of a wave. Gretchen swallowed and strained to raise her own weary voice to match Sara's. Power exploded as their voices combined—pure, clear, with a strength born of the gods.

The song they sang was not one Gretchen had heard before, yet she knew every word. And it filled her with power, bringing healing to her battered throat and peace to her heart. She could feel Kyros's arms wrap around her, and her heart filled with love for him.

Gretchen wasn't sure if the battle continued. Everything was drowned out by their song. The melody calmed and drifted away. The silence descended with deafening stillness.

The magic was broken when Sara's phone jingled.

Sara answered. "Xanthus. Are you all right? Oh no. How are you going to get him down here?

"Okay. We'll be right there."

Sara turned to Kyros and Gretchen. "Drakōn is hurt. There's a picnic area above. He said we should be able to find a road going in."

Gretchen stood, pulling Kyros up with her. When they reached the car, Gretchen pulled open the driver's side door.

"Are you sure you're fit to drive?" Kyros asked.

"I'm fine. Besides, I'm probably the only one here who's had more than a month of driving experience." She got in behind the wheel.

"You're probably right," Sara said.

They tore out onto the road and searched for a turn off. It was only about a hundred yards away. An old, wooden sign with faded lettering read Cauldron Cove Park.

Xanthus stood with Drakōn propped against him, blood dripped down his forehead. Looked like Xanthus had to knock some sense into the Dagonian. And from the looks of the wound, he'd hit him with the pommel—better that than the blade.

"Where's Aella?" Kyros asked.

"She fled like a coward," Xanthus answered.

"What about the people in the park?" Gretchen whispered—her voice weak and shaky.

He shook his head.

"What's that supposed to mean?" Gretchen asked.

"There are no more people in the park."

Gretchen looked around at the parking lot. There were a dozen cars parked there.

"They're all…"

"Dead," Xanthus said, solemn.

Kyros caught Gretchen around the waist when her knees gave out. She turned her head just in time to miss vomiting all over him. He gently pulled her hair back as she lost the entire contents of her stomach. "It's okay, baby," he whispered.

No, it's not, and it never will be again. These people are dead, and once again it's all her fault.

CHAPTER 25

Kyros was both fascinated and disgusted by the human reaction to the carnage. Every local channel broadcasted the story, interrupting their regular shows. Even international stations descended on the island. Every station replayed the scenes from the ravine over and over.

Kyros was sickened by how deeply enthralled the humans were by this story. But still, he and the others didn't seem to be any different. Here they were, watching the news, their eyes locked on the TV. The camera panned over to a woman on a gurney. "What happened?" the woman asked as she turned to the paramedic pushing her. "What am I doing here? How did I get hurt? Where's my boyfriend? His name is Jake. Have you seen him? Please, you have to find him." Her voice rose in volume with her plea.

The somber face of the female broadcaster flashed on the screen. "As you can see, the incident is baffling. No one seems to know what happened. The few survivors of this massacre have no recollection of how they came to be lying at the base of a cliff. As of yet, investigators have no suspects and no explanation as to what happened. Early indications showed it was a mass murder/suicide, but they are not ruling out hallucinogenic drugs. Speculations are that someone may have laced the food or drink, causing the hysteria." Kyros looked over at Drakōn. His eyes were literally on fire as he watched the TV screen. He looked as if he wanted nothing more than to rip Aella's head off with his bare hands.

"Turn it off," Gretchen said as she stepped into the room. What was she doing up? She should still be resting. He shouldn't have left her alone while she slept. He stepped to her side and wrapped her trembling body in his arms.

Sara lifted the remote and switched it off.

"She said thousands would die if I don't kill myself," Gretchen said as they sank down in the couch.

"She's insane," Pallas said. "Killing you won't save her now. There's too many who know she's alive. Besides, if she starts killing in the numbers she's threatening, she'll have the attention of not only Dagonians, but the gods on Olympus as well. They would not be able to overlook a mermaid killing thousands."

"It's happened before," Xanthus said.

"Mermaid killings?"

"Not mermaid—another demigod," Xanthus said. "Remember Paeton?"

"Oh yes," Pallas answered. "He drove his father, Apollo's, chariot too low and caught the hills on fire. He killed hundreds."

"Though his destruction was unintentional,"

Xanthus said, "Zeus struck him down with his lightning bolt."

"I can't wait for the gods to respond," Gretchen said—her voice weak. "I think I should do what she says."

"No." Kyros turned her toward him. "You will not. We simply have to kill her before she hurts anyone else." He turned to Xanthus. "Have you been able to get in contact with Triton?"

Xanthus shook his head.

"We'll have to move forward without him," Kyros said. "I remember where she was when I met her." He turned to Drakōn. The Dagonian still looked pale. The bandage on his head had a small spot of blood seeping through, but his mind was once again his own. "But I was not with her long," Kyros continued. "You were there much longer."

"Lucky me." Drakōn frowned.

"Do you think you can find her?" Kyros asked.

"Last I saw the witch, she was a hundred miles south-southwest of here. I'm sure she's moved again. She may be crazy, but she's not stupid."

"Then there's no way to find her?"

"I didn't say that," Drakōn said. "While I was with her, I noticed some strange behavior. It may be the clue to locating her."

"Stranger than her normal behavior?" Kyros asked.

Drakōn nodded. "She left twice daily—like clockwork. She never let on where she was going or who she was meeting. And we never traveled far. It's like she was anchored somewhere. Not literally, but something kept her close to one area."

"Her mermaid home, perhaps?" Xanthus asked.

Lying in Kyros's arms, Gretchen didn't say anything, but she shook her head.

"What is it?" Kyros asked her.

"I don't know...it's just...She never cared about coming home when *I* lived with her. She'd be gone days, or even weeks at a time. The only time she came to see me is when she was lonely or bored."

Straton had been leaning against a wall, taking everything in, not commenting. Kyros happened to be looking at him when Straton's eyes lit up with understanding.

"Not while you were a babe," Straton said. "She would have had to suckle you at *least* twice a day to sustain your life."

Gretchen sat up, shock registering on her face. "What are you implying?"

"Perhaps she's not alone."

"You mean, you think she has a baby?" Gretchen asked.

"I think it's a possibility," Straton answered.

Gretchen shot up to her feet. "We have to find her. We have to save her."

"We don't even know if she *has* a child," Pallas said.

"She does. Straton is right," Gretchen said. "It

makes sense. She was always afraid of being alone. That's why she kept *having* babies. Why she had me.

"You know…I haven't really understood it until now…" She seemed to be lost in thought, trying to figure something out. She looked over at Sara. "When Sara moved away, I was miserable. It wasn't that I didn't have any friends or family to connect with. It's just that I needed something *more*. I needed my best friend."

"What does Sara have to do with this?" Pallas asked.

Xanthus stood—his eyes bright. "Gretchen's right. When we moved out here, Sara also took it hard. I didn't understand why she was so unhappy, but I think I do now. Just a minute. I've got something you all need to hear." He left the room and came back seconds later, carrying a large book. Kyros recognized it immediately—the mermaid book.

Xanthus began to read. "The Mer are highly social beings, needing the company of others of their kind. If separated from other Mer for long periods of time, they will experience depression, anxiety, fear, paranoia, and/or insanity."

Kyros looked from Gretchen to Sara. "Did you both have trouble living alone, without others like you?" He wasn't sure if his question was too personal.

Gretchen answered first. "I spent half my life on a therapist's couch. That is, until I met Sara and got my act together.

Sara spoke up next. "I'd always blamed my

mother for making me miserable. Maybe she wasn't the real reason I was so unhappy."

"All this means only one thing," Gretchen said. Her face took on a glow of righteous indignation. "Straton's right, Aella has a baby, my baby brother or sister, and we need to save her."

Kyros nearly smiled, relieved to see Gretchen's spirit return. She'd been like a ghost of herself since coming out of the canyon. Looks like all she needed was a child to save.

"We will," Kyros said. "I promise." Even as he promised, he wondered how he'd be able to keep it. They'd have to track down the mermaid's lair. If they killed her without finding the location, they'd never find the child in time. But how did you get a mermaid to lead you to her home?

A noise from outside caught Kyros's attention. It sounded like the roar of an airplane, but it was louder than usual—and getting louder by the second. Soon, everyone noticed. Several stood, listening as the sound grew in volume. Kyros was the first to reach the door before they all poured out onto the front lawn. A large passenger airplane streaked down out of the sky.

"He needs to pull up," Sara yelled just before the plane slammed into the lighthouse. It knocked the structure over like a building block, and the plane broke apart before crashing into the ground. A giant fireball erupted in the distance, sending a mushroom cloud of smoke into the sky.

Descending

"Gods of Olympus," Straton gasped. "How many humans ride in those things?"

"Could be hundreds," Gretchen answered, sinking to her knees. Sara came up to her and put her arms around her.

"Do you think this was Aella?" Pallas asked.

Gretchen nodded, her face white. "She must have gotten to the pilot before it took off. This is *my* fault. She did this because of me."

"It's not your fault, Gretchen." Sara said.

"No, it's not," Drakōn said. "This witch would have no qualms of doing this for mere pleasure. You're just her excuse."

"We have to find her," Xanthus snarled. "We have to destroy her."

Each of them voiced agreement.

"We have work to do," Kyros growled, his hand clenched so hard he could feel his bones strain at the brink of cracking under the strain. He wanted nothing more than to take his fist, punch a hole in Aella's chest, and rip out her black heart.

⚡ ※

Gretchen and Kyros entered a yellow, rickety building with a private dock at its back. A dark man with grey-speckled hair and warm eyes stepped up to the counter. "Good morning, I'm Andre. What can I do for you?"

"I'd like to rent a boat—a fast one," Gretchen said. "And we'll need to transport seven passengers."

"Are you or your friend wanting to captain it yourself?"

She shook her head. "We'll need a captain."

"Are you looking for a tour? I have the tour schedule here. It's cheaper than paying for a private charter."

"No, we aren't doing a tour. We need to find a specific place."

"What kind of place?"

She looked at Kyros, and he shrugged. "We'll know it when we see it," she answered.

"You're in luck. We have one more boat left, and our best driver is available to take you anywhere around the island."

"We're looking to go a bit farther than Bermuda."

"How far you looking to go?"

"About a hundred miles south-southwest."

"How soon do you want to leave?"

"As soon as possible."

The man nodded and turned. "Hank."

"Yeah, what is it, boss?" A deep voice rumbled from the door behind the counter.

"I got a job for you."

A small, scrawny man stepped through the door. Gretchen wondered when Hank would appear. When the man spoke, his voice was low and deep. "What kind of job?"

"These people here are chartering a boat, and they need you to drive it for them. And they aren't looking to sail around Bermuda. They want to go into the heart."

"Into the heart?" Gretchen asked.

"The heart of the Triangle."

"Oh, right."

"That's gonna cost you more," Hank said. "The heart's a dangerous place."

"I understand," Gretchen said, feeling somber.

Andre looked at them intently as he spoke. "You aren't smiling. You believe in the legends."

Kyros's brows pressed together in confusion. Gretchen leaned toward him. "The Bermuda Triangle has a lot of mystery surrounding it—ships sinking, planes crashing, and people disappearing off boats…"

"Sounds like Aella has been busy over the years," Kyros said.

Gretchen nodded.

"Aella? Did you say Aella?" The old man's dark eyes widened.

"You've heard of her?" Gretchen asked.

He looked around, his eyes bouncing off the walls. "No. I never heard of her. I just remembered—the boat needs maintenance. It's not seaworthy. Hank, you get back to work."

"No wait, please!" Gretchen said as Hank walked out. "You're the only place that has an available boat."

"Sorry, I can't help you."

Gretchen swore under her breath. *I promised I'd never do this.* But, lives were at stake. "Kyros, I need you to wait outside."

He frowned at her. "I don't like leaving you," he whispered as he reached for his knife. "*I* can convince him."

"Don't you dare. I'll be fine. It'll only take a minute."

He scowled and nodded before he stepped out the door.

"Ma'am, I…"

Gretchen sang just above a whisper, but it was more than enough.

The man listened, but instead of the glazed, enamored look she usually got, his eyes widened in shock. "By gods, you're a mermaid."

"You…my voice doesn't affect you? Who are you?"

"I'm what some might call an oracle. And I'll tell you this," he said. "Aella is a beauty and a monster. She is the danger that lurks in the heart of the Triangle."

Gretchen strained to remember what she knew about oracles. It wasn't much. She'd convinced herself long ago that they were purely a myth. Obviously, she was wrong. But if she remembered correctly, they were something like a prophet for the gods. This oracle might just be what they needed to find Aella. "How do we find her?"

"Come closer," he said in a voice that commanded respect, a voice laced with power.

Gretchen's first reaction was to step back, but she wondered what this oracle might have to tell her. She reluctantly took a step toward him.

His hands shook as he raised them to her head. He pressed his palms again her temples and closed his eyes. When they opened, a jolt of fear shot through her. The eyes she was looking at were not his eyes. The irises were as green as a spring meadow and the whites as clear and luminous as a pearl. She'd never seen human eyes as flawless as these were. These were the eyes of a goddess.

"Ambrosia, daughter of death and sea." Gretchen gasped at the voice coming from this old man's lips. It was the voice of a woman, a voice so beautiful and compelling it put the legendary siren, Aella, to shame. "I have a message for you. The path that you travel leads to destinations unknown."

"What does that mean? Can't you tell us where to find Aella?" Gretchen asked.

"Aella is the least of your worries, but if you must know, follow the daughter of the sea king. She will lead the way. Kill the condemned mermaid quickly, for you are running out of time."

"Are you saying Sara will lead us?"

"Yes, she is a key, one of four needed to unlock the cage of the forgotten king, but you must hurry. Her mother is in great danger, and without her mother, she will never be able to open the lock."

"I don't understand what you are talking about. Are you saying Sara's mother, Nicole, is in danger?"

"You must hurry. Gather the daughters that join the four corners, and then go to the place where the mountain touches the heavens. There you must free the king by the fourth new moon. If you fail, the wind will drive fire across the land and the earth will crumble into the seas. All mankind will perish."

"You can't be serious." A vision opened to her mind. Fire raging, buildings crumbling, and her family lying crushed beneath debris as the crashing waves from the sea covered everything. She gasped at the sight, the horror stealing her breath and breaking her heart. And then the images were gone. Gretchen found herself on her knees, her breath heaving from her chest, her heart pounding like a drum against her chest. "May the gods have mercy on us," she breathed.

She looked up into Andre's face. His hands dropped and eyes closed. When he opened them, they were his own again, and they looked haunted.

"She showed you a vision, didn't she?" he asked, his voice raspy, weak.

Gretchen nodded, still stunned by the exchange. "Who showed me?"

"My patron goddess."

"Which goddess?"

"I cannot say."

"You can't say, or you don't know?"

"Both, actually." He smiled weakly. "What exactly did she show you?"

"You don't want to know. Just keep your family close, and if you have any unfinished business, you'd better get it finished."

Descending

He blanched at her words and nodded weakly. "Did she at least tell you where to find Aella?"

"Sort of." Gretchen frowned.

Andre frowned in return, and then his brows pinched together in confusion. "You know, you remind me of the last person to come in search of Aella."

"There have been others?" The words came out in a breath.

"Only one before you."

"When? Who was it?" Her voice rose.

"It was over two decades ago. A man with power that surpassed Aella came in search of her."

Gretchen's mind whirled. Who would be more powerful than Aella?

"What makes him so powerful?" she asked.

"His father is death."

"Hades?"

He shook his head. "No. D*eath*."

"I thought death was something that happened to you, not a person."

"Death is not a person; he's a god. He is also known as Thanatos. Strange, but your eyes are the same."

"What do you mean? I look like him?"

He shook his head. "There is death in your eyes."

Could he know I've killed before? She didn't like where the conversation was headed. "Listen, it's imperative that we stop Aella quickly. Can you please allow Hank to take us to find her?"

"No, I'll not allow my son to take such a risk."

"What now?" Her shoulders sagged. "It will take us much too long to swim there."

"You have others like you?"

"Not exactly like me."

His eyes widened as he looked toward the door. "They are descendants of Dagon—the Sumerian sea god, aren't they?"

She nodded.

"Strange companions for a mermaid."

"How did you know about them?"

"That's not important. The important thing is to stop Aella from killing others."

"It would help if we had a boat."

"You *do* have a boat."

"But you said—"

"That my son wouldn't take you, but I will."

Gretchen smiled. "You will?"

"Yes. I'm not thrilled about this journey, but I'll take you there."

"Thank you," she answered. She was relieved as she stepped out the door. The wind blew around her. Kyros stepped up to her, his eyes bright and anxious.

"Everything set to go?" Kyros glanced at Andre.

"Yes." Gretchen stepped close and whispered, "I have to warn you, Andre can't be compelled."

"Why not? Who is he?"

"He's an oracle."

Kyros's eyes widened as he looked at the rugged old man. "Did he say anything important?"

"Oh yeah. I don't know what in the heck she was talking about, but I've a feeling it's extremely important."

"She?"

"The goddess that spoke through him."

"Do you know which goddess it was?"

"I've no idea."

Kyros shook his head. "Normally, I'm supposed to kill those who discover our identity, but I doubt his patron goddess would be happy with me killing her oracle."

"You couldn't kill him anyway. He's the one taking us to Aella."

"Having an oracle for a guide is a good thing."

"I hope so." Gretchen looked at the gathering clouds and wondered.

CHAPTER 26

The wind whipped around and skipped over the waves as they climbed into the boat. Below deck, Gretchen found a cushioned seat next to Sara.

"Do you think we're headed in the right direction?" Gretchen asked her, remembering what the oracle had said—that Sara would lead them.

Sara was frowning at her husband when she gave a dismissive answer. "I sure hope so."

Gretchen wondered if she should mention the oracle's words. No. He never said she had to solicit Sara's help. Besides, knowing Sara like Gretchen did, Sara would freak at what the oracle said.

"Are you as nervous as I am?" Sara whispered to Gretchen.

"Probably."

"Just look at them. Shouldn't they be a little more somber and less like a child the night before Christmas? I mean, they look excited at the prospect of killing."

Xanthus had guns and other weapons lain out across a table. He and the other Dagonians were deep in conversation. Xanthus described in detail how to operate each weapon. Gretchen only half listened. She already knew how to shoot; she was more concerned with *who* she might have to shoot.

"I guess they enjoy their work," Gretchen shrugged.

"Doesn't it bother you?"

"Their behavior?"

Sara nodded.

"Not really. What I see are men who are excited about new weapons and are anxious to learn how to use them. It makes me feel more confident that they will be able to save my baby brother or sister."

Sara raised an eyebrow. "You've got a point."

"Besides, you know your husband. Have you ever met a person with a more protective nature?"

"No, I haven't." Sara sighed. "I think I'm just scared about what we'll find ahead. I really don't want to see more innocent people hurt."

"I don't either. And I'm sure Kyros and Xanthus are concerned as well. They just know how to compartmentalize it."

Sara nodded and Gretchen wondered if she should tell her about the prophesy. She looked her best friend up and down. Her hair laid limp again her head, and purple shadows darkened her drooping eyes. She looked exhausted. Now was not the time.

"Why don't you get some sleep?" Gretchen asked. "There may not be a chance to rest once we reach our destination."

"All right, but wake me before we get there."

"Sure."

Sara lay down across the cushioned bench. Gretchen caught Xanthus watching his wife with concern in his eyes. It was easy to see how much he loved Sara. Gretchen cracked a smile. Sara had had such a hard life. It was a thrill to see her find happiness.

Sara's breathing deepened within minutes. Gretchen searched and found a small spiral notebook and pencil. She wanted to write down what the oracle said before she forgot. She was a whiz when it came to remembering words, which was why she'd done so well in school. But even her memory wasn't infallible. She only had so much time before her mind muddled the words or forgot some of them completely.

The pencil scratched across the surface, giving her a clearer view of what the oracle said. The part about Sara leading them to Aella was easy enough to comprehend, though unbelievable. But the rest, about Sara's mom, about finding the daughters that join corners…Gretchen had no idea what that meant. Perhaps the others would know. But right now, Gretchen felt that this was not the time to bring this up. Their first responsibility was to kill Aella. The rest would have to wait.

Sara jolted up like she'd heard a shot, and Gretchen jumped in surprise. Sara's hands grabbed the cushion, crushing it in her grasp.

"Sara? What's wrong?" Gretchen rushed to her side.

Descending

Xanthus was there a second later. "Sara, what is it, baby?" He took her head in his hands, trying to get her to look at him.

Sara's eyes looked strange. Not strange like the oracle. These were still Sara's eyes, but they seemed to be taking in a scene that no one else could see. Color drained from her face.

"We have to change course." Her voice came out in a whisper.

"Why? What do you see?"

"We have to save them."

"Save whom?"

"They're lost. They're dying."

"Did Aella do this?"

"Yes, much too long ago. It's been over a week. They'll die."

Sara blinked. The vision seemed to disappear from her vision, and she looked at her husband.

"We have to save them, Xanthus."

"Who are they?"

"They're a family. Lost at sea. And they're dying. The smallest, a little girl, will die first, but the others won't be far behind. It's going to take us far off course, but we have to save them."

"Of course," Xanthus said, turning to Kyros. "I'll tell the captain we're changing course." He turned back to Sara. "Can you lead us to them?"

She nodded.

Gretchen's heart clenched when she realized,

Sara was now deciding their course. The oracle's words were coming true.

Xanthus and Sara made their way up to the bridge. Gretchen stayed behind. The bridge was barely big enough for two more.

Two hours later, Xanthus finally came down below. "I'm just getting Sara a coke. She could use some caffeine." He pulled a bottle from the fridge and turned to leave.

"Xanthus, I need to talk to you."

He must have heard the worry in her voice. He turned a sympathetic look on his face. "Don't worry about Sara. She's stronger than you think."

"That's not what I wanted to talk about. I need you to know what the oracle said about Sara."

Harsh worry lines flashed as Xanthus's jaw tensed. He looked terrified.

"Stop jumping to the wrong conclusions." Gretchen rushed to ease his fear. "He didn't say anything bad was going to happen to her." She pulled out the notebook and handed it to him. "Here, I wrote down every word that was spoken."

His brows pinched together as he read, and then his eyes widened in confusion. "Sara should be the one to lead us to Aella?"

"Yes, and do you understand the other part?"

"Some. We'll discuss it when Aella is dead." With that said, he was gone.

Several hours later, Gretchen stepped up to the

bridge. She'd told the others she wanted some air, but what she really wanted was to talk to the oracle.

Andre squinted at the sea. Gretchen followed his eyes. At first, all she could see was a flock of seagulls fluttering across the sky. Then she saw what he was looking at—a bump on the horizon.

"What is that?"

"I believe that is what we're searching for."

Minutes later, they pulled up alongside the raft. *We're too late.* The sight sickened her. A father, mother, and a little girl lay in the life raft—the child wrapped in the mother's arms, the mother wrapped in the father's. Their matted hair barely moved in the breeze. Their lips were cracked and caked in dried blood. Their skin was burned severely and flaking off their faces. Then a weak cough—it came from the little girl. The mother's arms tightened around the child.

"Are they alive?" Gretchen gasped, tears streaming down her face.

"Barely," Kyros answered as he rushed to get a hook to pull the raft next to the boat.

Pallas eased over the side and into the raft. The mother's eyes shot open when Pallas pulled the girl from her arms. "It's okay; we're here to help." The woman let her daughter go as a sob escaped her chest. The father jerked awake with a start. He too began to sob as words poured from his mouth. He was speaking a foreign language—one Gretchen was not familiar with. It was similar to German. Perhaps Dutch? And it sounded like the words of a prayer.

Minutes later, Straton was attending to them. Water seemed the best cure for their condition—both internally and in wet cloths draped over their blistered skin. He made sure not to give them too much to drink at a time. Gretchen was amazed how intuitive Straton was. He'd likely never treated dehydration before, but he seemed to know exactly what to do. The change in the family was no less than miraculous. The little girl chattered on and pointed to the large men standing around her. The parents looked stunned, but hopeful.

Kyros strolled over to Gretchen. "We're going to have to leave the ship and swim on from here. Land is in the opposite direction from where we are headed."

Gretchen nodded. "How long will it take us to swim there?"

He frowned, his brows pinching together. "Too long."

CHAPTER 27

Gretchen didn't argue. No one did. It was pointless. Andre needed to get the family to civilization, and they needed to go after Aella. Everyone else must have thought the same. No one else protested the decision to swim the long journey.

"Shouldn't Straton stay?" Sara asked.

"No," Xanthus said. "We may need him."

"Perhaps you and Sara should return with the others," Kyros said to Gretchen.

She clenched her fists. "Not a chance. I have to come."

Kyros sighed and pulled her into his arms. "I know. But you have to realize how dangerous this journey is."

"I'm not going back," she said.

"Everywhere Aella goes, death follows. I don't know if I could survive losing you," he whispered.

Gretchen sighed and answered. "You won't have to. My mother's only power is in her voice. I'm immune."

"I know, but we aren't."

"Actually," Xanthus spoke up, lifting his hand in the air. Pressed in his fingers, he held a small, grey ball. "As long as we keep wax in our ears, we are." He looked around to the others. "We can't chance hearing the mermaid's voice without a buffer."

Gretchen looked at the grey balls in Kyros's hand. "That doesn't look like wax."

"It's ambergris," Xanthus said.

"What's ambergris?"

"A waxy substance found in the intestines of sperm whales."

"Ew. I'm glad I don't have to put whale guts in *my* ears."

Kyros smiled. "Whale guts save lives," he said, putting the waxy balls in a pouch strapped to his chest.

Gretchen returned his smile. "Right."

The Dagonians took position around the mermaids as they swam. They traveled through the blue-tinted water, hugging the sea floor on their way. Darkness descended soon after they left. The Dagonians each had a lighted necklace—an orb on the end of a chain. Strangely, Kyros had two. The orbs cast a green glow on everything surrounding them—the sea floor, small fish, and floating speckles of plankton.

Gretchen's muscles burned trying to keep up with the Dagonians. Each of them was about two feet longer than she was. That extra length really made a difference.

They swam in silence for a couple of hours—Xanthus held Sara against his chest and swam with her in his arms. She appeared to be sleeping. Good, she needed her rest.

Descending

Kyros swam alongside Gretchen and raised an eyebrow. *He'd better not offer to carry me.* It was one thing for Sara to need help—she'd only learned to swim recently. Gretchen didn't need a ride; she was perfectly capable of swimming on her own.

Xanthus pointed into the distance. A rocky cliff rose from the sea floor towering above. As they neared, Drakōn and Amar shot off ahead, swimming toward the stone face. They disappeared inside a jagged, black shadow nestled in grey stone. It had to be a cave.

Moments later, five tiger sharks raced out of the entrance and disappeared into the inky sea. They entered the now-empty cave, and everyone hovered inside. Pulling the wax from their ears, Drakōn asked, "Why are we stopping?"

"I want everyone well rested when we confront Aella," Xanthus said.

"Are you kidding?" Drakōn asked. "When you trained us, you had us going full speed for a full day and then we battled through the night. We've been traveling at half speed for only two hours."

"Not all of us are trained warriors," Xanthus said.

"The females should have stayed behind," Drakōn said.

"We females may be the only thing standing between you warriors and death," Gretchen said.

Drakōn gave her a hard look. "You mermaids…"

Kyros swam to face Drakōn and snarled, "Watch

what you say, Drakōn."

Drakōn backed away. His narrowed eyes darted between Kyros and Xanthus.

"That's enough pointless arguing," Xanthus said. "I want *everyone* to get some rest."

Kyros returned to Gretchen, took her hand, and led her through a tunnel. They soon came to a rounded hollow that looked just big enough for the two of them.

"I shouldn't have said anything," Gretchen said. "Drakōn's been through enough already."

"What you said was true. Drakōn would be dead right now if it weren't for you. He owes you his life." Kyros pulled off the leather belts crossed over his chest, taking a metal hook out of his belt. It had a long, sharp spike on one end, which he slammed into the rocky wall. The spike drove deep into the stone.

"What's that for?" Gretchen asked.

"Do you want to wake up lost in these caves?"

"No, of course not."

"Well, then you'll need an anchor."

He wound a long, leather strap through the hook and looped Gretchen in the other end. "This is a bit wide, I'll—" she began to say.

Kyros cinched it up, until it was hugging her waist.

"Better?" he asked, smiling.

She nodded. "Where are *you* going to sleep?"

"I'm not going to sleep yet. Xanthus wants me on guard duty."

"But after?" She frowned, not wanting to be left alone.

"I'll come back here." His eyes softened as he moved in close. He chuckled softly. "Funny...you look a mess. Your eyes are shadowed, you hair is tangled, and yet...you're the most beautiful creature in the sea."

Gretchen reached up and tried to untangle her hair. Kyros caught her hand and brought it to his lips. Her breath caught as he kissed each of her knuckles, then he lightly kissed her injured palm and continued to nibble his way up her arm. Goose bumps broke out across her body.

"You taste amazing," he mumbled against her skin.

"I do?" Her voice cracked.

He pulled away—a hint of a smile on his face. "Yes."

She moved closer. He seemed to know what she wanted and leaned in to taste her lips, wrapping her in his arms. Gretchen was surrounded by him, his body, his heat, his scent, his taste...Everything about him intoxicated her. She wrapped her arms around his neck and moaned. His mouth moved against hers. Her body came alive in his arms. If she died at this very moment, she wouldn't know it. This was heaven.

He growled as he pulled away—much too soon. "I have to go."

She nodded. She wanted nothing more than to kiss him again.

Reaching behind his neck, he unhitched his necklace. "Here, so you won't be left in the dark." His fingers brushed her neck as he hooked it around her.

"Why do you have two?"

He fingered the necklace she wore. "This one belonged to my twin sister."

"What happened to her?"

He sighed, sadness shadowing his face. "She died, a long time ago."

"I'm sorry," she said.

"Get some sleep. I'll be back in a few hours," he answered, brushing his lips over hers. A swish of his tail and he was gone.

Sometime in the night, she awoke in his arms. Smiling, she pressed her head against his chest and once again fell into a dreamless sleep.

The morning came too soon. Though no longer sleepy, Gretchen was physically exhausted. Kyros brought her breakfast—an assortment of fish, speared like a kabob.

She ate heartily and finished just in time for them to leave. Though the swim was arduous, this travel was easier than her experiences hiking. On her last hiking trip, they'd gone over rough mountainous terrain, and had to ration water to make sure it lasted the two days they'd allotted. Here, she didn't have to worry about the rocky floor, and they had *plenty* of water.

"Do you see that?" Pallas asked, interrupting her thoughts.

She looked ahead and saw a faint glow in the distance.

"Could that be whirling?" Straton asked.

Kyros narrowed his eyes. "I don't think so."

"What's whirling?" Gretchen asked.

"It's a kind of plankton that gives off bioluminescent light," Kyros said.

They continued to move forward, but Gretchen could feel the tension in the water. The light ahead continued to grow as they approached. The water brushed over her body and seemed to cool as they approached the illumination. Something snagged at her hair, and she shook it off.

The glow that once seemed like a haze of light in the distance began to show a line on the horizon. The light appeared to originate from the other side of a drop off. Kyros jerked to a stop.

"What's wrong?" Gretchen asked.

The others began shouting. Then she heard an ear-piercing wail.

Kyros looked behind them. "Oh great gods," he breathed.

Gretchen followed his eyes and whooped in a gasp. A giant jellyfish had wrapped its tentacles around Straton. He thrashed his limbs. It took only a moment for his movements to cease. Gretchen had no idea the venom worked so fast. Drakōn raced toward Straton and sliced the creature's tentacles with his sword.

Gretchen raised her eyes toward the surface. Her

heart pounded in her chest—thousands more jellyfish were descending from overhead—their tentacles hanging down like an undersea willow tree forest. Only this forest could kill.

"What'll we do?" Her voice was weak and trembling in fear.

"Follow me," Kyros said. They raced around the poisonous tendrils. He weaved, snaking around, avoiding pain and death. Gretchen tried to see the path ahead of him, but it looked like tentacles and jellyfish everywhere. How he found a way through all the…A searing streak of pain sliced across her forehead. She cried out and turned away from the creature. Kyros stopped and turned his head toward her.

"Don't stop!" she shouted as she pressed her hand to her forehead. Ignoring her, he swam back. He clamped his arms around her, and they were moving again. Kyros skirted around them as they flew through the water. The tentacles thickened in the water as the darkness deepened. Kyros grunted as Gretchen saw a flutter of blue brush over his skin. She cringed, the pain in her forehead still stinging like crazy, Kyros had to be in a tremendous amount of pain. He grunted again, slowing to a stop. Gretchen looked around. They were surrounded by blue, green, and grey tentacles fluttering like shredded strips of fabric. They sank, avoiding the poison. Her gills burned behind her ears. Venom tainted the water. She couldn't see any way out.

Kyros kept his arms locked around her and shot

through the water at an inhuman speed. He used his own body as a barrier between her and the jellyfish, but her exposed arms brushed the tentacles. They sliced over her skin like hundreds of red-hot razorblades. Kyros's arms loosened, dropping away from her, and she slammed into a wall.

Strong arms grabbed her burning limbs. Pain clouded her vision, and she was having a difficult time thinking clearly. Somebody held her, and it wasn't Kyros. She could tell by his scent. *Where was he?*

"We have two more," she heard a voice shout in her ear. "Hurry, one of them is female."

Perhaps she should have wondered who the men were, but she was in so much pain that she didn't care. Her skin felt as if it had been flayed off her arms, and she wondered if she would die from the poison. She tried to open her eyes. A tortured moan permeated the sea as her chest rumbled. *Could that sound be coming from me?*

After several minutes of travel, her rescuer stopped. Then the coolest, most soothing caress she'd ever felt brushed over her skin. She began to sob at the relief. The pain—as excruciating as it had been—vanished. She looked up into an unfamiliar Dagonian face. His dark eyes were full of pity. His wild, red hair waved like a sea anemone in the current.

She looked around and gasped. They floated above the edge of an undersea city, nestled in a massive, deep-sea cave. Towering spires rose from the sea floor. Stone buildings stood, scattered among the spires. As they swam into the city, faces peeked curiously from windows and doorways. Gretchen looked above to see the ceiling high above. It was the largest cave she'd ever seen, large enough to keep an entire metropolis in its depths. The rocky surface of the cavern was pocked with holes. Some of the holes had round, glowing mounds that seemed to sparkle with light. The light emitted from these giant orbs made everything glow—the light settling down on the city like fairy dust.

"A mermaid," a voice screeched in the distance. "This one's a live mermaid."

Oh, thank heavens, Sara's okay.

The Dagonian's eyes narrowed as he looked Gretchen in the eye. He looked her over, his eyes lingering on her fitted dress and bare fin. "What does that make you?" His voice was course, with no sign of the pity he'd shown her before.

In that moment, Kyros was there, facing the Dagonian—his chest smeared with green goop. That must have been what they'd used on her. But they obviously hadn't finished applying it to Kyros. He still had bright red burns streaked across his skin.

"Get your hands off her," Kyros growled.

"What is she?"

"She's mine." Kyros's voice was so low and frightening, it even scared Gretchen.

The Dagonian let her go and backed away—obviously intimidated by Kyros. But still, he spoke again. "You have not answered my question? What is she?"

Descending

Gretchen swallowed as Kyros put his arm around her. He didn't answer the question.

"Bring the others here," another Dagonian shouted. Kyros and Gretchen were escorted forward.

"Whatever you do, don't sing," Kyros whispered in Gretchen's ear.

Gretchen locked eyes with Sara. Sara gave a weak smile. With Xanthus at her side, she looked apprehensive, but not frightened.

"Why are you here?" a Dagonian asked Xanthus. This Dagonian seemed to be the one in charge.

"We've come on Triton's errand," Xanthus said.

"…with a marked mermaid? And what of the other female?" the old Dagonian asked, looking at Gretchen. "She has strange clothing for a Dagonian. Looks like human clothing to me."

"She's not your concern," Xanthus said.

"Not my concern? I saved your lives, even after you brought these creatures to my city." He gestured to Sara and Gretchen. "Yet, you tell me it's not my concern?" He looked Gretchen over from head to tail. "What is your name?"

She opened her mouth to answer, but Kyros beat her to it. "Her name is Gretchen."

"Gretchen? That *does* sound like a human name. Looks like Triton has started breeding with humans again." The Dagonian swam up close to Gretchen. Kyros tightened his grip.

"So, young beauty, you're a mermaid, aren't

you?"

"She is not your concern," Kyros growled.

The Dagonian raised his finger, and his soldiers unsheathed their weapons. Kyros, Xanthus, and the others put their hands on their hilts but didn't draw their weapons.

"I'll tell you what my concern is," the old Dagonian said. "Five warriors swim into my city, armed to the gills, surrounding *mermaids*." He glared at Gretchen. "If that is not something to be concerned about, I don't know what is."

Gretchen could see more soldiers emerging from the crumbling city. They were multiplying by the second.

"We are hunting a third mermaid." Kyros said. "You might have heard of her, Aella."

"Aella?" The commander frowned. "No, I can't say I've heard of her."

The Dagonian had to be lying. According to Kyros, her mother was infamous among Dagonians.

"But there is one thing I do know," the Dagonian continued. "You and your mermaids are not welcome here."

"Like I said," Xanthus' eyes narrowed, "we are on King Triton's errand."

"And what errand would that be?"

"To hunt down and destroy Aella," Sara said.

Gretchen was surprised Sara could speak. She was growing bolder by the day.

The look the Dagonian gave Sara could have

melted rock. He snarled as he approached her. "I did not ask you, *mermaid*."

Faster than Gretchen could blink, Xanthus had pulled out his sword and had it pointed at the Dagonian's throat.

The Dagonian jerked back in surprise, holding his breath.

"If you even so much as look at my wife again, I'll slit your throat." His eyes burned in a fury that left no doubt in anyone's mind that he meant every word of his threat.

The Dagonian hesitated and nodded.

"I'll tell you what will happen," Xanthus snarled. "You will let us search your city and not interfere. If you don't allow it, you risk incurring the wrath of Triton."

Gretchen was impressed with Xanthus's courage. They were vastly outnumbered and with Triton AWOL, his threat was merely a bluff meant to intimidate.

Word must have filtered through the city. Soldiers flooded the streets. The commander looked at the numbers surrounding him, narrowed his eyes, and smiled. "Is that your final word?"

"Yes," Xanthus answered.

"Well, there you go," the commander said. "You've made my decision for me. You, the marked mermaid, and your Dagonians soldiers will leave. But the unmarked mermaid stays here."

Kyros pulled Gretchen behind his back. "You will not touch her." The words came out in a low growl.

The Dagonian commander laughed, full and loud. "How interesting. A Dagonian protects the mermaid." He swam toward Kyros. "You want to save this vile creature?"

Kyros glared at him.

"I asked," the commander bellowed, looking at the crowd. He turned to Kyros. "Do you want to save your mermaid?"

"Yes."

"Then you must fight for her."

CHAPTER 28

Gretchen felt as if she'd been dropped down into an undersea gladiator movie. A massive netted dome spread out, surrounding her. Only the net wasn't interlaced with rope—it looked more like stone seaweed had grown and tangled into a dome big enough that it could easily swallow the coliseum in Rome twice over. Dagonians surrounded the structure, peeking their faces through the gaps to get a view of the upcoming fight.

One large soldier held her still as another forced slimy black goop in her mouth. It tasted like motor oil and made her tongue tingle. Her whole mouth went numb. There went her voice. They dragged her across the arena to two tall, stone columns. Chains dangled from the tops. One soldier chained one of her arms to one column, while the other soldier chained her other arm to the other.

"Pity." One soldier frowned, looking her up and down. "She's a pretty thing."

"You can probably have what's left of her." The other soldier laughed.

"You're so disgusting," the first soldier said.

What's left of her? Gretchen didn't even want to

think what that meant.

The soldiers swam away and exited. The sounds of cheers swelled to a deafening volume. Looked like these Dagonians loved a good slaughter. At the other side of the dome, dozens of soldiers led Kyros into the arena. The commander swam above, smiling at the throngs.

He held a conch shell to his mouth and blew. The sound filled the arena, drowning out the cheers. When it stopped, there was silence.

"Dagonians of Triangle City, we have a special treat for you today. This Dagonian and his friends came to our city accompanied by an unmarked mermaid. When I offered to take this foul creature off their hands, they refused to give her up. It seems they've grown attached to her."

The crowd broke its silence to roar in disgust. "One Dagonian in particular threatened me as I tried to apprehend her. I've decided an opportunity like this could not pass us by. We will teach this Dagonian a lesson and kill both him and the mermaid."

At those words, the crowd went wild, cheering and shouting.

The commander turned to Kyros and smiled. "You are about to meet our city's crowning glory, the protector. You are welcome to try and save your mermaid, but you'll have to save yourself first. I give you our own Ketea, Colosso!"

The commander laughed as he and the other soldiers filed out of an exit.

Descending

What in the world is a Ketea? Whatever it was, Gretchen doubted she'd like it. Large, stone doors grated as they opened on the far end of the coliseum. At first, Gretchen didn't see a thing. Then, out of the darkness, slithered a large snake, then another, and another. There were over a dozen coming through the door. She was so focused on the creatures that she jumped when Kyros touched her. He smiled as he lifted his hand above him. What in the world did he find amusing in this situation? A sword sliced through the sea, coming straight at him. He caught it by the hilt.

"As soon as you get free," he said. "Go straight behind you. The others are attempting to open the doors." He thrust the blade into the chain at her wrist and pulled back, snapping it. Then he repeated with the other.

She tried to ask him what he was going to do, but it came out in an incoherent mumble.

He pulled her in for a crushing kiss. She couldn't feel a thing—stupid, slimy Novocain. As he pulled away, he smiled. "I'm just going to keep the Ketea busy."

He raised an eyebrow. "You know, next time I kiss you, it'd be nice if you'd kiss me back."

She tried to frown and had no idea if she'd succeeded.

Looking back, she saw it wasn't giant snakes entering the arena, but the tentacles of a giant creature with a head the size of a commuter bus. It emerged, its bulging, black eyes searching for prey. *You're going to keep that busy?*

"Don't worry," he said. "This is child's play. Gotta go." He shot through the water, heading straight for the beast.

Gretchen didn't know what kind of childhood he had, but it couldn't have been a good one.

She couldn't take her eyes off Kyros or the beast. The creature turned its body over to reveal a gaping mouth with giant, snapping jaws. Somewhere in the back of her mind, she could hear voices calling her name, but she couldn't possibly take her eyes off Kyros while he battled for his life.

He raced around the creature, slicing at its tentacle arms. The sword was so small in comparison to the creature that each slice looked like a mere paper cut. The Ketea swung its arms at him, pounding the ground, slamming the coliseum cage walls, missing him by inches each time. Finally, Kyros seemed to recover his desire to survive the battle. He swam away. But then he turned and raced straight toward the creature. Gretchen screamed as he reached the gaping mouth. The jaws snapped down, and he was gone.

He was gone. The creature had eaten him.

"Gretchen, come on. You've got to get out of there." She could hear Drakōn, shouting at her.

She looked up to see the monster bearing down on her. Then it hit her, she was about to die. She shook off her stupor and raced away. Drakōn's face showed through a window at the back door. She reached him as the beast slammed her against the door. Her head rang and everything dimmed. She fought to stay conscious. The door rumbled and finally opened, spilling her into Drakōn's arms.

Kyros is dead. She wanted to scream. *He's gone.* But her thick tongue wouldn't let the words through. Drakōn pulled her away. They shut the entrance and turned to her. An earth-shattering crash came from the door. It looked like the beast still wanted a taste of her.

As the others drew their swords and took position around the door, watching the beast through the netted wall, Gretchen searched for a weapon of her own. She spotted a sword propped against a wall. She grabbed it and waited alongside the others. The next time the beast hit the door, it broke open. She rushed forward, but Pallas caught her by the tail and pulled her back. "You don't want to do that. Don't worry. He'll be out soon."

She frowned at what he said. *He'll be out soon?* The creature thrashed around. It gave an eerie wail as it hit the side of the cage. It swam and slammed into the other side—bouncing against the coliseum walls. Finally, it hit the sea floor, twitching several times before its tentacles sank to the floor. He lay still, unmoving. The beast looked…dead.

One of the creatures eyes bulged as a tip of a blade came through. The eye came out completely, followed by Kyros. Gretchen met his gaze through a cloud of blood.

She dropped her sword and swam to Kyros so fast. If he'd been any smaller, she'd have plowed him over. He wrapped his arms around her as she sobbed.

"I told you I'd be fine." He pulled away, smiling. "Like I said—child's play."

There was so much she wanted to tell him, like he'd better never do anything as stupid as that again or if that was his kind of child's play, he must have had cruel parents. But she still couldn't speak—her mouth was tingling, though. She hoped that meant she'd get use of her voice again soon.

"Now let's go see if Xanthus has figured how to get us safely out of here."

Gretchen could hear the angry crowds above. *Right.* Getting out of here in one piece would take a miracle. She looked around to figure out where they were—in some kind of jail. Cells lined either sides of the room. The doors were sitting propped against a wall. Someone knew a little something about removing them. The bodies of dead guards floated in them.

Looking around, she said, "Bere's Saba an Xanbus?"

Kyros smiled. "What is that stuff they fed you? You sound ridiculous."

She punched him in the arm and frowned.

Kyros turned to Straton. "Where's Sara and Xanthus?"

"Xanthus left with Sara."

"Left?"

"You don't want to know."

All hints of amusement left Kyros's face. "Tell

me."

"That stuff they fed Gretchen didn't work on Sara, so they knocked her unconscious."

"They struck her? Oh gods, how did Xanthus react?"

"How do you think?"

"I can guess. So he took her away and left us to deal with the aftermath of his rampage?"

"I'm sure he'll be back."

"Well, unless he brings an army with him, it won't do much good. Did you see that angry crowd?"

"That's why we're locked in here and not out there."

A thunderous crash shook the door.

"They're trying to get in," Pallas said.

Another slam.

"Sounds like they're succeeding." Drakōn scowled.

At the next deafening blow, the door cracked.

"Is everyone armed?" Kyros shouted.

"Oh yeah." Straton smirked and gestured to the dead soldiers floating in the cells. "The guards here were generous enough to let us use their weapons."

"Be ready," Kyros said. "Our objective is *not* to fight, but defend. Our goal is escape. If we are separated, we'll meet up five miles due south of our final destination."

Grunts of agreement filled the water just before the door smashed open. Drakōn let out a shrill battle cry as he swam full speed toward the open door, his spear leading the way. The others quickly followed, not wanting to be trapped inside.

They pushed their way into the center of trained soldiers. The clash of metal and the roar of angry men filled the sea. Gretchen had her sword ready, but Kyros didn't give her a chance to use it. He wouldn't let anyone close to her.

He swung, sliced, dismembered, and moved forward. Turning, he swam straight at her. He passed her by—his body brushing across her arm and his fin scraping her skin.

She turned to see him block the strike coming at her from behind. Kyros's blade fluidly blocked, swept back, and returned, slicing off the Dagonian's head with no effort. It spun away, floating through the water. Gretchen covered her mouth as her stomach threatened to heave.

Two more came from either side. Gretchen took the one closest to her and raised her sword. She hadn't had much training with one. Most of the stuff her sensei covered was bare hand to hand. But she knew the basics of handling a weapon. A weapon in your hand was simply an extension of your arm.

The Dagonian narrowed his eyes and grinned at her—confident, too confident. He jabbed straight at her. She parried the blade, slammed her elbow into the Dagonian's nose, and followed with her sword, slicing it deep into his neck. He was dead a moment later. She turned away, unwilling to dwell on the fact that she'd just killed a man. She'd probably need hours of therapy later, but for now, survival was paramount.

She turned back to see how Kyros was handling his own attacker. The Dagonian that had gone after him was already dead, and Kyros was looking at her—his eyes bright with pride and relief.

And then there were four.

Kyros flew to her side. "We need to fight back to back."

She nodded—familiar with the tactic.

Gretchen fought like she'd never fought before. She'd always had fun training. Learning defense, offense, block, parry, nerve strikes—it was all fun and games. But nothing could have prepared her for how she'd feel in a real battle—the adrenaline pulsing through her veins, the desperate need to survive. Together, she and Kyros made short work of the four soldiers.

Then there were eight. Gretchen knew they were in trouble. These eight were fresh, their eyes bright. They'd simply been waiting their turn while Gretchen and Kyros fought. She was tiring. Her blade felt heavier with each swing. She didn't know how Kyros was holding up—probably much better than she was. But he needed his back protected. And the way she was faltering, she didn't think she'd be able to help him much longer.

Two men rushed Kyros, and he met them in a dance of death. He'd block one strike with the sword in one hand and another with the sword in his other, back and forth between the two. All the while Gretchen fought her own attacker. He dropped his blade down toward her head as she lifted her sword to block. His hand clamped around her throat.

She darted a glance to Kyros. He'd gained a third attacker on top of the two he'd already been fighting. He couldn't help her.

"This is the end of you, little mermaid," the Dagonian snarled inches from her face as she felt his blade press against her belly. And like an angel from above, a large bull shark descended and chomped down over her attacker's head. He shook his prey, severed the head clean off, and swallowed.

It circled her, caressing her body with his rough skin. "Thank you, friend," she sighed in relief as she reached out and hugged him. "You saved my life."

Movement came from the south. Like a flock of vultures ascending from the depths, thousands of sharks rose from the trench. Sara rode on the back of an enormous great white and Xanthus swam out in front, leading the way. And just like that, the battle was over.

Dagonians fled in fear. The ones who didn't escape quickly enough were finding themselves in the jaws of the mighty predators. Gretchen rushed to Kyros's side. "I need to gather the others. I'd hate to have any of you attacked by accident."

"It looks like Xanthus and Sara beat you to it."

Pallas, Straton, Drakōn, and Amar were being circled by Xanthus and Sara.

"I guess shark is permanently off my menu."

Kyros didn't sound too happy about it.

"Oh, they're terribly bad for you anyway," Gretchen said.

"Right." He frowned, shaking his head. "Come on. It's time to go."

They left with the sharks at their backs. The city would have a lot of cleaning up to do.

Kyros pulled Gretchen to his chest and swam.

"You know I can swim, don't you?" she asked.

"Gretchen, you look exhausted. You'll need your strength."

"And you don't?"

"I'm fine. This day has not been half as exhausting as a full day of training."

Gretchen shook her head and laid her head against his chest. "I don't envy your life, Kyros." She closed her eyes and relaxed in his arms.

Sometime later, Gretchen awoke to some of the most dramatic underwater seascapes she'd ever seen. High, stone columns towered around them, spouting bubbles of hot steam. There were hundreds of them. It looked like an undersea redwood forest. The darkness deepened as they swam deeper into the pillars. The water there grew stifling hot.

"Have you seen anything like this before?" she asked Kyros.

He frowned and shook his head. Gretchen couldn't help but wonder what they would do if the water got too hot to breathe. She brushed her fingers behind her ears, over her gills. They already seemed singed around the edges.

They kept to the sea floor where the water was cooler. Just as Gretchen was about to suggest they go back and try to swim around the forest, the water began to cool.

"I'm thinking it might have been better to have gone back and chartered a boat," she said.

"We don't need a boat," Kyros huffed.

"I *guess* not."

The darkness lifted as the forest thinned. Finally, they were out. The water felt so good and cool against her skin. Gretchen looked over at Sara. She had a nasty, purple bruise over her right eye. She probably had a splitting headache from it. Xanthus cradled her against his chest, stroking her hair.

"Are we going to stop and rest, or are we almost there?" Gretchen asked, frowning at her injured friend.

"Yes, we'll rest," Kyros answered. "We're almost to the outer perimeter. The others are scouting out ahead to get the layout of the terrain."

"What do we do while they're gone?"

"We wait."

They were gone for over an hour before Pallas returned.

"I saw nothing but flat sand and silt," Pallas said. "I sure hope the others had better luck."

Amar came back next. He shook his head and said, "Nothing."

Descending

Straton swam in with a smile on his face. "I think we have a winner. There's an island with an empty cabin."

"On land?" Kyros asked.

"Yes, on land. How many cabins do you know of in the sea?"

Kyros must have not thought Straton's question warranted an answer. He simply scowled.

"Well, Drakōn still hasn't come back," Kyros said. "Maybe he found someplace better. Like a cave."

"A cave would be better?" Gretchen asked.

Amar swam past her and mumbled, "He'd think the belly of a sperm whale was better than anything on land."

Gretchen whipped her head around at his retreating figure. *Did Amar just make a joke?* She was too stunned to laugh.

Drakōn came back with no news.

"Well, it looks like the island is where we're going."

"Wonderful," Kyros mumbled.

CHAPTER 29

C abin was an understatement. Kyros looked around inside the structure. It had six bedrooms, seven baths, and an eighty-nine inch projection screen with state-of-the-art electronic equipment.

"Okay, everyone," Gretchen shouted.

Surprised faces turned her way—his included. "Since we are staying uninvited in someone's house, we need to take care we leave everything just as we find it. Please respect this property and its owners. That being said, I think we need to figure out who is staying in what room. Xanthus and Sara will share a room, obviously. That leaves five bedrooms and six people. The beds are larger than the couches, and you guys are much larger than I am. I think it's best to have the rest of you take a room each, and I'll sleep on the couch out here."

"Absolutely not," Kyros bellowed.

The others nodded their agreement with him.

"You will not be sleeping unprotected out in the open."

"I'm not in the open; I'm in the living room of a house," Gretchen said. "Are you telling me one of you giants is going to sleep on this short couch?"

Descending

All of their eyes turned to the small sofa with the knotted, wooden armrests and frowned. "Look," she said, plopping down and stretching across the seat. "It's the perfect size for me."

Kyros frowned. She looked tiny on the sofa. Her skinny limbs appeared weaker than ever. He stomped over to her and scooped her off the couch as she squealed. He strode back into the hallway and through the nearest bedroom door. Stepping up to the bed, he dropped her. She squeaked and bounced against the mattress. "What are you doing? I'm not sleeping here."

"Yes, you are."

"But this is the biggest bedroom, next to the master."

"Good, it should easily fit both of us."

She turned over on her stomach and propped her head against her hands. "What about your vow to not touch me?"

"I won't touch you."

She nodded to the door. "This is not like the cave where anyone could see us. They'll think we are...you know."

Kyros narrowed his eyes and growled. Turning, he stomped out the door. If they were truly entertaining such wicked thoughts, he'd just have to set them straight.

They all looked up, stunned at his return. "So," Straton said to him, "*you* are going to sleep on this couch?"

"No. I'm sleeping with Gretchen."

Their eyes widened so far that they nearly popped

out of their skulls. "Xanthus is rather fond of Gretchen. I don't think he'll like this."

"We won't be having…" Kyros began. "That is…" *Hades, why is this so hard to say?* "You can assure him, Gretchen's virtue is safe with me."

With that said, he turned his back on their smirking faces and stomped back to the room. He found Gretchen forcing back a smile. She must have heard him bumbling at his friends.

"Go ahead. Laugh. I can tell you want to," Kyros said.

"No." She smirked. "I'm fine."

She looked over to the clock and said, "It's getting late. I need a shower to wash the salt water out."

Kyros nodded, relieved she was going to leave—allowing him a chance to collect his thoughts.

Gretchen stepped in and pulled the door shut. Soon, he could hear running water. His mind began to wander—Gretchen, standing in the shower, naked. No, he had to get his mind off her. And in order to do that, he had to get out of there.

He returned to the living area to find it practically deserted.

"Back so soon?" Straton asked.

"Uh, yeah. I couldn't sleep."

"I don't know if I could sleep either if a beautiful woman were naked in the next room."

"How do you know she's naked?" Kyros growled, wondering how he came by that knowledge.

"Retract the fangs, Kyros. She simply mentioned to Sara she was looking forward to a long, cool shower."

Kyros relaxed.

Straton stepped over to the couch and sat down. "You love her, don't you?"

Kyros glowered. "How do you know?"

"I'd have to be blind not to see it. You hover around her constantly. It's almost like you're ready to kill anyone who breathes on her wrong. Then there's the fact you fought a Ketea for her. You've sunk farther and faster than I would have dreamed possible for you."

"I guess it's pointless to deny it."

"Yeah."

"I intend to marry her."

Straton nodded. "I figured. Things are going to be rough on you until you do—especially if you insist on sleeping in the same room with her. You know Xanthus wouldn't take kindly to you shaming Gretchen before the wedding."

"I won't shame her. Hades, I love her too much to do that."

Straton nodded. "Should I congratulate you or give my condolences?"

Kyros smiled. "Either one would be appropriate."

Straton stood and stretched. "Well, this is as much male bonding as I can take. Besides, I feel like I've been chewed up and spit out by a Ketea. And you, my friend, actually have and boy, do you look it."

Kyros smiled. "I'll see you in the morning."

Straton walked through the hall, but turned back before he entered his room. "Kyros."

"What?"

"I know you were the one who put me on Xanthus's list." Straton's eyes were bright with unshed tears. "Thank you for coming to get me. You can't imagine what life was like at Panthon Prison."

"I'm glad I could. You, of all people, didn't belong there."

Straton nodded and stepped into his room.

Kyros awoke to the smell of burning flesh.

He looked around. Gretchen was gone. "Oh, not again," he mumbled, pulling Gretchen's pillow over his face. Her alluring scent was almost enough to mask the stench coming from the kitchen.

"Kyros," a voiced whispered through the door— Pallas? Straton? He wasn't sure. The door creaked open, and Pallas's head poked in. "We're sneaking out the back door to go hunting. Do you want to come?"

Hades, yes. But he simply had to talk to Gretchen. They couldn't take her trying to feed them dead flesh at every turn. "I'll come later. I need to have a talk with Gretchen first. Explain things to her."

"It's *your* stomach," he said before slinking down the hall.

"Explain what?" Gretchen's voice materialized as her head poked up from the side of the bed.

Kyros hollered as he flung back and scrambled to

his feet. "What in Hades? Where did you come from?"

"I was sleeping on the floor."

"The floor? Why?"

"Someone was tossing and turning all night. The second time I was bumped onto the floor, I decided it wasn't worth climbing back in so I curled up and fell asleep here." She smiled slyly. "What did you need to explain?"

"I guess I don't have to explain." He nodded toward the kitchen. "That's not *your* cooking?"

"Not unless I have Jedi cooking skills."

"Jedi, what?"

"Never mind. It must be Sara. And..." She narrowed her eyes. "I think I've figured something out. Dagonians don't like bacon, eggs, and sausage."

"What kind of animal is a bacon?"

"It's a pig. And the pig makes up the sausage too. You should try it. It tastes amazing."

"Nothing that smells like *that* could possibly taste amazing."

"Ah," she said, as understanding lit her face. "*That's* why you were all acting so strangely. And why you..."

"Why I what?"

"Why you kissed me. Desperate times, huh?"

"I took one for the team." Kyros smiled.

"You." She had a wicked grin on her face as she jumped up and pounced on him. He let her push him back on the bed. She clawed up and down his sides, poking him.

He cocked an eyebrow and cracked a smile. "What under Olympus are you doing?"

"I'm trying to tickle you." She frowned.

"What is a tickle?"

"You've got to be kidding me. Don't tell me that Dagonians aren't ticklish."

"I have no idea what you're talking about."

Gretchen frowned and blew out a breath, climbing off him. Kyros was having none of that and pulled her down, turning her over. "Not so fast, mermaid. I'd like to give this tickle thing a try."

"No!" she screeched. "No, don't tickle me."

He tried to mimic what she did and hesitated when she squirmed as he reached toward her side. "I'm not even touching you yet," he said, grinning as he enjoyed how she could laugh, writhe, and plead at the same time.

"Don't. Oh, please don't tickle me."

He reached again toward her, stopping just before he touched her. She yelped again.

"If you're reacting this much to the idea of me tickling you, I'm curious to see what would happen if I actually touched you."

"No, so help me. If you do, I'll never kiss you again."

"Added bonus." He smirked.

She slapped his chest. "Very funny."

Curiosity got the better of him, and he touched

her. She shrieked, ringing his eardrums. He softly clawed her side, and she nearly bucked him off the bed.

The door slammed open, and Kyros found a sword pointed at his throat. "Get off the mermaid." He followed the blade and found Drakōn on the other end of it. Seconds later, the others surrounded him.

"Stop! Don't, Drakōn," Gretchen breathed as she was wiping away tears.

Did I hurt her? The thought struck Kyros like a slap.

"Don't hurt him," she said. "He was only tickling me."

"He was doing what to you?"

"Tickling. It's what we humans do in play. To have fun. To tease."

"Why are you crying?" Kyros asked. He knew he wasn't helping his case, but he was concerned. "Did I hurt you?"

"No, of course not. Sometimes when a person laughs too hard, they cry."

"Yes, they do." Sara stepped into the room and pushed them back out the door, one by one. "Come on, you Neanderthals; you're embarrassing them. They were just having fun. Let them be."

She placed her hand on Drakōn's arm, which was still raised and pointing his sword at Kyros. "Come on, Drakōn. Kyros would never hurt Gretchen. It was all in play."

Hesitantly, he lowered his weapon and left.

"Sorry about the interruption," Sara said. She

ducked out the door and shut it.

"Well, that was…" Kyros began to say, until he noticed the bed was shaking.

He looked over to see Gretchen laughing. He smiled in return, and she laughed even harder. Seeing her laughing got him going, and his laughter followed hers.

When their laughter finally quieted, they lay back on the bed and looked at the ceiling. "I have to admit," Kyros said. "The looks on their faces were hilarious."

She laughed again. "Weren't they? And Drakōn looked like he was ready to run you through."

"At least I would have died happy."

"Would you have?"

He turned on his side and looked Gretchen over. She was so beautiful. Her hair was wild, her cheeks flushed, and her eyes searched his.

"I've never been truly happy until I met you. So yes, I would have died happy."

"You know what would make me happy?" She reached out and pulled him down for a kiss. His lips pressed down on hers, and he was in bliss. Her arms wrapped around his neck as he braced his body above her careful not to crush her. He explored her mouth. His hands burned to touch her body, but he held himself back. He wanted to say his vows before he took what was before him. She deserved that, deserved to be treated with respect and love. Not ravaged like a hormonally driven wild man. He wanted to show her how much he loved her, how much he cherished her. He wanted to show her she was worth waiting for, worth paying for.

He pulled back and smiled.

Gretchen growled. "Sometimes I wish you weren't so noble."

He brushed a kiss below her jaw. "Mmm. Me too. But you're worth it."

She chuckled.

"I can't wait forever, though."

She sucked in a quick breath. "I sure hope not."

"And since I can't protect your virtue indefinitely, I have a question to ask you."

"Yes?"

"Will you marry me, Gretchen?"

"Marry you? You're *asking* me?"

"I know, for a Dagonian, it's unorthodox to ask the bride to be. I would normally ask your father, but I know humans do things differently."

"No, I mean, you aren't just going to carry me off somewhere and marry me without my permission?"

He raised an eyebrow. "It's tempting. But no."

"You know, it's also customary for a man to get down on one knee to propose marriage."

Kyros moved to get off the bed. He was screwing this up. If only he'd studied up on how to offer marriage to a human woman. He never in his wildest dreams thought that knowledge would be needed.

"Kyros, stay where you are. I need to answer you."

He froze and looked back at her smiling face.

"The answer is yes."

A wide smile spread across his face. "You will?"

"And you don't have to carry me off and force me. You'll just have to carry me across the threshold."

"I'll carry you anywhere and everywhere you want."

"Careful what you offer; I just might take you up on that," she said, smiling.

He leaned in and kissed her again. As he pulled away, he had real worry etched in his face. "I do have a couple questions. What's a threshold, and how dangerous is it?"

CHAPTER 30

"**I**'m going with you," Gretchen said for the hundredth time. Her mind filled with the horrors her mother had wrought in the last two days. How Kyros expected her to just send him off to find her, she hadn't the faintest clue. She couldn't possibly let him go.

Kyros frowned. "I told you. We are not going to bring you and Sara into a situation blind. Once we find her, we'll need to scout things out. When we have the layout, we can plan our attack."

"Kyros is right," Xanthus said. "She'll be less likely to detect a smaller group."

"But why you?" she asked Kyros.

"Other than Xanthus," Kyros said, "Drakōn and I have the most experience in this area."

"I'd be going myself," Xanthus said, "but I have to be here to direct the operation."

"I should go. I can help," she said.

"Gretchen." Xanthus sighed as he stepped over to her. "How many times have you hunted down a killer?"

She didn't answer; she didn't need to. Still, she frowned at him.

"Kyros and Drakōn have gone after hundreds.

If you accompany them, you'll only be putting them at risk."

She stomped over to Kyros. "Fine, but if you get yourself killed, I'll never forgive you."

He stepped up to her and leaned in. "Gretchen—"

"Don't you do it," she interrupted. "You think I'd want to kiss you when you're acting like this? I…" she paused, glaring at him. She threw her arms around his neck and pressed her mouth to his. He enthusiastically kissed her back.

In the back of her mind, she heard a few grumbles and throats being cleared.

Kyros swept Gretchen up off her feet as she roped her arms around his neck. He nibbled from the corner of her mouth down to her neck. "If you don't come back in one piece, I'll never kiss you again." She spoke through ragged breaths.

"I'll come back," he said and groaned.

"In one piece."

"In one piece," he agreed.

He set her down, keeping his hand on her, making sure she was steady on her feet, before letting her go. She looked around, "Where did everyone go?"

Kyros chuckled. "I'm sure they had pressing matters elsewhere."

Drakōn appeared a moment later. "You ready to go?" he asked Kyros.

"Yes." Kyros stepped toward the door without a backwards glance.

Oh no, he will not. "Kyros, you aren't going to leave without kissing me goodbye, are you?"

Kyros turned back in surprise. "Gretchen, we spent the last ten minutes kissing." He stepped up to her, towering above. "Wasn't that enough?"

She shook her head. "No, I mean…no. You should always kiss the ones you love goodbye."

A smile spread across his face. "Is this a human thing?"

"No, it's a Gretchen thing."

He chuckled. "It is, huh?" He picked her up as he crushed his mouth to hers. This Dagonian never did things halfway. She'd only wanted a peck; instead, he once again made love to her with his mouth.

Drakōn cleared his throat before speaking. "Should we leave before or after the birth of your first child?"

Kyros smiled against Gretchen's mouth. "We'll leave now."

Kyros sat her down. "Goodbye, my love."

"Be safe," she answered.

He turned to the door and left.

Sara peeked in from the hallway with raised eyebrows.

Gretchen's shoulders drooped as she sighed. Sara stepped in the room, placing a hand on Gretchen's shoulder. "He's going to be fine. Xanthus said that, besides himself, Kyros is the most-skilled warrior in the entire sea."

"I know he's good, but…" She couldn't finish.

Sara tugged Gretchen over to the couch to sit down. "You love him. Of course you're going to worry."

Gretchen could feel tears building. "I love him so much. I don't think I could survive losing him."

"You won't have to. He'll be fine."

Gretchen nodded. She glanced at Sara as she tucked her legs up underneath her.

"I still can't believe you're walking around. I can't believe you're a mermaid, either," Gretchen said.

Sara smiled. "You didn't have any clue?"

Gretchen shook her head. "None. I didn't know mermaids could live on land with a tail."

Sara smiled. "What, you thought I would have shriveled up and died?"

Gretchen chuckled. "No. But, hiding a thing like a mermaid's tail must have been hard. It's too bad you didn't get land legs."

"Yeah, that would have saved me a lot of problems. But then, I probably wouldn't be the person I am today if my life had been easier."

"I know what you mean. I've spent my life trying to be as different from my birth mother as I possibly could."

Sara smiled. "Gretchen saves the world…"

"…one child at a time." Gretchen chuckled.

"Are you going to return to law school?" Sara asked. "They can't possibly believe you caused that man's death."

"I did cause it." Gretchen frowned.

"He deserved it anyway."

"Who am I to decide whether a person lives or dies?"

"From what Xanthus has told me, he and Kyros make that decision all the time."

"I don't think I want to hear it."

"Don't worry. It's all legal. They simply do their best to keep order in a place with dangerous criminals."

"Do you think there's a place for me down there?" Gretchen asked.

"There better be. That's where I'm going when this is all through. If there were no place for you, there wouldn't be a place for me either. Why do you ask? Are you thinking of leaving dry land?"

"Well, Kyros and I..." She hesitated, unable to prevent a smile from lighting up her face.

Sara sat up. "You what?"

"We're getting married."

Sara laughed.

Gretchen grinned. "What? You think marriage is funny?"

"No. It's just, he better hope you *do* decide to live down there. He's hated every moment of living on land. At least, he did until you showed up."

"Yeah, well, I may have said yes before I got a chance to think things through."

"But you love him."

"I do."

"What ever happened with Hal?"

Gretchen laughed. "I don't know what I was thinking dating him. Do you know that before we went anywhere, he'd insist on coming over and doing my makeup and hair? And then he went through my wardrobe and gave me fashion advice. Me! Can you believe it? Like *I* need fashion advice. I should have known he wasn't right for me when he started throwing out clothes of mine he didn't like. I mean, they were *mine*. He had no right. But I overlooked it. I thought it was just a creative genius being eccentric."

Sara shook her head. "It looks like you've picked someone as polar opposite to Hal as one can get. Can you imagine Kyros giving fashion advice? Or doing makeup?"

They heard a snort and looked up. Pallas stood in the doorway. He had his hands over his mouth. His shoulders were shaking.

"Pallas, were you listening in on our conversation?"

He cleared his throat and said, "Of course not. Only women feel the need to hear the insignificant details of other people's lives." He returned to his room, grumbling.

"Right," they both said at the same time. They turned to one another in surprise and burst out laughing.

"Oh, I haven't laughed like that since..." Gretchen began. "Since this morning."

And they were laughing all over again.

"We're acting like teenagers," Gretchen said.

"More like preteens," Sara chuckled.

"Ah, but it feels so good. The last few days have been…" Gretchen knew she didn't have to finish. Sara had been just as traumatized from the many deaths lately.

"Yeah," was all Sara said.

"Do you think we'll be all right? Going after your mom?" Sara asked a moment later.

"We'd better be."

Sara frowned, obviously not satisfied with her answer.

"I'd like to say we're going to have no trouble, but the truth is, my mom is smart. You can't survive two thousand years in hiding without learning some survival skills."

"Do you think you have a baby sister out there?"

Gretchen's eyes teared up. "Or a brother."

"How long has it been since you've seen your mother?"

"Fifteen years, the day I left her."

"You haven't seen her since?"

"Only in my nightmares. She was never a good mother. I've seen things so horrible, even years of therapy haven't been able to erase them."

"I always wondered what you needed therapy for. I've never seen you anything but happy, controlled, and confident."

"Yeah, I can put on a good front. Actually, that front is what saves me. If I can control myself, my world, I'm safe. Things got messy in Honolulu, and my careful control snapped. You know, that's what scares me the most."

"What?"

"That I'll lose control and become my mother."

"I know you well enough to know *that's* not ever going to happen."

"I'm not so sure. I can be pretty vicious when someone threatens those I love."

"Well, that's what makes you different."

"What?"

"You can love."

CHAPTER 31

Kyros and Drakōn swam north-northwest. They were following Sara's hunch. Drakōn remained silent at his side—of course, he never was one for chitchat. Kyros knew the Dagonian had to be struggling. Kyros had suffered enough in the short time he was with Aella. Drakōn had been with her much longer.

"Do you want to talk about it?" Kyros answered.

Drakōn didn't answer him.

"I didn't think so," Kyros mumbled and spoke up. "If there's going to be a problem keeping a cool head, I need to know."

"There's no problem."

"I hope not."

"There is no problem," Drakōn snarled.

"That's not what I'm seeing."

Drakōn whipped around and stopped in front of Kyros. "What are you seeing, Kyros?"

"I see someone who is on the brink of losing control," Kyros said.

Drakōn clenched his jaw. "I'm perfectly under control. I'm going to catch the witch and rip her heart out, or if my suspicions are right and she has no heart,

I'm going to tear her head off her shoulders. It's as simple as that. There is no problem, no conflict. If I see her, she's dead."

Kyros frowned at his posturing, but if anyone deserved to be upset besides Gretchen, it was Drakōn.

"Fine," Kyros said. "As long as it's understood we are also looking for a child—a babe."

"Any offspring of hers should be destroyed too."

Kyros roared and slammed his fists against Drakōn's chest. "Watch yourself, Dagonian. Panthon Prison would gladly welcome you back to its filth and despair."

Drakōn looked shocked for a moment before his eyes widened in understanding. He bowed his head. "My apologies. I wasn't thinking of Gretchen. It was wrong of me to speak so. Gretchen is nothing like her mother."

"And this babe will be nothing like her too."

Drakōn gave a curt nod.

Kyros swam on, putting Drakōn behind him. However, the Dagonian was not willing to be left behind.

"I do have information Gretchen might be interested in," Drakōn said.

Kyros furrowed his brows. "And what would that be?"

"Her father's alive."

Kyros stopped. "What?"

"Aella filled your head with lies. She wanted Gretchen to believe her father is dead, but he's alive."

Kyros shook his head. "Why would she leave a

Descending

human alive?"

"Her father's not human. He's a demigod."

"Do you swear by Olympus you speak the truth?"

"I do."

"Who is this demigod? Who is his father?"

"She didn't say. Only that he was immune to her voice."

"Promise me you will let me try to get this information from Aella before you destroy her."

"We shouldn't delay," Drakōn said. "Aella is dangerous."

"I know. But I know Gretchen would want to know who her father is."

Drakōn frowned. "I'll try to give you time. But if she's not cooperative, I will kill her—whether or not she divulges Gretchen's father's name."

Kyros nodded. "Okay."

They could see the place where the yacht had been anchored. "Sara has good instincts," Drakōn said. The coral lay scattered, broken by the anchor's drop.

"She swam that way from here." Drakōn pointed north.

"Yes, I remember. How long was she gone?"

"She'd be gone about two and a half hours."

"The destination is probably about an hour's swim from here."

"That would be my guess."

The ocean terrain was nondescript, and the trip uneventful. Still, they scoured the sea bottom, looking for any sign, any clue that Aella had been there. They came up with nothing.

Kyros heard a growl coming from Drakōn.

"Sorry. I'm a bit hungry."

"Perhaps we should stop and feed. Your stomach rumbling could give away our position." Kyros smiled. He looked around him and spotted a small lemon shark. "Strange, lemon sharks are schooling creatures. This one seems to be alone."

"That *is* strange."

Unbidden, Kyros's incisors elongated as he tasted the tantalizing flavor of the animal.

"What do you think?" Drakōn asked.

"I think we should look for other prey. After those beasts saved our lives in the city, I don't have much appetite for them.

Drakōn shrugged. "Sure."

A large bonefish swam in the distance. At nearly three feet long, it was more than enough to satisfy their appetites. "There," he whispered, pointing.

"You stay here. I'll get him," Drakōn said.

Drakōn set himself up in ambush. Floating low, the creature swam into his view above. He shot up and pounded into the fish, stunning it. He ripped it in two and handed the more flavorful end, with the head, to Kyros.

"Thanks." Kyros had nearly devoured his half when he noticed the lemon shark hovering near.

His stomach was stretched full, but not too full

to impede his search for the mermaid. He pushed the carcass toward the shark. "Go ahead. I know you want some."

The shark moved in and snapped his jaws at the meatiest part of the carcass. Kyros chuckled. "Well, don't be shy."

The shark continued to eat, seemingly unconcerned with Kyros's or Drakōn's presence.

"That creature's a strange one. Perhaps it has brain damage."

"Yeah, we might want to keep our fingers to ourselves. I'd hate to lose a digit or two."

"I agree."

They swam on, hoping beyond hope that their reasoning would pay off. Kyros wanted nothing more than to destroy the greatest threat to Gretchen's life.

"Kyros," Drakōn whispered. "Look."

He glanced behind Drakōn and found the same lemon shark following them. He shook his head. "Great, now we have a pet."

"I knew you shouldn't have fed it."

Kyros stopped to turn around and shush it away, but it kept going, nearly touching them as it passed by. Kyros frowned. "Don't tell me we're going the same direction?"

The shark circled back and stopped for a moment before he continued on the same path.

"Does he want us to follow him?" Drakōn asked, stunned.

Kyros shook his head. "Sharks aren't intelligent enough to act like this."

"Actually," Drakōn said, "they were pretty well organized when Sara brought them up from the depths to the Dagonian city. Could this one be under the influence of a mermaid?"

Kyros and Drakōn drew their swords.

They followed the creature, searching for an ambush—any kind of a threat. The water brightened, growing shallower. He looked ahead and found the ground rose in the distance. It rose so high that it disappeared above the surface. It was an island.

He wondered if the shark meant them to leave the water. But the shark turned. He was circling around the island. They followed.

The far side of the island was rocky, barren. The shark continued its way around the shore. And they were back where they started. And the shark kept going, circling the island again.

"This is pointless. He must mean for us to go to the island." Kyros swam forward and surfaced. Drakōn followed closely behind.

They kept moving forward as the waves battered their backs. Kyros pulled himself forward, dragging himself onto the beach and waiting for the change. Each time his body went through it, it seemed to hurt less. It still hurt like Hades, but not as much as the first time. Drakōn roared as his own body made the change. They pulled a pair of shorts out of their belts and slipped them on.

They trudged up the beach and looked at the island. It was small with towering palm trees and thick shrubbery. He walked down a path.

"I don't know why we followed a stupid shark," Drakōn said. "Why would a mermaid choose to live on land?"

Kyros raised an eyebrow. "I don't know. Perhaps to escape the sea creatures that wanted to kill her?"

Drakōn cracked a smile and shrugged.

They walked along the path and entered a tropical forest. They were just cresting the first hill when they saw it—an old, wooden mansion in the distance.

"I thought she lived in a cave?" Drakōn said.

"*Gretchen* lived in the cave. Her mother was rarely there with her. Perhaps this is her second home."

"I don't think we should approach the house in the open in broad daylight," Drakōn said.

"You're right," Kyros said. "She's sure to see us coming."

"She's probably not home," Drakōn said. "I bet she's sinking an ocean liner even as we speak."

"Or compelling a man to kill his brother," Kyros said. "Speaking of which, is Robert still with her?"

"No. He split while I was there."

"He split? Do you mean...?"

"Don't ask. I'd rather not think of what she had me do to him. Speaking of which, let's get in the earplugs before she has me do to you what I did to Robert. Believe me; you are not worth the splitting headache it takes to resist."

"I know what you mean."

From then on out, they had to rely on hand signals. They couldn't chance speaking loud enough to be heard.

When darkness fell, it was time to go in.

CHAPTER 32

"They should be back by now." Gretchen stepped over to the window and looked out—again. Xanthus patted her shoulder. "These things take time."

"They probably found her," Pallas said. "Otherwise, they would have come back to sleep and resumed the search tomorrow."

"We need to help him," Gretchen shouted.

"It's nightfall," Xanthus said. "Searching at night would not be effective. We'll find them at daybreak."

"I should have gone with them to begin with," Gretchen said. "Why did I let you talk me into staying behind? I should be there. I'm immune to her."

"With the wax, Kyros and Drakōn are immune too."

"Yeah, until she traps them and removes it. Gah! I'm going. I have to help them." She stomped toward the door, stopping when Pallas and Straton stepped between her and the exit.

"Let me pass."

"I'm sorry, Gretchen." Pallas said. "We can't."

She narrowed her eyes. If only Xanthus wasn't

immune to her voice. She wouldn't be able to go unless she could restrain him. There was exactly zero chance in that happening.

"Gretchen, we just have to be patient," Xanthus said calmly. "We'll go after them in the morning."

"By morning, they could both be dead," she said. "Please Xanthus, I have to go."

He sighed, resigned. "And you *will* go—in the morning."

"Fine." She turned on her heel and stomped to her room. Tears were burning in her eyes. Entering, she slammed the door. She pressed her ear against the door. If she had to, she'd go alone. She saw the maps, the area they were searching. She could find her way there.

"Pallas, you take watch outside her window." She heard Xanthus giving orders through the door. "Straton, you watch her door. I wouldn't put it past her to go alone. You'll have to stop your ears in case she tries to sing."

Oh great. Xanthus was a mind reader.

She threw herself on the bed. Kyros's scent surrounded her. The morning had started off so well—with laughter, kisses, and a marriage proposal—but now she might be a widow even before she got married. Tears came unbidden to her eyes and spilled onto Kyros's pillow.

He'd better not die on her.

※ ※

Kyros led point as Drakōn took up the rear. Infiltration on land was much less complicated than in the

Descending

sea. In the sea, you had to be aware of your surroundings above, below, and all around. On land, you just had to search the area surrounding you.

Kyros pushed the wax deeper in his ears. He might have difficulty getting them out, but that would be better than hearing the song of a mermaid—especially Aella. The view of the home was obstructed for a while, but when it came back into view, there were lights on in the house.

Kyros signaled Drakōn to proceed with caution. They slinked up to the house and peered through a window. The house was furnished, clean, and looked more well kept than it seemed from the outside. He could see no sign of Aella...but wait. A shadow crossed the door, and a woman stepped into the room. Kyros knew at once it was not Aella. This woman was thick, white haired, and she was dancing or rather, shuffling, around the room.

Drakōn pulled on Kyros's arm. He shook his head and frowned. Kyros understood how Drakōn was feeling. This was not what they were looking for. Drakōn pulled out his earplugs, and Kyros followed suit.

"This cannot be the right place," Drakōn whispered.

"This doesn't seem to fit Aella. Still, I think we should question the old woman."

Drakōn nodded. "I'll do it."

Kyros looked over the muscle-bound, scar-faced Dagonian and shook his head. "No, I'd better go in first.

We don't want her to die of fright. She's human, and she's old. Her heart may be weak."

"All right, you go in. I'll watch from out here."

Kyros nodded and stepped up to the door.

He pressed the doorbell, and the sound of tinkling chimes rang out. He waited for several minutes before the woman cracked the door open. The first thing he noticed was the light spilling through the crack, the small chain keeping the door from being opened all the way, and the rifle pointed at his stomach.

"What are you doing here? This is a private island."

Kyros's mind raced for a believable story. "Our boat broke down on the water. We were lucky enough to find your island. Can I please come in so I can call my wife? She's got to be worried sick."

"We? You're not alone?"

"Um, no. A friend came with me. He's staying with the boat."

"Okay, you can come in. But I'm keeping my Winchester close. If you're thinking to rob me, you'd better think again. I'm a crack shot."

"I wouldn't dream of it."

"The phone's in the kitchen. You're welcome to it."

Kyros stepped inside the door and pulled it closed. "I do have to ask. There was a woman with us. I'm worried she might be lost at sea."

Her eyes narrowed. "What woman?"

"She's got dark hair, striking blue eyes, beautiful…"

The old woman shook her head, but her tight curls didn't move a bit. "No. I haven't seen anyone who looks like that. Course I don't *ever* see anyone. We don't get visitors here." She led the way into the foyer.

"Who's the we?" Kyros asked.

The old woman turned and answered. "Me and my grandchildren."

"How many grandchildren live here?" He glanced around, looking for any signs an infant was there.

"It's just me and my grandson." Her eyes darted around. The woman seemed distressed. Still, Kyros kept up the questions.

"But you said, 'grand*children*.'"

"Yes. I've had other grandchildren live here. They always leave too soon."

"They don't visit long enough?"

"No, Aelle——" She breathed out an exaggerated huff. "And now I've said too much. My old, addled brain will be the death of me."

A thunderous boom exploded in Kyros's belly. He doubled over in pain and sank to his knees just as Drakōn burst inside. Another boom, and Drakōn slammed back against the wall and slid to the floor——crimson blood streaked across flowered wallpaper.

Somewhere in the house, a baby began to cry.

"You should have made your phone call and left."

The old woman shook her head. "Now, you're probably

going to die."

She opened a closet and pulled out a rope. "This rope is most likely overkill. Your shots are fatal without treatment. But I don't want to take any chances, though. You both look as strong as an ox."

She crept forward carefully with the rope dangling from her fingers. "If you try anything, I won't help you."

"Help me how?"

"Dress your wounds, of course."

"You shot me, but you're going to treat my wounds?"

"What do you take me for, a monster?"

"I take you for someone who shoots innocent, unarmed men."

"Well, that was something that couldn't be helped. You asked too many questions."

This woman was either crazy, or she was compelled. Given the situation, he was guessing compelled. He gave a desperate look to Drakōn and shoved wax deep in his ears. Drakōn did the same.

Kyros looked down at his belly. His blood flowed from his wound. If he were to survive this, he would need the old woman's help. He put his bloody wrists together and offered the woman his hands to tie. Moments later, both he and Drakōn were tied up—the woman sure knew a thing or two about knots. He hoped she knew as much about treating injuries. The way she shoved wads of red, herb-soaked cloths into his wound gave him serious doubts. The stuff she gave them to drink burned like Hades, but he drank obediently. It was either trust her, or die.

She looked down on them tied up like pretzels on the hardwood floor and frowned. "I wish you would stop bleeding on my floor," she said, as if they had the power to obey her. "Blood is impossible to get out of this porous wood. Well, I guess it can't be helped. Neither of you look like you could take a single step. And I sure as certain am not strong enough to drag you into the kitchen.

"I've got to go and soothe my grandson. You stay right here and don't try anything funny, or next time my bullets will be in your heads."

The woman lumbered up the stairs.

Well, this was just perfect. They went looking for the most-wanted criminal in the sea and ended up getting shot and captured by a decrepit, little old woman. Kyros' ego was going to suffer terribly from this...*if* he survived. The room began to fade in and out—probably from loss of blood. He looked over at Drakōn. He looked to have fallen asleep with a snarl on his lips.

Kyros tried to squeeze his hands out of the knots. They only seemed to tighten with his effort. Blackness seeped into his vision as his stomach took a lurch. *Come on, Kyros. You've battled Krakens, Leviathans, Keteas...you can't be defeated by an old woman.*

Kyros awoke to the peal of laughter. Pain exploded in his gut, and he curled forward, trying to protect his injury. He looked up to see Aella standing above him. *Did she just kick me?*

"Kyros…So good to see you again." The voice seemed to come from far away. He must still have wax in his ears. "I see you've met Rhonda. She joined me a short time ago. Well, it's short for me anyhow. Sixty years goes by like that." She snapped her fingers. "Especially when you're almost four thousand years old."

"The old woman…She's the one that cares for your children. That is, until you decide to slaughter them."

"There's no need for such harsh words. I don't *slaughter* my children; I just send them off to the Fields of Asphodel or Seas of Elysium—depending on whether they have legs or a fin. I'm sure they're perfectly happy there."

"How many have you killed?"

She frowned. "Oh, now, that's not something I keep track of."

Kyros looked over to his friend. Drakōn was stripped and beaten. Blood pooled around him, and his face was as white as silt. Kyros couldn't tell if he were dead or alive.

"Oh, I'm so sorry about Drakōn. He was your friend, right?"

"You killed him?" Kyros snarled, his anger rising.

"Oh no, he's not dead. I'm sorry. Did I give you that impression?" She giggled.

Kyros scowled. She knew exactly what impression she'd given. You couldn't believe a word the mermaid said.

"No. I'm not going to kill Drakōn—yet. I have special plans for him. Although, perhaps I might consider you. You are just as good a prospect."

"Prospect for what?"

"To father my next child."

"Your next…? But what about the baby upstairs?"

She barked out a laugh. "Oh that one, he's worthless. True, he has a perfectly wonderful fin, but the child has no gills. He's a merman who can't breathe underwater. Have you ever heard of anything so ridiculous? That's what I get for breeding with a human. You never know *what* you're going to get." She flipped her hair in exasperation. "I'll be getting rid of him as soon as I get pregnant."

"You never cease to amaze me."

She raised an eyebrow.

"How can a woman so beautiful be so revolting?"

"Oh really." She stepped over to him and kicked him across the face. He heard, more than felt, his nose break. Blood filled his mouth.

He spat it out onto her feet.

"Oh, now, that's just gross. And you call *me* revolting. You Dagonians are so uncivilized."

He shook his head. "Are you serious? *You* are calling *us* uncivilized?"

"Absolutely. I have no idea what Ambrosia sees in you. She could do *so* much better."

"Her name is Gretchen."

"Such a crude name. The name I chose for her

was much better. You know, she was my most-perfect creation. She had all my greatest gifts, and she also wielded the power given by her father."

"I thought her father was a pathetic human."

Aella smiled slyly. "Oh, you can't believe everything you hear."

"Who was her father?"

Her smile widened. "You think when you get out of here you can go and tell Gretchen, and she'll have a nice reunion with her daddy?"

Kyros narrowed his eyes.

"Well, you might want to rethink that. Anyone who walks with him, walks the path of death. Her daddy is a dangerous demigod. There are few in the land of the humans who equal his power. Why else would I keep a child alive as long as Ambrosia? The trouble was that I couldn't find someone as appealing as her father. And then, what were the chances I could bring forth another child as powerful as his baby? I waited a full year before having another one after she left. A year!"

"Who is her father?" Kyros repeated.

"Why, he is the son of death himself."

"Hades?"

"Oh great gods, doesn't anyone pay attention in school these days? Hades is the god of the Underworld. Thanatos is death himself."

"So Gretchen's father's name is…"

"Thane."

"That's anticlimactic. He sounds like a weakling."

She smiled. "I'm sure you'll be thinking that as he sucks your soul from your body and thrusts you down to the Underworld."

She pulled her hair back into a ponytail. "I think we've had enough chitchat. It's your turn now." She turned her head toward the stairs. "Rhonda!"

"My turn?" Kyros asked.

Rhonda shuffled in, carrying a long, leather whip with shards of glass embedded in the strap. Aella took the whip and gave a flick of the wrist. It snapped against the wall, leaving deep gouges.

"I've had my fun with Drakōn; now it's your turn."

This was not going to be pretty.

CHAPTER 33

The morning sun took its time getting there, but as soon as Gretchen could see a glow through the window, she shot out of bed. She threw on some clothes, yanked a brush through her hair, brushed her teeth, and raced out the bedroom door in less than one minute.

She was relieved to see Xanthus was already waiting to speak to her. "I need you to understand how things are going to work. You will stay close to Pallas and follow every order given you."

"By whom?"

"Each of us. I don't want arguments, only cooperation. I'll not tolerate you putting yourself in danger. Do you understand?"

"Are you serious?"

Xanthus frowned at her. Obviously, he was serious.

"Okay, I'll do what you say as long as I agree with you."

"No, you will do what I say whether or not you agree."

"You've got to be joking. Listen, this is the twenty-first century."

"Don't give me that. I've studied you humans long enough to know you. This is a military operation. Even in the twenty-first century, soldiers must obey orders without question."

"I'm not a soldier."

"If you're coming with us, you *will* play by a soldier's rules."

Gretchen huffed. "Fine."

Each of the Dagonian men buckled straps across their muscled chest and slipped daggers, knives, and other weapons she'd never seen before into their scabbards.

Gretchen stepped up to Xanthus. "Do you have any weapons that would work for me?"

He frowned and handed her a long, narrow blade. "Don't cut yourself."

She held it for a second and cracked a smile. Flipping the blade around, she held it against her own arm, blunt side toward her flesh. She launched into a complicated kata, slicing and dicing the air so fluidly that Bruce Lee couldn't have done better.

Xanthus raised an eyebrow. "That's as beautiful as it is deadly. You'll have to teach me sometime."

Gretchen's surprise at his words distracted her for a moment—allowing the knife to slip from her fingers. She sank down into a twist stance, caught the handle, and came back up in another fluid kata. "I'd love to," she answered.

"Impressive."

She smiled, proud he didn't notice her blunder.

He stepped in close and whispered in her ear. "Nice save, by the way."

Oh great. He noticed.

"Okay, everyone," he announced. He went into commander mode, talking about maps, tactics, and all the best ways to kill a mermaid. Who knew there were so many things to consider?

Sara stepped out into the room, wearing a dark, fitted dress and a leather strap around her waist with scabbards holding several knives. Xanthus's face darkened.

Gretchen stepped over to her friend. "Sara. What are you doing?"

"I won't be left behind."

"This isn't like you. I took you to see *The Hobbit* and you couldn't even stay for the whole thing. How do you think you'll do in a real battle?"

"Gretchen, I've already seen a real battle, several in fact."

Gretchen nodded, frowning at the memories.

"I know I don't know how to fight, but I'm not a weakling. I'm valuable. Like you said, I have a sight. I can tell when bad things are about to happen. I can warn us of danger."

"All right, I'll support you. But…"

"But what?"

"How do you intend to convince Xanthus?"

"I already have."

"Oh, so that's why he looks so angry. He's already lost the battle."

"He's lost one battle, but I'll help him win this war. We will get Aella. She'll never kill again."

※ ⵣ

Gretchen popped her head above the surface of the water and searched the shore. She couldn't see any sign of Kyros and Drakōn from there.

"Are you sure this is where they went?" Xanthus asked.

"No, I'm not sure. I'm just telling you what I feel," Sara said.

One by one, they rose from the water, stepping out onto the small island.

Gretchen scanned the beach and saw something—footprints in the distance. "Look," she shouted. She pointed to the telltale signs of Kyros and Drakōn. She sprinted to it.

When she got there, she dropped to her knees and touched the large prints. "It's got to be them. You Dagonians have huge feet." She looked up at Xanthus, who was sniffing the air.

"It's them," Xanthus said.

"You've married a bloodhound," Gretchen whispered to Sara.

"You've no idea." Sara answered.

"There's a house on that ridge." Pallas pointed in the distance.

"He has to be there," Gretchen said as she

stepped forward. Xanthus's hand reached out to stop her. "Kyros and Drakōn were most likely captured. We probably don't want to take their same path. We need to find another way in."

They took the long—really long—way around. Coming around the backside of the house, they stopped among the foliage. They could see the house with little chance of being spotted. There were several lights on inside.

"Pallas," Xanthus whispered. "You and Amar split up and see if there are any open windows. But don't go in—just come back and let us know."

They both nodded and slinked stealthily toward the house.

Gretchen looked over to see Sara gnawing on her bottom lip. Gretchen stepped up to her and took her hand. "It's going to be all right. We have the numbers, the element of surprise, and our voices."

"I know. I guess old fears don't die easily."

"Bravery isn't about not *having* fear," Gretchen said. "It's about not letting it rule your actions."

Sara jerked a nod. "I know. I keep telling myself that. Don't tell Xanthus, but I'm kinda freaking out."

Gretchen looked over at Xanthus. He was looking back at Sara, frowning.

"I think he already knows."

"Oh great, he already isn't happy I'm here." Sara looked down, avoiding Xanthus's gaze.

"That's 'cause he loves you," Gretchen said. "And

he's a tad overprotective."

"I guess I'm glad for that at times like this."

"Yeah, he won't let anything happen to you."

"I know."

Pallas burst through the bushes and made straight for Xanthus. He told Xanthus something that turned his expression murderous.

Gretchen let go of Sara's hand and strode toward them. "What is it?"

"I don't think you want to know," Xanthus growled.

"I don't care what you think. Tell me."

"Pallas said he got a look at Drakōn and Kyros through a locked window."

"And...?"

"They're both beaten severely...Pallas couldn't even tell if they're still alive."

Everything in Gretchen's vision glowed red. Her anger, fear, fury, and desperation churned in her head as she marched toward the house. She was going to kill that mother of hers with her bare hands. So help her, she would show no mercy and slaughter her in the most painful way possible.

Xanthus grabbed her shoulders and yanked her back. "What in Hades are you doing? You're going to get yourself killed storming in like that."

"I don't care. I'm going to kill that mermaid. She's not going to get away with it this time. She's destroyed enough lives. I won't allow her one more—

least of all mine. She can't have Kyros. I love him!"
Gretchen sobbed. "Why does she do this? How can she
be so cruel?"

Sara's arms came around her. "I don't know."

"I loved her too, once," Gretchen sobbed.

"Of course you did," Sara said.

"She didn't care," Gretchen said. "The only
reason she kept me around is because she hates being
alone. She didn't love me. She didn't even like me.
Everything I cared about, she destroyed. She destroyed
it because it caused me pain. And my pain was her
entertainment.

"But I escaped her. I left. I made a life. I was
happy. I had a future. Kyros and I were going to get
married. And now she's killed him. She's succeeded in
destroying me. I'm not dead, but I may as well be."

"No." Sara turned Gretchen to face her shook
her hard. "No, she hasn't succeeded. Gretchen, you need
to snap out of this. You're stronger than this. You're the
strongest woman I've ever known—much stronger than
I am. Now, I know you've had the worst mother in the
history of the world, but you can't let her have that kind
of power. You've got to fight. You don't *know* if Kyros is
dead. Don't you give up on him. He wouldn't give up on
you.

Gretchen kept her head down and nodded.

"Now pull yourself together," Sara said. "We've
got a mermaid to kill and Kyros and Drakōn to save. And
we aren't going to tear in there without a plan, and we're

definitely not going to curl up in a fetal position and give up without a fight. We're going to make a plan, carry it out, and kill that witch."

Gretchen choked back a sob and wiped her tears. She looked over at Xanthus, who was beaming at his wife. Gretchen looked up at Sara. She glowed with power and confidence. Gretchen always knew Sara had it in her. Of course, as strong as Sara was proving herself to be, Gretchen felt like she'd finally shown everyone how weak she truly was. "I'm sorry. I just...sometimes it's hard putting up a strong front. It's a constant fight for me. I'm not as tough as you think I am."

"Yes, you are," Sara said. "And don't let me ever hear you say you aren't. You're the toughest woman I know."

Gretchen straightened her spine and blew out a breath. "I'm sorry. Xanthus, you won't have any more trouble from me."

"Gretchen, don't apologize. You're stronger than any warrior I've ever known."

Gretchen couldn't bring herself to smile, but she appreciated his words. No one had ever given her greater praise. She knew Xanthus didn't need a thank you, but she gave him a nod of acknowledgment.

Xanthus gathered them in together. "Okay, Pallas, what did you discover?"

"From what we could see, there are only three individuals in the home—Aella, an old woman, and an infant."

Gretchen gasped. "So it's true. She has a baby in there—my brother or sister."

Pallas nodded. "A boy. And he has a fin, not legs."

A brother? Gretchen's heart immediately went out to the babe. She knew what it was like being mothered by the spawn of evil.

"I suspect Kyros and Drakōn underestimated the old woman," Xanthus said. "We will not be making the same mistake. If she gives you any resistance, kill her at once."

Gretchen swallowed. Kill an old woman? If it came to that, she hoped she wouldn't be the one who had to kill her.

"I'll be going in alone," Xanthus said. "Pallas, you and Amar will watch the exits and make sure the mermaid does not escape."

"Yes, sir," Pallas said.

"I will give my life if needed," Amar said.

"Let's make sure that's not needed," Xanthus said.

"Agreed." Pallas smiled.

"Straton," Xanthus said. "You'll stay here. We need your healing skills. We can't chance having our healer wounded or killed."

Straton nodded.

"Gretchen and Sara, you'll wait here with Straton. Amar you need to lay down a perimeter of gasoline completely around the home. If we don't come out in fifteen minutes, Straton, you'll need to set the house on fire."

"What?" Gretchen whispered harshly.

Sara, at the same time, moaned, "No."

"This mermaid must die. If we can't accomplish what we've come for in fifteen minutes, it means we've failed and have been captured. Sara and Gretchen, as brave as you both are, you are not warriors. I will not allow you to put yourself in mortal danger. If I fail, there is little chance you'll succeed. And Aella cannot, under any circumstances, be allowed to survive. If we cannot kill her, the responsibility will fall to you."

"What about your lives?" Gretchen asked. "What about the others? What about Kyros and my baby brother?"

"Don't assume the worse."

"Assume the worst?" Sara said. "You just did assume the worse when you told Straton to burn all of you alive."

"Please be reasonable. If we fail, we fail. Don't make a bad situation worse by letting the mermaid escape to continue slaughtering innocent lives. Gretchen, Sara, promise me you'll not interfere with Straton."

Gretchen pursed her lips together, unwilling to agree with him. Sara was giving them the same reaction.

Xanthus scowled at them. "If neither of you give me your word, I'll set the fire now."

"What? You wouldn't," Gretchen challenged.

"You think I want to? You'd give me no choice. If you're asking me to choose between the life of my wife or the life of soldiers—friends or not, I'll choose my wife's a million times over."

"Xanthus," Sara said. "You agreed to bring me. You said I could help."

"I did *not* agree to put you danger. Your being this close to the place of battle is beyond what I'm comfortable with. Do not ask me to allow more!"

"It's my choice," Sara said, raising her voice.

"No. It's not."

"Then you lied to me."

"When did I?"

"When we got married, you promised me you'd never give me orders. You said you'd always give me a choice."

"This is different. You could get killed in there."

"If I'm willing to put my life on the line to help those innocent men, you should respect that choice."

"Sara, I will not. I cannot." He pulled her in close. "If anything happened to you, moro mou, I could not survive it."

"And you think I could?"

Xanthus looked tormented. "Will you agree to my conditions?"

She frowned as she thought hard. "I will...*if* you promise me one thing."

"What would you have me promise you?"

"That you will do *everything*, and I mean *everything*, you can to survive."

"I promise I will do everything I can to survive."

"You'd better." Sara jumped into his arms and kissed him passionately. "That's to let you know what's waiting for you when you get back."

"I'll be back to collect on that promise," Xanthus growled.

Gretchen fought back tears. She wanted more than anything to embrace Kyros and show him how much she loved him. But he might be…No, she wouldn't go there. He was alive and she'd bring him home, nurse him back to health, and marry him so she could kiss every inch of his beautiful body. But first, they needed to save him.

With Sara's arms still wrapped around him, Xanthus glanced at Gretchen. She kept her mouth shut. Unlike Sara, Gretchen wasn't about to make any promises. She had a feeling Xanthus knew what she was thinking. But he didn't say anything. It appeared he wasn't going to try and stop her. His primary concern was for his wife, and he'd already gotten her word.

Xanthus stepped away from Sara. "Okay, soldiers. Let's move in."

CHAPTER 34

Kyros felt as if every bone in his body were broken and his flesh torn to shreds. How he could still be alive after such a beating, he had no idea. Aella had honed her skills and knowledge on how to inflict pain and suffering over the ages. She was a master.

Kyros pried his one good eye open and looked around. He was still in the living area—probably because he was too big for Aella or her grandmotherly minion to move. Drakōn lay unmoving in the same position he had been in hours ago.

"You have to come!"

He could hear Aella's voice coming from the kitchen.

"I know, I'm sorry. I didn't mean to raise my voice. It's just that my situation is desperate. The Dagonians are on their way. They'll kill me."

Aella came into view through the kitchen door with a phone to her ear. She stomped forward, turned, and stomped back.

"Leaving will not solve the problem. They'll just follow. Listen, I know you don't care if I live or die, but there's something I have to tell you, something that *makes* this situation your concern. When you and I were together, something happened."

Another pause.

"No, not that. Don't be crude. It was something that should have never happened. But it did, and I can't regret it." There was silence, and Aella spoke low. "I got pregnant."

There was a pause, and she said, "Thane? Are you there?"

There was a low rumbling, and a crack of thunder that caused the house to shake. Dark mist entered the living room through the kitchen door and filled the house with shadows that brushed Kyros's skin like the kiss of death.

A voice that seemed born of Tartarus filled the home. "If you are lying, you'll wish the Dagonians had gotten to you first."

"I'm not lying." Aella's voice shook. "I swear on the River Styx. I'm telling you the truth. You have a daughter. Her name is Gretchen."

"A daughter? Why did you wait until now to tell me?"

"I…I knew you were angry with me. I was afraid you'd take her."

"Believe me, I would have. No daughter of mine should have to be raised by a mother as cruel and heartless as you."

"But I love her."

He laughed. "You are not capable of love, Aella.

I should have destroyed you when I found you."

"You wouldn't kill me. After everything we've been through—"

"After everything you put me through, I should have summoned my father to claim your soul."

"But then Gretchen would not be here. And she is. She's in danger."

Kyros didn't know Thane's voice could have gotten any more terrifying than it was, but somehow, the demigod pulled it off. "What kind of danger?"

"She's traveling with the Dagonians. They've convinced her they care about her. She's leading them to me."

"Why can't you handle these Dagonians yourself? Why summon me? And don't tell me you wanted to unite me with my daughter. I know you better than that."

"Their leader is immune to my voice, and they are accompanied by two mermaids."

"I assume one is my daughter. Who is the other?"

"A new daughter of Triton."

"You want me to kill a daughter of Triton? Do you know what Triton would do to me?"

"You don't have to kill her. Just their leader, Xanthus. Once he falls, the others will be easy prey."

"I've heard of Xanthus. They call him the Nightmare of the Deep, and he's usually accompanied by a Dagonian just as formidable—Kyros Dionysius."

At his name, Aella giggled. "Kyros is far from formidable. Would you like to see what I've done to him?"

Descending

Kyros watched as a demon stepped through the shadowy mist. He towered above Aella, who walked at his side. His eyes sent a jolt of fear into Kyros's bones. The demigod's irises were silver ringed with black, and they glowed against his dark presence. This was Gretchen's father? It looked like she got her looks from her mother. He looked from Kyros to Drakōn.

"You did this to them?" he sneered.

"Yeah, you're not the only one who knows how to inflict pain."

"What did they do to warrant it?"

"Haven't you been listening to a word I've said?"

He turned his glowing eyes on her. "You forget yourself, mermaid."

"I think *you* forget who *I* am. I am a daughter of Triton. I…" Her voice choked off, and she slapped her hands across her throat. Her mouth opened wide as she tried to draw in a breath.

Thane leaned in, sneering at her. "Your father banished you and left you to die."

Thane released her, and she dropped to the floor. She gasped, trying to catch her breath.

"Enlighten me," he said. "What did they do to warrant this?"

"They've been trying to kill me!"

"If I recall, Dagonians have been trying to kill you for thousands of years. How did they find you?"

"I was in the wrong place at the wrong time."

"She's lying," Kyros's voice came out in a forced

whisper.

Aella kicked Kyros in the head, making it snap back. The room went dark; he wasn't sure if it was him losing consciousness again or the demigod's mist.

"I think you've caused this soldier enough pain," Thane said. "Tell me what he…" Thane stopped speaking, and silence descended.

"The Dagonians are here," he hissed.

"Oh gods, Thane, you have to stop them. You can't let them hurt me."

"I care nothing for you or the Dagonians. My only concern is for my daughter."

"But how will your daughter feel if you let her mother die?"

"Fine," he snapped. "Just stay behind me."

"I know you're there, Dagonian. Come out now, and you might survive."

"Who are you?"

"My name is Thane, son of Thanatos."

"We have no quarrel with you. We've come for Aella. Her death has been ordered by Poseidon."

"And what of my daughter? What business do you have with her?"

"Your daughter?"

"Gretchen."

Kyros could almost feel Xanthus's horror and confusion. He was confused himself as to why Aella brought Gretchen's father here, knowing she was trying to kill the very daughter he might want to save.

"I was not aware she was your daughter. We still have no quarrel with you. Gretchen is safe with us, but her mother seeks to kill her."

Thane whipped around and grabbed Aella by the throat. "Is this true?"

"No," her voice rasped. "He lies. You have to believe me."

"I don't have to believe anything." He threw Aella to the floor and turned toward Xanthus as he stepped into the room.

"You will give me my daughter, or I will destroy each and every one of you."

"I have a solemn duty to protect her. I will not give her to someone I know nothing about."

"I am her father."

"So Aella says, but you do not seem the fatherly type. Gretchen has been through enough pain in her life. I will not turn her over to you until you prove worthy of her."

"Give me my daughter, Dagonian, or you will die."

"Gretchen stays with us."

"Then die." Thane pulled a long, black sword from his cloak and sliced toward Xanthus's head. Xanthus blocked the strike with his own sword, and sparks lit up the room. Xanthus sliced at Thane's stomach, and he parried and struck back.

"We do not need to fight," Xanthus said as he blocked the blade. "I am not your enemy."

"When you come between me and my daughter, you become my enemy."

"Just because you are her father, doesn't mean she is safe with you. Her own mother seeks her life."

"Lies! How could a mother want the death of her own child?"

"Aella has killed many of her own children."

"And your lies continue to grow."

"She has an intense fear of being alone, but she also fears discovery. She continues bearing children only to kill them. Gretchen told me this herself." He spoke as they met blow after blow. Kyros could see neither Thane nor Xanthus was putting his heart into the battle. It was more like they were battling as an afterthought to the debate. "Aella has tried to have Gretchen shot, she attempted to compel Kyros, the Dagonian who loves her, to slice her open and spill her guts. She tried to force Gretchen to turn herself in by compelling others to kill themselves."

"And you expect me to believe that this mermaid is capable of that level of evil?"

"I expect you to believe the truth. You know Aella. You know she lies. Who should you believe? Someone who has proven an honorable warrior willing to risk his life to protect an innocent mermaid? Willing to risk his life to protect your daughter? Or a being who has lied, deceived, and killed at every turn?"

The blows stopped. Both warriors dropped their weapons. "I seek the answer from my own daughter's lips. I promise you, I will not take her against her will."

A thunderous pop beat into Kyros's ears. Thane's mouth dropped open in surprise as blood seeped from his chest through his robe. He collapsed on the ground, groaning in pain.

"All I asked for was a little help." Aella stepped over to Thane—rifle in hand. "I asked you to protect me, to believe me. But no, you believed this murderer over me."

"You were going to kill me either way, weren't you?" Thane coughed.

Aella gave a dainty shrug and pointed the gun in Xanthus's direction.

Xanthus scowled at her.

"Well, I guess I'll have to take care of him myself." She raised the gun to Xanthus's head.

Kyros knew he was about to see his friend die— the friend that had been by his side for the better part of eighty years. He had to do something to stop her. He pushed himself up and staggered to his feet. His body screamed at the effort. "You're a coward, Aella."

Aella turned to him and snarled. "What did you say?"

"I said you're a coward. Oh, and you're a pathetic, needy, sorry excuse for a daughter of Triton. I can see why he hasn't helped you in all these years. He was ashamed of you."

"Kyros, what are you doing?" Xanthus asked.

"I'm telling her the truth." He turned back to

Aella. "You're plenty brave when you think you have the upper hand. But when you're cornered, you cry for help. Just like a child."

"Shut up! I'll kill you," she screeched.

"Go ahead," Kyros said, "kill her."

"What?" She turned around just in time to see Xanthus's hand fly toward her chest. He thrust so powerfully that his fist pounded a hole into her. Aella looked down in horror at Xanthus's hand buried in her chest. She watched him yank his hand out. Her heart was beating in his fingers.

Kyros stepped up behind her and grabbed her shoulders. "Give Hades my best." She glanced back at him, in confusion. Her eyes rolled back as she collapsed. Kyros caught her and lowered her slowly to the ground.

"I don't know what I ever saw in that mermaid," Thane said, his face pale as the moon.

Kyros's strength left him, and he dropped to his knees. Xanthus was at his side immediately. "Hades, Kyros. You look like death."

"He looks nothing like my father." Thane coughed out a laugh.

Xanthus shook his head. "Are you going to be okay?" he asked Thane.

"I'll survive," he answered. "It takes a lot to kill a demigod—especially the son of death. A shot to the chest isn't enough to do it. But still, it hurts like Hades."

"Don't worry about me, Xanthus," Kyros said. "I've only been beaten to an inch of my life."

"I'm not worried about you. You're too stubborn to die."

"I wish *I* were dead." Drakōn spoke from across the room.

Kyros looked around and smiled. "We are a sorry lot. Xanthus, it looks like you're the only one that came out of this unscathed."

"Not for long if we don't get out of this house. I ordered Straton to burn it down if I didn't return."

"You did what?" Thane growled.

"We couldn't let the mermaid escape. Even at the cost of our own lives. She's killed far too many innocents."

"Well, you three can get out through the front door. I have my own way out."

"What about Gretchen?" Kyros said. "I know she'll want to meet you."

"We *will* meet. But I have a few things to straighten out before I'm fit to step in as her father. Until then, take care of her."

"I swear it," Kyros answered.

CHAPTER 35

H e wouldn't wait another minute. As much as Gretchen pleaded, Straton was determined to follow Xanthus's order.

"It has to be done," Straton said. "I've already given them five extra minutes."

"Fine, you do what you need to do, and I'll do what I need to do."

She sprinted off towards the house as Straton called, "Gretchen, I'll give you five more minutes, then I'm setting the fire.

She crept up behind a bush at the back door. The wooden steps up to the door were old and broken. Aella probably had someone watching it, or some kind of trap set. Gretchen skirted the house, peering into windows. And that was when she saw heard it—a baby crying. She looked up to see an open window on the second floor. To the side of the window was a rickety lattice with an old, dead rosebush laced through it.

She glanced at her watch, noting she only had three minutes left. She needed to climb in, grab the baby, find Kyros, and get them out.

It would take a miracle.

Descending

She grabbed a hold of the thin lattice and took her first step up. The wood cracked and splintered, her foot dropping down. *How in the world am I going to make it all the way to the top?* She took a deep breath and tried a different spot. That time the wood creaked, but held. Another step. *Crack, break.* Darn it. "It's okay, Gretchen, just try another," she whispered.

She took another step, and it held. The thorns from the rosebush were prickly and sharp as needles. She did her best to avoid them, but still got more scratches with every handhold. Her injured hand had healed incredibly fast, but with the pressure she was putting on it, she could feel the new, tender skin split apart and blood trailed down her hand.

When she was about halfway up, she felt as if she'd reached a milestone. She twisted her arm around and looked at her watch—one minute left. It had taken her two minutes to get this high. At that rate, Straton would set the fire while she was on the dry, dead-leafed lattice. She'd never seen anything that looked more flammable.

The baby increased his volume as if he could sense her doubt. Scowling, Gretchen made her way up, cracking slats and scraping skin along the way. Finally, the windowsill was within reach. She pulled herself up and breathed a sigh of relief just before the face of an old woman appeared in the window.

The woman thrust Gretchen backwards. Gretchen tried to keep hold of the sill, but her fingers slipped as she fell. She clawed at the branches, attempting to stop her freefall. She caught a branch and grabbed it like a lifeline, squeezing so hard thorns pierced her hands. Ignoring the blood dripping down her wrists, she pulled herself back up.

The old woman was there again, with murder in her eyes.

Gretchen opened her mouth to sing. Her voice was weak, and her throat dry. The lady looked confused as she pushed Gretchen back and tried to peel her hands off the windowsill. Darn. Her throat felt as if she'd swallowed dry sand.

The grey-haired woman pushed Gretchen's forehead and back she went again, this time catching herself on the lattice. And the baby continued to cry. How could she possibly get in with the woman trying to push her out?

Another slat broke, and she scrambled to get on another. "Please, let me in." Gretchen knew reasoning with the woman was pointless, but still she tried. "That's my brother. I need to save my brother."

Doubt crossed the woman's face before she screamed and collapsed to the floor. Gretchen didn't waste a moment as she flung herself through the window.

"No," the grandmotherly woman snarled as she threw herself at Gretchen. For a little old woman, that lady sure could body slam. Gretchen was sandwiched against the wall. She pushed, and the old woman fell back.

"Lady, I don't want to hurt you. I just want my brother."

"You can't have him. I can't allow it."

"Yes, you can."

The woman picked up a picture off the dresser and swung it at Gretchen's head.

Gretchen jerked back; the heavy, wooden frame grazed her cheek.

"I won't let you have him. He's my grandson. I won't let him go."

"You'll let him go when Aella tells you to."

The old lady stopped fighting and opened her mouth to speak. Once again, she shrieked.

"Aella will never let you keep him forever," Gretchen said. "Do you know what she does to her babies?"

The woman's tear-streaked face looked up at her. "What do you mean?"

"She kills them. I've seen them. Their skeletons. Hundreds of them. Tiny babies, little toddlers, and young children."

"You lie!" The woman collapsed forward, screaming.

Gretchen heard a whoosh and looked out the window. Orange flames licked the sky and spread up and over the window. Straton had given her more time, but it still wasn't long enough. The house was surrounded by flames.

"I'm telling the truth. This baby and I are the

only ones left of her children. She's been trying to kill me too."

"You're not Aella's." The woman was rocking back and forth on her knees, sobbing.

"I am." The flames were now licking the walls.

"What is your name?" The old woman clutched her head so hard that her fingernails pierced her skin. Blood dripped down her face.

"Gretchen."

"Aella never had a child named Gretchen."

"I changed my name. It used to be Ambrosia."

"Ambrosia?" Her pained eyes held a spark of remembrance.

"Do I know you?"

"I took care of you until she took you away."

"I don't remember you."

"You were just a baby, but you were mine."

Gretchen nodded. Could this woman have been like a mother to her?

The old lady pulled herself off the floor and swayed as she moaned. If only Gretchen could take the pain away, but her throat was getting drier by the moment. The last of the moisture in the air was sucked up by the approaching flames.

The woman moaned, pressing her hands against her head until Gretchen thought she might crush her own skull. "Will you take care of little Nikias? Don't let Aella have him."

Gretchen's heart beat into her throat as the

woman inched toward the window. She seemed to be waiting for Gretchen's answer. "I will."

With that, the old woman rushed into the flames, shrieking as she threw herself out the window. Gretchen gasped.

She was gone. Dead.

The flames thickened and crawled through the window, licking across a nearby rug. The heat became unbearable. Gretchen rushed to the crib and grabbed the crying infant. Taking a blanket, she draped it over the child's head. The baby seemed so tiny—too tiny. The flames were on her heels as she ran out the bedroom door.

She flew down the stairs, looking for Kyros and the others. As she leapt to the floor, she looked around. To her right was a living area, with blood smeared all over the floor. Aella lay at her feet. Her were eyes glassy, and her chest had a gaping hole in it. And her heart lay still, several feet away. Sadness tugged at her. This woman was the first face she'd ever laid eyes on. She'd laughed with her and bore her mother's tears of loneliness. She remembered wanting more than anything for her to love her. True, Aella was a monster, but she was also her mother. And that kind of bond left a mark on one's soul.

Gretchen blinked away her tears and looked back to where she'd come. The fire was making its way down the stairs. She heard a crack just before a chunk of the ceiling collapsed behind her. The baby whimpered.

"It's okay, baby. I've got you."

Gretchen raced to the front door and reached for the doorknob. It singed her fingertips, and she jerked her hand back. She went to the nearest window. Flames danced on the other side of the pane. Smoke billowed in the room. She dropped to her knees, coughing and sputtering.

"Kyros," she yelled. "Xanthus…anyone!"

Crawling on her knees, she made her way to the back of the house. There was a door. She didn't even try that one. The smoke billowed through the cracks. She looked up at the window. Through the smoke, she could see the flames. Fire completely surrounded the house. A few orange flames began to crawl their way through the crack in the door.

Gretchen coughed as she looked for a fire extinguisher. The baby began to cough through the blanket. There was no extinguisher, but there was a sink with a sprayer hose. She crawled over to the counter and placed the baby on the floor as she stood, grabbed the hose, and turned on the water. She sprayed the fire as she sank back to the floor, picked up the brother she never got a chance to know, and pulled him against her chest.

This was how she would die—in a fire. At least she could take some solace in the fact that everyone else made it out. She wondered for a moment how she'd actually go. Would she succumb to the smoke? Would the house collapse on her? She didn't even want to consider being burned alive.

She leaned down and kissed the lump under the

blanket as tears poured from her eyes. "I'm sorry, baby. I tried to save you. I'm so sorry."

CHAPTER 36

Kyros sighed and staggered to lean against a tree. They'd made it out just in time. The fire rushed the perimeter of the house, devouring the gasoline and overgrown grass. It made trails of flames up the side of the home, curling paint and climbing the porch posts. Several dry bushes caught so quickly that they roared and crackled. Black smoke billowed to the sky, dimming the sun from view.

His eyes searched for the only person who mattered—Gretchen. He wanted nothing more than to embrace her, to lose himself in her arms. He dreaded telling her they were unable to save her brother. Xanthus had tried to go back in after him, but a wall of flames blocked his path. There was no way in.

Where was she? Through the roaring of the fire, he heard something that chilled him. A woman was screaming—from inside the house.

Forgetting his injuries, Kyros raced over to Sara and Straton, who was treating Drakōn's injuries.

"Where's Gretchen?"

"I don't know," Sara said. "She disappeared while Straton was pouring the gas around the house."

Descending

"Could she...?" Kyros looked at the burning house.

"She couldn't be." Sara shook her head, her eyes wide with fright. "She knew Straton was setting the fire."

He heard it, his name. Gretchen was screaming his name from inside the inferno.

"Great gods, she's still in the house," Straton said as Kyros raced toward the flames.

Just as he was about to reach them, Xanthus rushed him from the side, slamming into him. The pain of the impact against his injuries caused his legs to buckle.

"Let go of me, Xanthus. I *have* to go in there."

"It's suicide. There's no way in."

Kyros pounded Xanthus's chest, pushed him off, and scrambled toward the house.

Xanthus pulled him back. "Kyros, if you want to save Gretchen, you can't just run in there. You won't be able to help her if you're dead."

"How? How am I going to get in there?" Kyros looked up to the structure. It was completely engulfed in flames—except for the upstairs window above the porch roof. At that sight, hope lit his heart. "There, I'm going in there."

"How will you reach it? There's fire burning below it."

Kyros looked around and saw just what he needed—a tall tree standing in front of the house. He immediately began to climb. "Xanthus, get the others. You'll need their strength."

Xanthus looked from the tree to the house. "This plan is only slightly less crazy than rushing head on into the flames."

"Just hurry," Kyros shouted.

Kyros was just reaching the upper limbs when Xanthus came back with Amar and Pallas. Dagonians are much stronger than humans. But still, the trunk was more than a foot in diameter. Xanthus, being the tallest at nearly seven feet, pushed from above while Pallas was below him and Amar was on the bottom.

"Okay, push!" Kyros shouted.

At first, the tree didn't seem to budge. The Dagonians were pushing so hard, their faces bloomed red and their muscles bulged. A crack pierced the air, and the tree swayed. Another crack and the tree toppled forward. Kyros felt as if he were free falling just before he crashed against the porch roof. It buckled under the weight, sinking about a foot down, but it held.

Kyros scrambled onto the roof and dove through the window. He was met with a cloud of smoke. Breathing in, he coughed out, sputtering. He wouldn't last long in this. Rushing forward, he made his way to the door. Outside the room was even worse. Over the crackling roar of the fire, he could hear a baby crying. If he knew Gretchen, she'd be with the baby.

"Gretchen…I'm coming. Stay…where you are." He spoke through coughs.

He stepped forward, toward the burning stairs. He had to go down. He took his first step and the stair cracked beneath his foot, sending him stumbling down and landing with flames on his back. He jumped up as the heat burned him. He moved so fast, his open wounds flared in pain. He looked down. Blood soaked through the bandages, seeping down his legs.

"Kyros, is that you?" He'd never heard a more beautiful sound. Gretchen called him through the black clouds billowing from the kitchen.

"Yes baby, I'm coming."

He ran into the kitchen and slammed his knee into a chair. "Where are you?" he asked, and then hacked so hard he could barely take in a breath.

"Down here. You need to get down. The smoke is thinner down low."

He dropped down and was met with clearer air. Looking up, he glanced across the floor. And there she was, holding a crying bundle in one arm and a sprayer hose in the other.

"Oh gods, Gretchen." He crawled forward and wrapped his arms around her. "I found you."

She threw her arms around him. His stomach lurched at the pain her embrace caused him, but it was so good to feel her. She felt so alive.

"I'm so glad you're alive," she said.

"I was thinking the same about you."

She pulled away, smiling. Then she looked at the inferno surrounding them. "Do you have any idea how we are going to get out?"

"I don't know how, I just know we are." Kyros's

foot heated, burning him as he pulled it back. Gretchen turned the spray on the flames, and they retreated as steam rose and was immediately sucked up by the dry air.

There was a crash from somewhere in the house, and it shook. This place was going to collapse around them. "We have to go," he said.

"There's no way out."

"If we stay, we'll die for sure. Let's go."

Gretchen let go of the sprayer hose and crawled forward. Kyros took position over her and the baby as they crawled, blocking her from potential falling debris.

The flames moved in, heating the air so hot that Kyros's lungs burned.

Another crack. Gretchen screamed as the upper floor landed in their path. Then more rumbling and the entire house shook.

"Kyros, Gretchen…are you there?" Xanthus's voice called from the right. The clouds in that direction were different, grey, not black. Kyros got sprayed with water. It felt so cool against his burned skin. As the grey clouds cleared, he could see Xanthus standing in a giant hole in the wall.

"Oh, thank the gods, Xanthus. We need more water."

"I'm giving you as much as I can."

Kyros pulled Gretchen to her feet, and they raced toward Xanthus. Fresh, cool air hit him like a deep-sea current, cool, crisp and life giving. They continued to run until they were well away from the burning house.

Descending

He looked back in time to see the entire structure fall down behind him. Then he collapsed to the ground.

CHAPTER 37

Gretchen dropped to her knee beside Kyros and cradled the babe to her chest.

"Let me through," Straton said.

He dropped down on his knees at Kyros's side. "He should have never gone in himself. He'll be lucky to survive this."

Terror gripped her heart as Gretchen whipped around and said, "You will not let him die."

The baby in her arms coughed and cried some more. His cries were not right; he was hoarse. She lifted the blanket off his head and saw a tiny, soot-covered face. He coughed again.

"He doesn't sound right," Sara said. Gretchen hadn't even noticed she was there.

"I know." She looked down on the tiny boy. He seemed so much smaller than any other baby Gretchen had ever seen. He lifted his fisted hand to his face and sucked on it.

"He needs to see a doctor."

She looked over at Straton, who was taking care of Kyros's injuries. Worry gripped her heart in her chest. What would she ever do without Kyros? Tears sprung to her eyes. The baby coughed so hard he couldn't seem to take in a breath. The blanket slid off him, and his pale, little, grey tail curled in the breeze.

Pallas stepped forward, his eyes glued to the tiny child. "I've never seen a babe before. I didn't know they started out this small."

"You may need to take him for a swim," Xanthus said. "It sounds like he's got smoke in his lungs. He probably needs oxygen."

Kyros was once again coughing.

"Kyros, you can't be moving like that," Straton said as he pushed him back. "You're causing your wounds to bleed again."

"He doesn't have gills," Kyros said, his voice grating like sandpaper. He hacked again.

Gretchen's eyes widened. "No gills?" she breathed.

"Good grief, what are you going to do?" Sara asked.

"I don't know." Gretchen answered. "How do we even get him off this island? He can't breathe underwater."

"I saw a boat," Pallas said.

"Where?" Gretchen asked.

"In the trees. Over in that direction." He nodded his head.

"I'll go with him and check it out," Xanthus said.

The baby squirmed and gnawed vigorously on his fist.

"I think he's hungry," Gretchen said.

"I think you're right," Sara said.

Xanthus and Pallas came back with a small rowboat.

"Oh shoot," Gretchen said. "I was hoping it had a motor."

"Are you kidding me?" Xanthus said. "You don't need a motor. We can push it."

"What about Kyros and Drakōn? Should they ride too?"

"No, they're better off in the water. Straton and Amar can care for them."

"Are they going to stay here?"

"No, once Straton has them stable, he and Amar can bring them."

Xanthus and Pallas carried the boat to the water and Gretchen climbed in, holding the baby. Sara followed.

Gretchen and Sara didn't talk much on the journey. They just sat, with the wind in their faces, listening to the infant cough.

"I'm worried," Gretchen finally said.

"About the baby?" Sara asked.

"About them both. What if Kyros—?"

"Don't even go there, Gretchen. We just need to take things one at a time. Don't borrow trouble."

Gretchen nodded.

"Life sure is different than I thought it would be," Sara said.

Descending

"Tell me about it. I thought I'd be a power attorney in Honolulu—saving children."

Sara smiled. "You *are* saving children. Only this one is your own brother."

Gretchen had a ghost of a smile.

"Are you going to go back to do another internship?"

Gretchen shrugged. "Probably not. I have Kyros and this baby to think about. My life isn't my own anymore." And the fact that the world would be destroyed if they couldn't decipher the oracle's message weighed heavily on her mind. An internship seemed insignificant in comparison.

"Does that make you sad?" Sara asked.

Gretchen shook her head. "No." Tears welled in her eyes. "I love Kyros and my brother more than anything. I just want them to be okay."

She looked down into the tiny face of her little brother. He'd fallen asleep. He looked like an angel—a skinny, wrinkled angel.

"He needs a name," Gretchen said.

"Did Aella give him one?"

"It doesn't matter. I don't want him to have anything she gave him. She doesn't deserve that."

"Have you thought of any names for him?"

"Are you kidding? When have I had time to think of baby names?"

"Sorry I asked."

"I was thinking Donovan."

Sara smiled. "You *have* thought of it."

Gretchen smiled back. "Yes, I have. Donovan would fit him. It means strong survivor."

"That does fit him. Who came up with your name?"

"That's a long story, but my name fits me too. Gretchen means pearl. Life gave me a piece of dirt, but I'm making it beautiful, one layer at a time."

"That's profound."

The baby coughed again, and Gretchen looked down on his little, frail body. "I don't think Aella fed him well."

"Undoubtedly. A baby this small is supposed to eat a lot more than twice a day."

"He needs me. He needs a family." Gretchen brushed her finger over his little tail.

"Life will be difficult for him if he stays like he is. I know from personal experience. It was hard living as a freak."

"You weren't a freak."

Sara raised an eyebrow.

"Well, *I* wouldn't have called you a freak," Gretchen said. "Do you think your dad might help him?"

"Of course he will," Sara said. "If he can. I must confess, I'm worried about him."

"Your dad?"

"Yes."

"He still won't answer you?"

Sara shook her head. "I hope he's okay. What if

something terrible has happened to him?"

"Gretchen, he's a god. They can't die, can they?"

"I don't know. I don't think so."

Gretchen looked up, and the island of Bermuda was coming into view. "Xanthus and Pallas sure can swim fast."

"Yes, they can," Sara said.

"Well," Gretchen said. "We'd better figure out a story to tell the doctors and police."

"Police?"

"They'll undoubtedly be called when the doctors see Donovan's condition. I have no idea how to explain his tail."

"Gretchen. You can make the doctors believe anything you want."

Gretchen smiled. "I keep forgetting that."

CHAPTER 38

Gretchen laid sleeping Donovan in the bassinet. She marveled at his tiny face, his little, round head covered in white/blond fuzz, and his adorable tail, which flapped when he was upset. He looked healthier than he had three days ago, when she rescued him. His cheeks were fuller, his skin was pinker, and he ate constantly.

Gretchen scratched at the seaweed wrapped around her palm. She peeked under the seaweed wrap and cringed. If only she hadn't reopened the wound and then got it all cut up on the rosebush. She'd be lucky if it didn't scar.

Gretchen strolled into the living area of Xanthus's home and hesitated.

Sara and Xanthus were wrapped in each other's arms, kissing on the couch.

"You guys do realize you have a bedroom here, right?"

Sara jumped and rushed to untangle herself from Xanthus. He locked his arms around her and held her tight as he smiled.

"Um, yeah," Sara answered.

"Listen, I'm going to see Kyros. Donovan is asleep. He'll probably be asleep for about an hour."

"Don't worry about him. We've got things covered. Your baby is in good hands."

Gretchen tried to smile, but she just couldn't bring herself to do it. Her heart wasn't in the mood for pretenses, so she answered with a nod.

She hiked out to the cave and dove into the water. Kyros and Straton were on the bottom, about twenty feet down.

Kyros was cradled in a sleeping harness—his face still shockingly pale.

"Any change?"

Straton shook his head.

"But he's been out for three days. Drakōn's been up and around for more than a day."

"Well, Kyros's injuries were more severe than Drakōn's.

"What will I do if he doesn't come back to me?" Gretchen was tired and weak with exhaustion. She hadn't gotten more than a few minutes of sleep at a time. Between caring for a baby recovering from smoke inhalation and malnutrition and worrying about Kyros, she just couldn't sleep.

"He's healing nicely, Gretchen," Straton answered. "He'll be fine. His body just needs him to rest. Give it more time."

"How's your injury?" Straton asked.

Kyros's eyes opened. Gretchen shrieked—her

heart racing. He looked pale, close to death, but he was looking at her. "Kyros, oh my gosh, you're awake!"

Kyros looked her up and down, and his eyes landed on her hand wrapped in seaweed. He narrowed his eyes.

"What's wrong?" she asked. "Are you hurting? Do you need me to get you something?"

He shook his head and raised her hand up.

"What? You're worried about this?"

He pursed his lips and gave her a hard stare.

"It's nothing. I don't know why Straton is fussing over it. I just got some scrapes when I climbed up a valance with a rosebush."

"She reopened the wound in her hand," Straton said, earning a glare from her.

"But it's almost all healed now," she said, stretching the truth a bit.

"How are you feeling?" Straton asked Kyros. "How's your throat?"

At those words, Kyros's eyes widened.

"Oh, don't worry," Straton said. "You'll be getting your voice back soon. Your windpipe was burned. It's a good thing you have your gills. When your trachea closed up and your lungs filled with fluid, you would have died without them."

Kyros reached out to Gretchen and pulled her forward, wrapping his arms around her.

Straton cleared his throat. "I've got some errands to run. I'll be back soon to check on you."

Descending

Gretchen broke down in his embrace, sobbing as she held onto him. She never wanted to let him go again.

He held her, absorbed her pain, and kissed her head, her forehead, and each of her cheeks, before his lips settled on hers, kissing her gently.

This kiss was different from all the other kisses they'd shared. There was no desperation, no burning passion, only love and comfort. Gretchen felt as if he were caressing her soul. As he broke off the kiss, she settled her head in the crook of his neck.

"I love you, Kyros."

"Love...you..." he said with great effort.

"Straton said for you not to talk."

He shook off the order. "Marry...me...now."

"What? Now? Don't you want to wait to heal?"

"Now..."

"You've just awoken from a coma. Besides, I don't even have a dress."

"Don't...need..."

"Okay, I will. Just stop talking. You need to save your voice."

He grinned and relaxed. "Baby...needs...a family."

"Shhh. Yes, he does." Gretchen smiled, relieved he seemed to understand that their lives had changed. They had a baby to care for.

"You're going to love our baby," she said. "He's so beautiful, so sweet. He's a perfect little angel."

"Like...you."

Kyros pressed his lips to hers. Gretchen reveled in the fact he was alive, and he loved her. Nothing else mattered. Despite all the confusion and threats looming overhead, not any of that mattered at this moment. What mattered was that they would face them together. Her life was his, and his was hers. And the future was theirs to share together.

ACKNOWLEDGEMENTS

To Rebecca, Courtney, Dyan and Marya. Without you, I'd still be a woman sitting in my pajamas, plucking away on my laptop. Now I'm an author plucking away on my computer in my pj's.

ABOUT THE AUTHOR

I'm a mom who writes books in her spare time: translation—I hide in the bathroom with my laptop and lock the door while the kids destroy the house and smear peanut butter on the walls. ;) I was born in Utah but lived in Salina, Kansas until I was 13 and in Garland, Texas until I was 18. I'm now back in Utah—"happy valley". I'm married to a wonderful husband, James, and we are currently raising 6 rambunctious children. My interests are reading, writing (of course), martial arts, visual arts, and spending time with family.

CPSIA information can be obtained at www.ICGtesting.com
Printed in the USA
LVOW09s1700221114

415118LV00002B/3/P